BY MONICA MURPHY

One Week Girlfriend Series

One Week Girlfriend
Second Chance Boyfriend
Three Broken Promises
Drew + Fable Forever
  (e-Original Novella)
Four Years Later

FOUR
YEARS
LATER

FOUR
YEARS
LATER

A NOVEL

Monica Murphy

BANTAM BOOKS TRADE PAPERBACKS | NEW YORK

A Bantam Books Trade Paperback Original

Published in the United States by Bantam Books, an imprint of Random House, a division of Random House LLC, a Penguin Random House Company, New York.

BANTAM BOOKS and the HOUSE colophon are registered trademarks of Random House LLC.

LIBRARY OF CONGRESS CATALOGING-IN-PUBLICATION DATA
Murphy, Monica.
Four years later : a novel / Monica Murphy.
pages cm
ISBN 978-0-8041-7682-8 (pbk.)—ISBN 978-0-8041-7683-5 (eBook)
1. Alienation (Social psychology)—Fiction. 2. Mothers and sons—Fiction. 3. Life change events—Fiction. 4. Young women—Fiction.
I. Title.
PS3613.U7525F68 2014
813'.6—dc23
2013044026

Printed in the United States of America on acid-free paper

www.bantamdell.com

9 8 7 6 5 4 3 2 1

This book is for the readers. I hope you all love Owen and Chelsea as much as I do.

People cry, not because they're weak. It's because they've been strong for too long.

—Johnny Depp

FOUR
YEARS
LATER

CHAPTER 1

It doesn't matter what people think about you. It's what you think about yourself that counts.
—Unknown

Owen

I wait outside in the hallway, slumped in a chair with my head bent down, staring at my grungy black Chucks. The closed door to my immediate left is composed mostly of glass, hazy and distorting, but I know who's inside. I can hear the low murmur of their voices but I don't really hear the words.

That's okay. I know what they're saying about me.

My counselor. My coach. My sister. My brother-in-law. They're all inside, talking about my future. Or lack thereof.

Tilting my head back, I stare at the ceiling, wondering yet again how the hell I got here. A few years ago, life was good. Hell, last summer life was *really* good. I was on the team. Running on that field like my feet were fire and I couldn't ever be stopped. Coach approved, a big grin on his face when he'd tell me, *You're just like Drew.*

Yeah. That made me proud as shit. I idolize my brother-in-law. He makes me feel safe. He understands me when Fable never, ever could. Not that she doesn't try the best she can, but she's a girl. She doesn't get it.

Thinking of girls makes my heart feel like it's made out of lead. Solid and thick and impenetrable. I haven't been with a

3

girl since . . . I don't know. A few weeks? I miss 'em. Their smiles and their laughter and the way they gasp when I dive in all smooth-like and kiss them. Their soft skin and how easy it all was. Clothes falling off and legs and arms tangled up.

Being on the football team meant I could get all the tail that I could ever want. But if I don't have the grades, I can't stay on the team. If I can't stop smoking weed, then I'm kicked off the team. If I get caught one more time drinking at one of the bars while I'm underage, I'm definitely off the fucking team forever. Zero tolerance, baby.

None of us practice what the team rules preach.

The glass door swings open and my college counselor peeks her head out, her expression grim, her gaze distant when she stares at me. "You can come in now, Owen."

Without a word I stand and shuffle inside the room, unable to look at anyone for fear I'll see all that disappointment flashing in their eyes. The only one I chance a glance at is Drew, and his expression is full of so much sympathy I almost want to grab him in a tackle hug and beg him to make it all better.

But I can't do that. I'm a grown-ass man—or so Mom tells me.

Fuck. There's my biggest secret. I can hardly stand to think of her, let alone when Fable is sitting right next to me. She would flip. Out. If she knew the truth.

She doesn't know. No one knows Mom is back in town and begging me to help her. She asks me to get her weed and I do. She gives me beer as payment and I drink it. Handing over all the spare money that I make.

I'm working at The District, where I'm a waiter when I'm not in class or at practice or supposed to be studying or whatever the hell. I'm making decent money, I'm on a football scholarship, and Drew plays for the NFL, for the love of God, so Fable and Drew have no problems. They live in the Bay Area, he plays for the 49ers, and he's one loaded motherfucker.

But I refuse to take a handout from them beyond their helping me pay for school expenses and my house, which I share, thank you very much, to ease the burden. Mom blew back into town last spring, when my freshman year was winding down. Knowing I have a soft spot for her, that I'm easily manipulated by her words.

Your sister's rich, she tells me. *That little bitch won't give me a dime, but I know you will, sweetie. You're my precious baby boy, remember? The one who always watched out for me. You want to protect me right? I need you, Owen. Please.*

She says "please," and like a sucker I hand over all the available cash I have to her.

"We've been discussing your future here at length, Owen," my counselor says. Her voice is raspy, like she's smoked about fifty thousand packs of smokes too many, and I focus all my attention on her, not wanting to see the disappointment written all over Fable's face. "There are some things we're willing to look past. You're young. You've made some mistakes. There are many on your team who've made the same mistakes."

Hell yeah, there are. Those guys are my friends. We made those mistakes together.

"Your grades are suffering. Your sister is afraid you work too much and she called your boss." *Holy. Shit.* I can't believe she did that. But hell, the owner is her friend and former boss, Colin. He'll rat me out fast, I guess, even though he doesn't really work there any longer. He and his girlfriend, Jen moved on right after I graduated high school. They're in Southern California now, opening one restaurant after another, all over the place.

"What did my boss say?" I bite out, furious. My job is mine and no one else's. It's the only thing that gives me freedom, a little bit of pocket money that I earned all on my own. Not a handout from Drew. Not an allowance to keep a roof over my head and my cell phone bill paid.

It's money that's mine because I earned it.

"That you're working in excess of thirty hours a week." Dolores—that's my counselor's name. She sounds like a man and she's ancient. She's probably worked at this college as long as it's been around and considering it was founded around the turn of the twentieth century, this bitch is old as dirt. "That's too much, Owen. When do you have time to study?"

Never, I want to say, but I keep my mouth shut.

"All your grades have slipped tremendously, but you're failing English Comp. That's the class we need you to focus on at the moment," Dolores the man-lady says.

"Which I can't believe," Fable says, causing me to look at her. Ah hell, she's pissed. Her green eyes—which look just like mine—are full of angry fire and her mouth is screwed up so tight, I'm afraid she's going to spit nails. "You've always done so well in English. Once upon a time, you actually liked to write."

Once upon a time, I had all the hours in the world to write. Well, not really, but I could carve out enough time to get the words down. It was therapeutic. I copied Drew at first with it. The guy used to always scribble a bunch of nonsense that made my sister look like she wanted to faint, and I wanted to do the same. Not faint or make my sister faint, but touch people with my words.

So I became a carbon copy of Drew Callahan. I played football, I wrote, I studied, I tried my best to do the right thing. I'm a little more outgoing than Drew, though. Girls are my thing. So are my friends. And beer. Oh, and weed.

All of that equals not doing the right thing, despite my intentions.

I tried to kick the drug habit, as they call it. And I did. But then Mom came back around, and now I have a smoking buddy.

That is all sorts of fucked up.

"I don't have any time," I say with a shrug.

"Right. Working a job you don't even need, you little shit." Fable hisses the last word at me, and it stings as if she's lashed at my skin with a whip. Drew settles his hand on her arm, sending her a look that says "chill the hell out."

So she does. He has that sort of effect on her. The two of them together are so perfect for each other it's kind of disgusting. I miss them. I'm alone, adrift in this town I grew up in, going to school here because this is what I wanted. Independence from them.

Now I wish I'd moved with them. Gone to Stanford like they originally wanted me to. Well, like Fable wanted me to. Drew told her not to push. The more she pushes, the more I pull away.

And I did. With the Stanford thing, with the move-in-with-my-sister-and-her-husband-in-the-big-ass-mansion thing. All of it, I said no to.

I'm one stupid asshole aren't I?

"We've found you a tutor," the counselor says, pretending as if my sister's outburst hadn't happened. "You're going to meet with her in an hour."

"I have to be at work in an hour," I start, but Fable butts in.

"No, you don't. You're on probation."

"Probation from work?" I turn to her, incredulous. What the hell is she talking about?

"Until you get your shi—your *act* together, you're not working. You need to focus. On school more than anything," Fable says. When I open my mouth to protest, she narrows her eyes. I shut the hell up. "They're benching you on the team, too. You need to move fast before you lose everything. I mean it."

Shit.

Chelsea

The classroom is quiet and smells like old books and chalk dust, even though I bet there hasn't been a chalkboard in here for years. We're meeting in one of the original buildings on campus, where the air is thick with generations of students past and everything is drafty and old, broken down and historic looking.

I feel very shiny and brand new, and that's a feeling I haven't had in a while. I'd almost forgotten what it was like. I got my hair cut yesterday—splurged for the blow-dry treatment, too, so it falls in perfect waves just past my shoulders. Waves I don't normally bother to make happen since my hair is boringly straight. I'm wearing a new pair of jeans and a cardigan sweater I picked up at Old Navy yesterday with the 30-percent-off coupon they emailed me. Mom would be proud of my newly found thrifty ways.

I don't have a choice. Being frugal has become a way of life.

Now I'm waiting for the new student I'm going to tutor for the rest of the semester. It's already October, so we don't have much time to turn his grades around; not that I'm worried. I'm good at my job. So good, I get the tough cases, and supposedly this one is extra tough.

I've been a tutor since I was a freshman in college, and considering I graduated high school over a year early and I'm now a junior, that's going on three years. I have a lot of experience. I'm not bragging when I say I'm smart. I'm what some people might call a prodigy.

More like I'm too smart for my own good.

All I know about the guy I'm going to tutor is that he's a football player and he's failing English. Considering I don't pay attention to any of the sports teams at my college, I have no idea who he is beyond his name. My first instinct is that he's a punk with a chip on his shoulder who hates the idea of being tutored by little old me.

Whatever. I don't let it bother me. I'll simply collect my check every two weeks and send what I can to Mom. I've dealt with plenty of punk athletes in the past who are resentful that they have to do schoolwork in the first place. More than one whined at me in the past, "Who cares about my grades? I just wanna play ball."

They think they can get by on playing ball and that's it. Doesn't matter what ball it is, either. Football, baseball, basketball . . . if they're good at it, they think they're invincible. They believe it'll take them so far they'll never need anything else.

Relying on one thing and one thing only for your happiness, your expenses, your entire life, doesn't work. Mom is living proof of that.

So am I.

Glancing at my phone, I see my new student is almost ten minutes late. I'm only giving him fifty minutes, then. I have to go to my other job after this and don't have time to wait for him. I work some nights and weekends at a crappy little diner downtown and I don't really like it there. The boss is an arrogant jerk and the customers are grouchy. But the tips are decent, and I need whatever dollars I can get.

We're two broke girls, Mom and I. Dad left us with nothing.

I hate him. I sorta hate guys in general. Once, when I was almost fourteen and suffering in high school as the young kid no one liked with hardly any friends, I went through a stage where I believed I was a lesbian. I told the few friends I had, I told my parents, I told everyone who would listen to me that I liked girls. I never told them the reason why I'd decided I was a lesbian.

Sixteen-year-old Cody Curtis had stuck his tongue down my throat, his rough, inexperienced hands roaming all over me one Saturday night at a birthday party gone wild, and I almost gagged. I decided right then and there if that's what boys do to girls, I would have no part of it. I'd rather become an ostracized lesbian than deal with guys who wanted to grab my butt and lick the roof of my mouth.

Funny thing was, no one believed me. Not my parents or my friends. They all thought it was a stage. Especially my best friend, Kari, who *knew* Cody stuck his tongue down my throat and how much I hated it.

They were right. It was a total stage that wasn't really a stage at all. More like a front. But I've never been comfortable around guys. They give me even a hint of attention and I think they have ulterior motives. They want something from me I don't want to give.

My body. My mind. My soul.

They'll take everything, then destroy me. Walk away without a backward glance. Look at Dad. He's done it time and again. He leaves. My mom cries. He comes back. She gives in. He decimates her, piece by piece, until she's a broken crumble of human spirit on the ground, and then he's gone. This time for good.

I'm the one left who has to pick up the pieces. Glue her back together and tell her she's strong. She's tough. She doesn't need him. We *both* don't need him.

But I'm lying. I think she does need him. And I need him, too, only to keep her together more than anything else. I don't love him, not anymore. He stomped all over that love until he made me resentful.

Seeing what he does to Mom makes me really wish I'd stuck to that lesbian deal. Or maybe I should just become asexual. That would work, too. I like it here in my little world that makes sense, with school and tutoring and plans to go on to get my master's degree. I can be whatever I want. I don't need a man to define me. Kari's afraid I'll never want to graduate college because I like school too much. She thinks something's wrong with that.

It's hard to confess to her how scared I am of the real world.

A creak sounds, startling me out of my thoughts, and the classroom door swings open. A boy struts in—there's no other way to describe his walk. It's all effortless grace and smooth movement. He's tall and broad, and with a menacing glower on his face. A face that is . . . holy wow, it's beautiful.

All thoughts of returning to my so-called lesbian ways are thrown right out the window. If I'm as smart as I claim to be, I'll go chasing after them and snatch them back up. Pretend this gorgeous boy doesn't exist.

"You my tutor?" He stops just in front of the table that I'm sitting behind and I leap to my feet, pushing the chair back with so much force it falls to the side with a loud clatter.

My cheeks are hot, but I ignore the fallen chair as though

11

I didn't knock it over. I am the biggest dork on the planet. "Yeah. You're Owen?" I wince. *Yeah*. I'm supposed to bring up his English grade and I can't even utter a proper yes.

"Yeah." He flicks his chin at me. It's a firm chin and jaw that's covered in golden stubble that doesn't match the color of the hair on his head. That's brown. A rich, golden brown, though, that hints he could almost be a blond if he sat in the sun long enough. "I don't have time for this shit, though. I gotta go to work."

Oh. Not even a minute in and he's blowing me off and cursing at me. *Jerk*. "You're late."

"I know. Told you I don't have time."

"I don't think you have a choice." Turning, I bend over and grab my chair, righting it. When I turn back to face him, his gaze quickly lifts to my face, as if he'd been checking out my butt, and I swear my cheeks are on fire.

More over the fact that I actually liked catching him most likely checking out my butt.

What is *wrong* with me?

"I really don't need your help," he says, his gaze locking with mine. "I'm usually pretty good at English."

I'm at a loss for words just looking at him, which is pitiful. His eyes are green. A deep, intense green that is so beautiful, they're almost painful to stare into. A girl could get lost in eyes like those. I bet a thousand girls before me already have. "Really?" I ask, my voice full of contempt. "Because according to your teacher, you're failing."

His generous mouth sets into a hard line, the lush fullness that could be considered almost feminine if he didn't have all those harsh angles in his face to offset it disappearing in an instant. "This is such bullshit," he mutters, running a hand through his hair, messing it up completely.

It's a good look for him. That I'm even thinking this makes me want to punch myself. Where did my lesbian plans go? My asexual plans? Shoved aside because of a good-looking guy sauntering into a room full of attitude and doing his best to get away from me?

I'm not one of those girls. I'm smart. Boys don't interest me and I'm okay with that. I have a protective shell that's surrounded me for years, but I had no idea it was so thin.

He's shattered through it with one look of his too green eyes and he doesn't even know it. I refuse to hand over the power.

"Why don't we sit down and go over everything," I suggest, settling in my chair and scooting it close to the table.

He doesn't follow my lead. Still standing above me, he's so tall, his shoulders so broad, he's all I can see. I tilt my head back, hating how it feels like he has the upper hand. Hating more how he looks down at me like I'm nothing. Like he could walk away right now and forget I even exist.

Which he probably could.

"Can't we just say I come and see you every week and you get paid and we pretend everything's fine? You turn in your little reports and I turn in my assignments, take my barely passing grade and call it good?" he asks as he reaches out and grips the back of the chair he's standing in front of. His fingers are long; they curl around the edge of the chair so tightly his knuckles turn white. He's tense.

Great. So am I. "Um, that would be lying. And cheating," I say slowly, letting my words sink in.

"So? I can make this happen. I just need to catch up on my assignments, right?" He makes it sound so easy.

"You failed three tests already," I point out, not even bothering to look at the sheet that breaks down his epic fail-

13

ure of English Advanced Comp. I studied it before he arrived. Memorized it, really. "You're also taking a creative writing class and you're close to failing that one as well."

"I thought . . ." His voice trails off and he exhales, his nostrils flaring slightly. "I thought it would be easy."

"Apparently not." I raise a brow, proud of my calm, cool demeanor. Inside, my nerves are starting a riot in my belly.

"I'll pay you extra," he blurts. "I can't . . . I gotta work." His offer shocks me, and all I can do is blink.

"Maybe . . ." I take a deep breath. "Maybe we could meet at another time? Is that the problem? Does this time not work for you?"

"It doesn't. Not at all." He shakes his head. "I don't want to do this. No offense, but I don't have time for this shit."

And with that final statement, he turns on his heel and leaves.

CHAPTER 2

It's so much safer not to feel, not to let the world touch me.
—Sylvia Plath

Chelsea

I hate working at the diner. It's located in the not-so-great part of downtown, next door to a bar where the college students definitely don't hang out. But considering it's open twenty-four hours, the last of the college bar-hoppers tend to trickle in around two thirty in the morning, starving and drunk.

I'm working until four only because I don't have morning classes, so I can go back to my apartment and crash for a few hours. Kari, my best friend and roommate, is rarely there. She has a heavy schedule like me and she used to have a boyfriend. She stayed at his place, smoking joints and having sex all day and night with him, but then he dumped her.

I thought it was the best thing that ever could have happened to her. That guy was a loser. My friend picks the worst type of guy every single time. It's like she prefers the bad boys. The ones who make her feel good sexually.

I know this because she loves to tell me all about her sexual escapades in graphic detail. I think she likes shocking me, which is fine. I actually soak up all those details and wonder exactly what the big deal is about sex.

It sounds kind of horrifying. Awkward. Painful. Demeaning. It makes me happy that I choose to be alone.

Mom hates that I work at the diner and tries as often as possible to convince me to quit, but I can't. I need the job to pay for the extra expenses my scholarship doesn't cover. I work two jobs and go to school full time. I'll be a senior next year and then after that, I want to get my master's in education. Not here, though.

I can't wait to leave this town. It's so not my scene. I can get into a college much closer to home, Walnut Creek. Well, we *used* to live in Walnut Creek, until we lost pretty much everything we had. Mom now lives in an apartment in Concord. She made me stay here so I wouldn't have to face the scandal every day.

Her words, not mine.

Tonight the diner is quiet, but it's Wednesday, so that's normal. I shuffle from table to table, serving up giant plates of fries or nachos to the tables full of students. Breakfast to the two old dudes just off shift from the electrical plant, endless cups of coffee to the two guys who came in earlier to study for some crazy test they have coming up in less than six hours.

The usual.

That's why I'm shocked when the door swings open approximately sixty minutes before my shift ends and in walks Owen Maguire with two other guys as big as him, though not as good-looking.

Crap. I hate that I even think like that.

I've never noticed him in here before, but who knows if I would have. I'm usually not thinking about hot guys. I'm usually just . . . working.

But this guy is different. I meet him once and I can't forget him. His defiance is irritating, but his face . . . his eyes . . .

"Well, check you out." His voice draws my attention and

I snap my head up, our gazes locking. He's smirking at me, a little wobbly on his feet, and I know in an instant he's drunk.

Must have a fake ID to get into the bars, considering he's only nineteen.

"Hi." I flash the three drunk boys a brief smile before letting it fade. "Want a table?"

"Sure do," Owen says, his smirk growing. I want to slap it off his face.

Or kiss it off.

Ignoring my disturbing thoughts, I lead them to a table, stepping away when Owen seems to get right up into my personal space. "Nice uniform," he murmurs just before he slides into the booth.

I can smell beer on his breath and I wrinkle my nose. I'm wearing an ugly black polyester waitress uniform that is the dowdiest thing on the planet. It's not like I'm trying to impress anyone, so I've never really had a problem with it before.

Yet for whatever reason, now I want to shed it like a snake sheds its skin. Just wiggle out of this ugly, unflattering dress and toss it in the trash. I hate that he's seen me like this.

But I like seeing him.

"Something to drink?" I ask, casting my gaze at all three of them, not letting it linger on Owen. He might get the wrong idea, and I need his respect if I'm really going to be his tutor. I have a strong feeling that's not going to work out, but a girl can hope.

You are not hoping. You'd rather not deal with him at all.

I'm such a liar.

His friends order Cokes and Owen asks for coffee, which surprises me. I leave the table and go behind the counter, preparing their drinks and ignoring the way my shaky knees want to knock together. I'm overreacting.

I both want him here and need him gone.

Irritation fills me at the way I'm thinking. Boys don't affect me. I don't care what he thinks, what he wants. So why is he making me feel all shaky and uneasy? I talked to him for ten minutes tops, and then, as if there's some sort of magnetic pull between us, he shows up where I work. Smiles at me like he thinks it's funny that he's found me. Says rude cute things like *nice uniform* in that deep, rumbly voice of his, the one that sent a shiver down my spine.

I am acting like such a total girl, I'm beginning to hate myself.

Forcing myself to pretend he doesn't matter, I go about my usual routine. I deliver their drinks, then take their order. Deliver it to the cook, then head back out onto the floor so I can wipe down the empty tables, refill napkin dispensers, and take money from the customers who are leaving one by one by one. Until the restaurant is pretty much empty with the exception of me; the cook; the other waitress, Paula; and Owen and his friends.

I take them their food, noting that Owen likes his coffee with a ton of cream. Why I want to store that bit of info for later like a squirrel stores nuts away for winter, I don't know. It's dumb. He makes me feel dumb.

And I don't even know him. He doesn't care about me. I'm that pain-in-the-ass girl he's supposed to go see twice a week for an hour to bring up his grades. The one he tried to pay off so she'll pretend she's tutoring him and he won't have to deal with her.

Jerk.

"Anything else?" I ask them minutes later as I drop the check on their table.

Owen slaps his hand against the piece of paper and drags it toward him. "I think that's it."

"Great." I smile, but it feels brittle. "I can be your cashier or you can pay at the register."

"Hey, what else can you be for us, huh?" one of Owen's friends asks, making the other one laugh.

My cheeks are hot again and my mouth is open. I'm gaping at them like a dying fish, and thankfully Owen rushes to my defense. "Shut the hell up, Des." He glances up at me, all traces of the buzzed foolish boy who first walked in here gone. "He's drunk. He doesn't know what he's saying."

"I know exactly what I'm saying," drunken Des mumbles, clamping his lips shut when Owen shoots him a deadly stare.

"It's all right," I say, backing away from them slowly. "Take your time."

I turn to flee from their table when I hear someone slide out of the booth, strong fingers curling around my upper arm and stopping me from leaving. He's standing directly behind me, the warmth from his body seeping into mine, and I go completely still. Willing myself not to react, not to say something stupid and embarrass myself.

Look what he's doing to me just by touching my arm. This sort of thing doesn't happen to me. I don't care about boys. I've been kissed a measly three times in my life, once by Cody Curtis the tongue thruster, and he definitely doesn't count.

So twice. Twice I've been kissed, and I'm a virgin. A freaking virgin. Owen Maguire has "player" written all over him. I'm nothing to him.

So why is he touching me? Talking to me in that husky, low murmur of his that slides over me like slow, warm honey?

". . . need to talk to you. About this tutoring thing," he's saying, and I wrench myself out of his grip, irritated that I didn't pay attention to what he said at first.

"Just meet me Monday afternoon as scheduled and we should be good to go." I turn to face him, a fake smile plastered to my face, and he stares at my lips for a long, breath-stealing second before he finally lifts those too-pretty green eyes up to meet mine.

My lips are tingling as if he actually kissed them. *God.*

"I don't even know your name," he murmurs.

Owen

What am I doing? Why do I even care about her name? I don't know her. I don't *want* to know her. I'd never seen her in my life before today. We had our brief encounter this afternoon where she told me no and pissed me off. Now here she is again.

Wearing a really fucked-up black uniform that's shapeless and does nothing for her but make her look bad. Her hair is dark, dark brown and her eyes are a wide, innocent blue. She looks completely untouchable, like no girl I've ever been interested in before, and I'm asking for her name like I care or something.

"It's Chelsea," she answers, and I turn it over in my head. Over and over. Again and again.

Chelsea. Chelsea. Chelsea.

"I was, uh, hoping I could meet up with you tomorrow so I could get my assignments from you." Man, this is awkward. We're standing in the middle of this shitty diner, where Des and Wade can overhear every single thing I'm saying to Chelsea the innocent tutor with the blue, blue eyes and the pink, pink lips. They don't even know what's going on. I'm going to hear an endless amount of crap once we leave this place.

"Tomorrow? Friday?" Her delicate brows draw downward and her entire face scrunches up like she's adorably confused. Which she is. Adorable.

Dude. Cut with the "adorable" shit.

"Tomorrow is Thursday," I remind her.

"No, today is Thursday, considering it's almost four in the morning."

"Right." She makes me feel like a dumbass. I don't like it. "Can we meet later this afternoon, then? I need to get those assignments, especially if we're not going to see each other again until Monday."

A lot can happen between now and Monday. Shit, I can't even begin to consider all the possibilities. I feel like I'm walking on a tightrope, weaving this way and that, just waiting for the right amount of wind to send me toppling over and plummeting to my death.

This is what my life has turned into. The push and pull. The wanting to do right and instead falling into the same old habit of doing wrong. I want to tell Fable the truth. I want to tell Mom to leave me alone.

I know, deep in my heart, I will do none of that. I will keep going. Keep up the pretense of right and wrong. Of living two lives. One where I'm the good brother who does what Drew and Fable want me to do. And then there's the other, where I'm the "good" son who slips his mom some money when she comes around asking for it, which is all the time. Then smokes a joint with her and begs her to buy him some beer.

Sometimes, I really hate myself.

"I have class all afternoon." She sniffs and lifts her chin, all haughty virginal princess. I have no idea if she really is a virgin, but she just screams untouchable to me. "And I have a tutoring appointment at five."

"How about after?" I chance a glance over my shoulder to find my friends watching me, curiosity written all over their drunk, tired faces. I turn back to face Chelsea to find her studying me, like she's trying to figure me out.

Good luck with that. *I* can't even figure me out.

21

She heaves out a big sigh, which expands her chest, making me notice her tits. They seem decent enough, but I can't really tell with that ugly uniform she has on. And I hadn't really checked them out when I first met her, though I had scoped out her ass.

It was nice. Looked real good in those tight jeans she wore, too.

"If you can make it quick, I'll meet you then. Say around six fifteen? Same room we met in before?"

Relief floods me, making me feel like a pussy. I don't give a shit about my grades, but Fable is gonna kill me if I don't get my act together. "I can do that."

"Okay." She takes a step backward, her foot poised to turn around. "I'll see you later, then."

"See ya," I say to her retreating back, not moving at all as I watch her walk away, pushing through the swinging door that leads into the kitchen.

I hear my friends snicker behind me and I turn to see Wade and Des climbing out of the booth, stumbling over their feet. The food in their bellies did nothing to calm their drunken asses down and for whatever stupid reason, that pisses me off. I wasn't as wasted as they were when we first got here and my buzz is pretty much gone. Finding Chelsea working here helped take it away.

My *drunken* buzz. Seeing her, touching her arm even for that brief moment, gave me another sort of buzz I'd rather ignore.

"So who is this chick?" Wade approaches me first, followed by Des.

I shoot them both a look that says shut the hell up, and we exit the diner into the cold, early fall night. The house I share with Wade isn't too far from the downtown area since we live pretty close to campus, and we start our trek down the side street that leads to our neighborhood. Des will crash on our couch like he always does.

"Remember how I said my counselor wanted to meet with me?" I ask, stuffing my hands in my jeans pockets. I blow out a breath that I can see and hunch my neck lower in my hoodie to ward off the chill.

"Yeah." Des makes a skeptical noise. "What the hell was that all about? Like, whose counselor ever wants to meet with a student?"

"Is she hot?" Wade asks. "Don't tell me the sexy little waitress is your counselor, dude. 'Cos she's hot."

Irritation fills my veins, making my blood ignite. "No, the waitress is not my counselor, you dumbass. My counselor's name is Dolores, and I'm pretty sure she's two hundred years old."

"That waitress was nowhere near hot," Des says, kicking at a rock. It skitters across the broken sidewalk and lands on the side of the road. "Did you see what she was wearing? Black polyester sucks."

"How the hell do you know that she's wearing polyester? What, are you in fashion design now?" Wade sneers.

Fuck. These two love to go round and round. Wade is my oldest friend. Des is one of my newer friends. They claim to like each other, but sometimes . . .

I wonder.

"Knock it off," I tell them both, not in the mood. When am I ever in the mood to hear them fight?

"So who is she?" Des asks. "The not-hot waitress wearing polyester."

I wouldn't call her hot. But she's definitely not ugly. She's . . . sweet. All clean, wholesome innocence. I bet if I

23

looked close enough, she'd have a sprinkle of freckles across her nose. "I met with my counselor, and Coach and Drew and Fable were there."

"Your brother-in-law was there?" Des's mouth hangs open. He's in awe of Drew. Wade's not, because he's known him forever, but Des and I only became friends early in our freshman year of college. The fact that my brother-in-law plays for the 49ers sends most guys into a dumbstruck stupor.

"I'm failing a few classes," I say, my voice grim. "They got me a tutor. The waitress?"

"Is your tutor," Wade finishes for me, shaking his head. "Man, you need to keep clean. No more dope for a while."

Weed. It's been my problem for years. I've been smoking since I was in junior high, back when we lived with my mom and she didn't give a shit what we did. Once Fable took over, she forced me to quit. Drew made me *want* to quit. But then . . .

I fell back into my bad habits. I can't help it that I like how I feel when I'm high. Nothing gets me down. My troubles don't weigh heavily on my soul. And I've got them. Troubles. Most of them I created myself.

Some I didn't ask for at all. One, specifically, is my mom. She's like that fly that keeps hovering around you and no matter how much you swat it away, it comes back. Bigger and louder than ever.

Yeah. That's her. A nagging, fat, irritating-as-fuck fly.

"You probably shouldn't have gone out tonight, either," Des says.

Since when did these two idiots turn responsible? "Listen, I'm gonna have to lay low for a while. Catch up on my homework, retake a few tests, and bring my grades up." I can't believe I'm saying this. I was totally against it earlier. Only because the tutoring sessions were screwing with my work schedule, and I need that money so Fable doesn't know I'm giving most of it to Mom.

But I talked to my boss earlier, before we went bar hopping. Got everything straightened out and a new schedule. I can do all of it. No problem. The tutoring is temporary anyway. Once I get my grades back up, I won't need Chelsea's help any longer.

"You're gonna be busy," Wade says. "No time for chicks."

"When do I ever make time for chicks?"

"A few weeks ago, when you brought that one girl back to the house. I know you thought I was asleep on the couch, but I heard you bang her brains out," Wade says with a laugh.

Sneaky, sick fucker. "You were listening to me bang her?"

She'd been loud. Lots of *ooh, touch me right there* and *yeah, I like it just like that.* All of it had felt incredibly fake. Like she was putting on a performance and thinking that was what I wanted. I went with it. Encouraged her, even, with all the essential dirty talk she seemed to crave, but I hadn't been into it. I hadn't lasted long and when it was over, I kicked her out quick.

I can't even remember her name.

"It couldn't be avoided. She was a screamer." Wade nudges Des in the ribs and they break into laughter.

Bastards.

"I get more pussy than the two of you put together," I say, irritated that I'm making that some sort of claim to fame.

"Considering Des is gay, that's not saying much. Ow!" Wade rubs his arm when Des socks him in it.

Same old shit, different day. Getting drunk and walking home. Name calling. Bragging about pussy.

I'm getting sick of it. Sick of my life. Sick of *me.* I need a change. I need to leave.

I'm talking to Fable about it tomorrow.

CHAPTER 3

You're not a bad seed. You're just a flower waiting to bloom.
—Chelsea Simmons

Owen

"You know I would love it if you came here, but Drew's traveling a lot with the team for games and I've been going with him," Fable says, her voice full of regret.

I clutch my cell phone tight and close my eyes. I'm still in bed. It's past one o'clock and I have a class at two. I need to get my ass moving. "You travel even with the baby?"

My niece, Autumn, is their whole world. She's three and a half months old and the cutest thing I've ever seen. She makes these little cooing noises whenever she sees me, which isn't often enough. She looks just like Fable. Drew loves nothing more than holding his little baby girl in his arms and walking out in public like that. Paparazzi take pictures and they appear on the Internet, making girls swoon.

Those photos make Fable swoon, too. It's some crazy shit. Who knew women love a dude holding his baby?

"*Especially* with the baby. Who knows how long I'll be able to do this? Autumn will get older and next thing you know, she'll be in school or whatever and I won't want to go on the road with her. I'm taking advantage while I can." Fable grunts a little; I can tell she's juggling the baby because I hear Autumn's little whimper. "God, she's greedy."

I don't even want to imagine what Fable's doing right now. "I sort of screwed up my meeting with the tutor," I admit.

She sighs. "How?"

I tell her what happened, then finish by letting her know about my meeting with Chelsea tonight. That appeases Fable, but I can hear the weariness in her tone when she tells me not to blow this off and that I need to stick with it. I can't run away from my problems by coming to live with them and blah, blah, blah.

Huge mistake, thinking I could call and ask her if she'd let me stay with her for a while. I get off the phone quick and toss it on my bedside table. Close my eyes and let my thoughts drift . . .

To the tutor. Chelsea with the big blue eyes and long dark hair. She hates me. And I should hate her. She's one of those smart rich girls and I'm just one of the local scrubs who got picked up on a scholarship. Yeah, Drew is rich and he's taken care of us—hell, he's made more money now that he plays for the NFL than his dad ever did, and I benefit from that—but I can't forget my roots. Where I came from.

Mom suddenly hanging around again reminds me of those roots all the time.

A girl like Chelsea would view being with me as slumming. Get with the rough bad boy and keep me her dirty little secret. And I bet she's never slummed in her entire life. I probably scare the pants off of her.

Don't you want to scare the pants off of her?

Hell, yeah. Though I shouldn't. She's not for me. Not my type.

My phone buzzes, indicating I have a text, and I grab it, groaning when I see it's my mom:

I'm in front of your house. Are you home?

Hell. She is the last person I want to deal with right now. Or ever.

Crawling out of bed, I pull on a T-shirt and slip on some jeans, head toward the front door, and throw it open to find her pacing the sidewalk. She looks twitchy.

Great.

"Owen." She smiles, but it doesn't light her eyes. Has it ever? "Are you just getting out of bed? You shouldn't sleep in so late."

Her attempts at mothering make me want to laugh. She's a total joke. "I have class in less than an hour." I don't want her hanging around too long. She'll end up asking for more, more, more.

She always wants more.

"What do you want?" I ask her when she doesn't say anything.

Mom flinches and sighs. "Fine, we're gonna get right to the point? I need money."

Sure she does. She always does. Her part-time job doesn't pay much. I can't even believe she's holding down a job, what with her crappy track record. When she bailed on us, she'd been unemployed, spending a lot of time with her loser boyfriend Larry and basically living at his place or their favorite bar. That had been over four years ago.

Now here she is. Like she's never left. Though somehow the tables have turned and I'm the one who takes care of her. Funny, considering she never really took care of me or Fable. "How much?"

"Two hundred?" She winces, as if she hates asking, but

it's all a lie. She has no problem whatsoever asking me for cash. She thinks I'm an endless money train, thanks to Drew the stud football player Callahan. And that's a direct quote, spit out with so much venom and bitterness I recoiled when she said it.

Yeah. Mom and Fable do *not* get along. Hell, they don't even talk. Drew's never met Mom. And Mom has never seen her grandbaby, though she knows Autumn exists.

My family is fucked up in every which way you could think of.

"I don't have that kind of cash," I say.

Her eyes go wide. Dull and green. Her overdyed hair is yellow and fried at the ends. She looks like hell. Fable would flip the fuck out if she knew I've been talking to her, giving her money for months. "What do you mean, you don't have it? Your sister's husband is a goddamn football player for the NFL! He's loaded!"

I press my lips together. Here she goes, even though she knows Fable doesn't know we're in contact. "Drew doesn't give me money."

"He keeps you in this house. Bought your brand-new car. Paid for your education."

"I earned a scholarship fair and square. This house is a shithole, but I wouldn't let Drew pay for some expensive place I don't need. And he gave me that car when I turned eighteen." I cross my arms in front of my chest, hating that I have to defend what I have. She looks at Fable and me and all she sees is dollar signs.

"I need it." She's whining. "You're telling me you really don't have two hundred to spare?"

"Not till I get paid," I say, which is the fucking truth. I live on my own terms as much as I can. My extra spending money is what I make at the restaurant. It doesn't come out of Drew's bank account. I gotta man up sometime.

"When's that?"

"Friday."

She glances down at the sidewalk and kicks at it with her beat-up Nikes that have seen way better days. Like five-years-ago-plus better days. "Tomorrow then? Can I come by and get it tomorrow?"

"Sure," I bite out. "And bring some beer, would you?"

"How can I bring you beer if I don't have any money?" She glares at me. Those dull eyes sharpen with an edge of anger, that thin mouth set in a firm line. She's the unhappiest person I've ever met. Mean for mean's sake. Selfish and dumb, she makes the worst choices I've ever witnessed.

I'm scared as hell that I'll turn out exactly like her. The choices I make are terrible. I know better. Yet I keep doing it.

Like mother, like son . . .

"Come by tomorrow afternoon and I'll give you extra so you can go grab some beer," I suggest. That way I won't be tempted to go out to the bars. I'll stay home and drink a few brews with Wade and invite Des over. Maybe call one of the few hookups I have saved in my phone. Get a little drunk, get naked for an hour with a willing female, then slap her on the ass and send her away.

Fuck. I'm a pig.

"Only if you score me a J," she throws back at me, and I grimace.

Des is my weed source. He can score me an entire gallon Ziploc bag of joints if I ask him for it. "Whatever. If that's what you want."

"Smoke it with me? We could talk. Like we used to." She sounds hopeful, and I want to be sick. This is her idea of bonding with her baby boy. The two of us passing a joint back and forth, getting high.

We did it a few times when I was thirteen. Before she ditched us. That's our little secret. I never told Fable.

She'd die. Worse, she'd want to kill Mom.

"Maybe." I shrug, and her eyes go even dimmer if that's possible. "I gotta get ready for class."

"Class." She sneers. "Have fun."

"Will do." I watch her walk away, staying on my front porch long after she disappears.

Our relationship is a mess. I hate that I keep this a secret. It's eating me up inside. I want to tell Fable, but she'll be furious. I'd love to confide in Drew, but he'd tell her. He'd have to. She's his wife. And he's so loyal to Fable, he'd freaking die for her if that's what it took to keep her safe. To protect their relationship.

So I can't do that to him. Can't expect him to keep a secret like that. It's too much.

Instead, I let it fester inside of me. Growing like a noxious weed, its long, grabby tendrils moving through me, within me, wrapping around my arms and legs and gut and heart and brain, clutching me hard in its grip until my secret is all I can think about.

I need a fucking distraction, and quick.

Chelsea

I dressed for him. So ridiculous, but I went through my closet meticulously. Pushing aside each hanger, dismissing everything with harsh words I utter out loud. Easy to do since I'm alone, as usual, and no one is around to ask me what the heck I'm doing.

Old. Ugly. Cheap. Bad color. Frumpy. Makes me look fat. Makes me look sickly. Makes me look like a slut.

The last one I pull out is the slut shirt. I wore it on my eighteenth birthday. Kari dared me to buy it and I did. Back when I believed I could still afford frivolous purchases, though the financial ax fell less than a month after.

It's black. A halter top that dips low in the front, with a drapey neck and completely backless. I wore it that night at the restaurant Kari took me to with a few friends. I felt so daring, so grown up. We ate a bunch of food, then went back to someone's house and got drunk on cheap beer and wine. That's where I had my second kiss. A true make-out session on a couch and everything with a boy whose tongue wasn't as disgusting as Cody's, but who really didn't know how to use it.

At least, I don't think he did. Not that I have much to compare it to.

God. I'm so pitiful it's freaking painful.

I shove the slut shirt back into my closet and keep going. I can't look like I'm trying too hard. Like I'd wear a halter top to school on a Thursday afternoon. I mean, really? But my wardrobe is seriously lacking, considering it's mostly full of T-shirts. So boring.

I settled on a cute pale yellow shirt I got last summer on clearance and throw my favorite black cardigan over it. My favorite pair of faded jeans. Gray Converses I snagged at Target, which means they're not *real* Converses but close enough. I skip through classes with a restless energy that hums just beneath my skin. I finally recognize it as anticipation.

If he knew, he'd laugh at me—I just know it.

My one tutoring session before Owen's is a nightmare. My energy isn't in it and my student, a senior named Wes who's been on a downward spiral with English since his freshman year, knows it. So he screws around and gives me crap, spends way too much time texting and not enough time listening to me until I finally end the session ten minutes early.

Big mistake. Now I'm left waiting around for Owen Maguire for twenty-five minutes instead of fifteen. And considering how late he was yesterday, my wait will probably be longer.

Feeling like a first grader told to take a nap, I cross my arms on top of the table and rest my head on them, closing my eyes. I didn't get much sleep last night, so I'm super tired. I doubt I'll sleep now, I rarely take naps or anything, but what else am I going to do to pass the time? Pace the room? Wait out front for him to finally show?

Sounds like torture.

I let my mind float. I think of Mom and how she wants me to come home. She misses me. I'm her only child and she's super lonely. Her friends don't come around much now that she's in Concord and Dad is in jail. She's got no one. She likes to tell me that every time we talk. No one but me.

But I can't afford to go visit her whenever she wants me to and I want to save up for Thanksgiving, when I have a week off. That makes more sense. Somehow, I need to convince her of that.

But how am I going to get a week off from my job at the diner? The tutoring comes to a stop because it's school break, but it will still be busy at the diner. I haven't even dared ask my boss for any time off yet, which is dumb. I need to prepare early. I need to stop being such a chicken . . .

I need to stop thinking about boys with pretty green eyes who think I'm a joke. I saw the amusement in his gaze at the diner. He probably laughed about me with his friends when they left. They might have asked who I was, and I bet he said *she's nobody.*

Nobody.

I've always been nobody.

Why can't I be someone's somebody? I'm lying to myself when I say I'd rather be asexual or a lesbian or whatever other silly scheme I come up with. I want a boy with a sexy walk and glittering green eyes to like me. I want him to whisper sweet words in my ear that make me shiver. I want him to touch me. I want to know what it feels like to be cherished. Just once . . .

"Hey."

I recognize him, recognize that one softly spoken word. Look at how he even haunts my dreams. His deep, rumbly voice moves through me, making me tingle, and I let loose a soft sigh. A sigh that turns into a barely there whimper when he touches my hair, his fingers tangled in the strands.

"Wake up, sleepyhead." His tone is tinged with amusement, and I realize I'm not dreaming.

His voice is real. His fingers in my hair are . . . real.

Crap.

I lift my head and blink my eyes open to find him standing right above me, a smile curving his lips, his hand nowhere near my hair. Did I imagine that? "Wh—what are you doing here?"

"I'm supposed to meet you here, remember?" He peers down at me as if I've lost my mind.

Maybe I have.

"What time is it?" I push the hair out of my eyes, my vision fuzzy, my head foggy. I must have really fallen asleep.

"Six fifteen. For once, I'm right on time." His smile grows and he leans his hip against the table. "I figured you'd appreciate that."

He showed up on time to please me. And guess what? It

does please me, more than it should. I'm such an easy target. "I fell asleep."

"Clearly."

I rub my forehead. "I don't usually do that."

"Maybe you should more often. I think you were sleeping pretty hard."

Wariness fills me and I stiffen my spine. "Why do you say that?"

"Well, you have crease marks on your cheek." He reaches out and traces them, his fingertips so light on my skin a shiver steals through me.

I cannot believe he touched me.

His hand drops and he pulls out the chair next to mine, settling in it like he belongs there. He's not sitting across from me the way I usually meet with my students; he's right next to me and I can feel his warmth, smell his intoxicating scent. Like smoke and spice, fresh air and crisp apples. He smells like fall.

Fall has always been my favorite season.

"You have those assignments?"

His question knocks me out of my distracted state and I pull a folder from the pile I have stacked beside me, the one that's labeled *Maguire, Owen*. I flip it open and hand him the sheet of paper I copied for him earlier. It lists all the assignments he's missed so far and the ones he's completed, which aren't many. "Here you go."

The paper lands in front of him and he studies it, his brows crinkled with concentration, his lips pressed together. I stare at him unabashedly because I can. As though maybe I'm supposed to, because hey, I'm his tutor. I need to watch over him and make sure he understands what's going on, right?

"Can I make up the tests?" His deep voice wraps around me, making me warm, and I nod, staring into his dreamy eyes.

"Yes."

He keeps staring at me as if he's waiting for me to say something else, and I realize I do have more I need to say.

"You must finish the assignments leading up to the three tests you've missed first." Leaning over, I point at the four assignments he missed that are listed before the first test. "So you turn those in, then you can complete the test."

"What about these?" His index finger joins mine on the sheet of paper, tapping on the missing work just below the first test, his finger almost but not quite brushing mine.

I hold my breath, count to five. My insides are a fluttering, riotous mess, all because our fingers are close to each other on a piece of paper. "Same thing. Turn in the work, then take the test." I sound all breathy and girlish. Like I'm trying to flirt, which I'm not.

Owen Maguire just puts me into a breathless, girlish state.

"Mmm-hmm." He glances back up at me and our gazes meet. A lock of hair has fallen over his forehead and I want to push it back. Test its softness. Why is he looking at me like that? There's no amusement, no mocking, no anger in his gaze. He's looking at me as if he might . . . like me.

Yeah, right—you have completely lost your mind.

"You'll help me?"

"That's my job." I nod.

"You'll meet with me twice a week? Monday and Wednesday?"

I nod again. "Yeah." Clearing my throat, I sit up straighter. "Yes. I will."

He smiles. I like his smile. His teeth are straight. His lips are temptation. "Then we have a deal, Chelsea. See you Monday."

Before I can say goodbye, he's up and out of the chair, fleeing the room in a rush. I can almost believe he was never there in the first place.

Almost.

CHAPTER 4

*See the light in others, and treat them as if that is
all you see.*
—Dr. Wayne Dyer

Monday #1

Owen

My weekend dragged on for what felt like forever. Friday,
after making sure my paycheck was direct deposited into my
account, I cruised to the bank and took out some cash, then
texted Mom to meet me. I handed over a stack of twenties
and she took them greedily, her eyes wide, her mouth curved
in what I suppose was a smile.

Later she brought over two twelve-packs to the house and
we got high together, though really I only took one puff. It
bothers me, doing that with her. I'm to the point where I can't
stand it. And I only smoke with her when no one else is around.

I don't need the guilt, or the weird looks. Wade knows my
relationship with my mom is twenty flavors of fucked up, but
Des doesn't. He thinks my life is sunshine and roses.

Irritated with everything going down in my life, especially
Mom, I got her to leave pretty quickly and she went without
protest, happy because she was high as hell and had a pocket
full of cash.

I made a mental bet with myself she'd be back within a week, needing more.

Wade, Des, and I hung out together all weekend when I wasn't working, and considering my boss cut my hours because the owner said he had to, I was glad to be working at all. We drank beer, watched shitty movies, and talked about nothing in particular. The usual. I wanted to forget my troubles. The fact that I wasn't able to play in this weekend's game ate at me, though I tried to not worry about it. Still, I was pissed when Wade was gone, playing without me.

Looking for a distraction, I was glad when a couple of girls came over late Friday night. But I realized quickly that I didn't want to deal with them. I don't remember their names, even though one sat on my lap, stroking my hair, whispering in my ear how hot I was and how much she wanted me. I let her do it, my attention focused on the shit movie rather than her, and I know it pissed her off. I wasn't into her. So she left me and went and sat on Wade's lap.

Pretty sure he scored with that one.

I worked Saturday night. The rush of the dinner crowd kept me busy, my brain occupied, which I needed. My shift was till eleven but I stayed later, past midnight because it got so busy, and I helped out wherever I could. The tips were extra good and I stashed the cash in a secret spot in my closet, in the pocket of one of my old jackets. Fabes taught me that trick.

Hopefully I'd be able to hang on to some of the money and not have to give it all up to Mom.

Each night I lay awake in bed for way too long, thinking about my tutor. Chelsea. It's as if I can't stop thinking about her, which is pointless. Stupid. Remembering how I found her resting her head on the table, fast asleep. Her pink lips parted, her breathing even, looking like a dark-haired angel. She'd been incredibly still, fascinating to watch, and doing so made me feel like a voyeur. Seeing her like that felt like an incredibly intimate experience I had no business being a part of.

And when I touched her? I don't know what made me do that. Her brown hair looked like silk, and I wanted to see if it felt like silk, too.

It did.

When she stirred, I yanked my hand back as if I'd just touched fire and got burned. No way did I want her knowing I had my fingers in her hair. She'd probably freak out. I don't think she likes me much.

I make her uncomfortable and sick asshole that I am, I like it. I pushed her on purpose last Thursday. Wanting to see a reaction, needing to see her cheeks turn pink and her lids slide down so they were covering those too-blue eyes. She has thick, dark eyelashes and a sprinkling of freckles, just like I thought.

Never knew I had a thing for freckles, but I've come to realize I might.

You don't even know this girl. What gives?

When did knowing a girl ever matter to me before?

Sunday I didn't do shit. Slept in, lay around in bed until finally Wade asked if I wanted to order a pizza for dinner. I agreed and pulled out the assignment sheet Chelsea gave me while we waited for the delivery guy. What I needed to do to catch up and get my grade out of the gutter wasn't that bad. Answer short essay questions about books we were supposed to have read that I haven't yet. Or questions asking for our opinion on a certain topic—simple stuff that I could handle. I found one of the assigned books for cheap and downloaded it on my phone.

After I wolfed down half the damn pizza I worked on a

few of my assignments, feeling like I'd actually accomplished something when I finished two of them. I thought of how much that might please Chelsea and that spurred me on, making me finish another assignment after I skimmed the other assigned book, which I finally found under my bed.

Now here I am moving down the crowded hall, pushing through the throng of students, anxious to reach the room where I know Chelsea's waiting for me. I'd put on jeans and a brand-new black T-shirt I picked up in a pack at Walmart, throwing one of my favorite old flannel shirts over it because it got damn cold outside. The sky is gloomy and gray; I think it might rain, and I wonder how long the decent weather will last before summer leaves us for good.

I finally find the room and see that the door is closed. Approaching it, trepidation fills me. What am I doing? Why do I look forward to seeing her? She's nothing. Nobody. She's not even that attractive.

Liar.

Fine. She's cute. But nothing special. I don't understand why I feel this way.

Clutching the door handle, I push it open and walk inside. She's sitting at the same table, hunched over her cell phone and tapping away at the screen. Texting someone, no doubt. I wonder who.

A friend, a family member, a . . . boyfriend?

I don't like the idea of her having a guy and I sort of find it hard to imagine, too, though that makes me sound like a dick. But she gives off that untouchable vibe. Chicks like that normally don't interest me whatsoever. *Fine, you don't want me to touch you, let alone look at you? No problem.*

So why does seeing Chelsea make me want to touch her all over?

Focus, asshole.

"Hey." Her soft voice breaks through my thoughts and I glance up, meet her gaze to see she's smiling at me. Seeing that smile shoots a zing straight through my heart, but I ignore it. "You made it."

Flicking my chin at her in greeting, I settle in the chair across from her, not right next to her like last time. I'd done that to rattle her before. It had worked. But not today. Today I'm thinking we need to act like she's my tutor and I'm her student.

"I completed a few assignments," I tell her as I unzip my backpack and dig through it, pulling out the three assignments I worked on last night. "Here you go." I hand them to her.

Chelsea's entire face brightens as she takes the papers from me, our fingers grazing, her gaze roving over each page as she looks through them. "I'm so glad you did this. Did you go to class?"

I nod. It had been kind of hard, because I was behind in assignments and it was difficult to keep pace, but I pretended to keep up as well as I could. "Went to my Creative Writing class, too."

"That's the one class I'm looking forward to working on with you. I've heard it's your secret talent," she says, grabbing her phone so she can shove it into her backpack before she opens up my academic file.

"I have lots of special talents." When she glances up to look at me with a frown, I raise my brows at her, trying to look like an egotistical ass.

She rolls her eyes. "I'm sure," she says sarcastically, but her cheeks are tinged with pink, giving away her discomfort at my dirty joke. *Cute.* Most girls would flirt right back or call me out on it.

"So what do I have due in the Creative Writing class?" I

may as well get it out in the open and make it happen. The faster I can get through this, the faster I can get rid of her and get on with my life.

"You could start on these shorter assignments. They're quick and should be easy for you." She hands me a sheet of paper and I take it, glancing over the missing assignments and the requirements they have before I turn them in.

Great. I need to actually create and keep a portfolio of my writing for the entire semester. Considering I'm already about six weeks behind, I have a lot of catching up to do. At this rate, I'm never going to get back on the football team.

Fuck that.

"Can I ask you a question?"

She glances up at me with startled wide eyes, her lips parted. "Um, sure."

"Do you really think I can catch up on all of these assignments quick enough so I can get back on the field and play the rest of the season?" My heart feels like it's nearly stopped as I wait for her answer.

Chelsea sinks her teeth in her lower lip, flicking her gaze away from mine. "I . . . don't know. You have a lot of missing assignments."

"Will you help me?" I clear my throat, hating how hopeful and pleading I sound. I don't beg. If shit doesn't go my way, I let it go.

But I can't let this go. School, football, my sister's approval . . . I need it. I want it.

"I *am* helping you." Chelsea smiles, her voice soft, her eyes filled with this sparkly glow that's pretty damn mesmerizing.

"I know. You are. Can you help me more, though? Like with the portfolio and stuff? Maybe I can see you more than just twice a week?"

She blinks, looking at me as though I've lost my mind for making the suggestion. "I don't know . . ."

"I'll pay you," I interrupt.

"Of course you'll pay me," she retorts, making me smile. Okay, my tutor is a little feisty. Good. I was hoping she had a backbone. "It's just that I have a pretty packed schedule."

"Tutoring around the clock, huh?" I lean back in my chair, curious to hear what's keeping her so busy.

"Well, no. Not exactly."

"Heavy class load?" I suggest.

"Definitely that." She nods.

"Your social calendar is jammed with upcoming events." I don't even know where I'm coming up with this crap. "I'm guessing you're part of a sorority, right?"

She laughs, scrunching her nose. "Not quite. And no, I'm definitely not in a sorority."

"Steady boyfriend who never lets you out of his sight?" Okay. I threw that last one out because I had to fucking hear it. Does she have someone? Even a casual someone? I'd like to know. Why, I'm not exactly sure, because I don't have plans on ever doing anything with this girl, but I'm curious.

Her cheeks turn this rosy pink as she drops her head, studying my open file with rapt attention. I know it can't be that interesting. "No. No boyfriend."

Relief surges through me, which is absolutely ridiculous. I should not care.

"How about you?" she asks. "Do you have a girlfriend?" Her voice shakes on the last word and I stare at her, willing her to look up, but she doesn't.

"Nope. No girlfriend," I mimic her answer. She lifts her head at that and I find myself momentarily lost in her gaze. Stupid. "Why do you ask? Hoping for a chance?" I smirk at her like the asshole I am, because I can't help myself.

She grimaces. "Yeah, right."

Ouch. I bet she looks at me and sees a dumb jock, which is kind of true. She probably likes brainy, skinny dudes who study all day and never make a sexual move on her. They probably make her feel safe.

I am the farthest thing from safe for her, especially when I look at her and all I can think about is what she looks like naked.

Fucking get over it, Maguire. This chick is not your type.

"I have another job, I'm taking sixteen units this semester, and my tutoring schedule is the heaviest I've ever had," she explains. "So it's going to be sort of hard to fit you in for extra help. I'm sure you're busy, too."

I am. But not at the moment, what with my reduced work schedule and my temporary suspension from the football team. "Not as busy as I was last week, that's for sure. Listen." Leaning forward, I rest my forearms on the table, trying to get close to her so I can get my point across. "I've got to accelerate these tutoring sessions. I need to get back onto the team. I—"

"Why?"

I lean back. "What?"

"Why do you need to get back on the team?"

Because I want to get in my sister's good graces again. I don't want Fable mad at me anymore. And maybe if I'm too busy, Mom will eventually give up and stop hassling me. That last one is pure bullshit. In my dreams Mom will stop coming by and begging for money. "They need me."

She studies me closely and I'm tempted to look away, but I hold my ground. I have the distinct feeling she doesn't believe me, but what do I care? "Then write about that."

"What?" I ask again like I'm stuck on repeat.

"Write about how much your team needs you. There's

your first piece for your portfolio." Chelsea smiles, looking awfully pleased with herself. "And you're welcome."

Chelsea

He is *waaay* too good-looking. Sitting this close, asking me super-uncomfortable questions like whether I have a boyfriend. I mean, talk about awkward. Why does he care? And because he asked, I had to ask back, under the pretense that I want to know how busy he is.

Please. I'm dying of curiosity to know if he has a steady girl, because he's definitely good-looking enough to have one. He's a total catch, though maybe not so much on the intelligence part.

Well. That's a lie. I've looked at his academic file. I probably know it by heart. He's smart; he's just not applying himself. Something's distracting him and I don't know if it's football or whatever, but he's barely bothering going to class.

Right now, he's tapping away at the keyboard of the laptop he pulled out of his backpack a few minutes ago. That was sort of fun, suggesting the story idea. Here he was, trying to wheel and deal with me, convince me to meet with him more often, when really the guy just needed to focus and actually work.

"You should go to class, too, you know," I suggest out of the blue, causing him to peer at me from above his laptop. "That all counts toward your grade. The more absences you have, the worse your grade becomes."

"It's gonna take more than me showing up in class to improve my grades enough to get back on the team quick, and you know it," he says, annoyance tingeing his voice. "I'll consider your advice, though."

"Good." I nod, feeling stupid. And I never feel stupid with

anyone. I'm the smart one. I've been told more often than not that I'm the one that makes others feel dumb. Uncomfortable. Or they flat-out don't like me, think I'm some sort of freak of nature with the too-big brain and the thieving father.

Blowing out a harsh breath, I push all thoughts of my dad from my head and slap Owen's file shut, grabbing a textbook out of my backpack and setting it on the table with a loud thump.

Owen doesn't even glance up from his laptop screen, his fingers tapping rhythmically on the keyboard, and I'm glad to see him getting into it. This is what he needed. A push, the realization that hey, he'd better get to work before he fails and ruins everything.

He can handle it, though. I know he can.

I flip open the textbook and start reading, feeling bad that I'm giving him no real direction, but what else am I supposed to do? He's the one who needs to do the work. There's nothing else I can do but wait him out while he writes. So I may as well work on my own assignments to pass the time.

It's either that or stare at him unabashedly while he works.

Stealing a glance at him, I drink him in, my breath stalling in my throat at the sight before me. His brows are furrowed in concentration, his mouth scrunched, those pretty green eyes narrowed as he stares at his laptop screen. His fingers keep up an impressive pace and he looks up, catches me staring at him.

His fingers pause and I hurriedly look down, staring unseeingly at the words in front of me while deep inside, my heart is racing a bazillion miles a minute.

He doesn't resume typing for a while and I slowly start to realize it's because he's still staring at me. I can feel the weight of his gaze pressing on me, burning my skin, making me want to squirm in my chair. I refuse to look back up, resting my elbow on the table so I can prop my cheek on my fist, hiding my face from his eyes.

"Must be real interesting," he drawls. "What you're reading."

There's no hiding for me. He can see right through my act.

"Fascinating," I murmur, not even sure what the heck I'm reading, since the words are all blurry thanks to my gonehazy vision. All I can think about is him. Owen. Watching me and teasing me, the scent of his cologne and soap and shampoo and whatever else he uses tickling my senses. That spicy, autumnal scent that's driving me crazier the deeper I breathe him in.

"What's it about?"

I still refuse to look at him. "Shouldn't you worry about your own work?"

"Sorry." Now he sounds irritated. *Great.* "Just trying to make conversation."

"Don't you want to get a move on this stuff so you can get back to playing for your team?" I finally drop my hand and look at him. Really look at him, and I can tell my words affect him.

He doesn't need to antagonize me when he should be using his time much more wisely.

"You're right." Heaving a big sigh, he starts typing again, his fingers going clackety-clack upon the keys. "Keep me on track, Chelsea. I think I'm going to need it for the next few weeks, months, whatever. Need *you*."

Those two words pound a restless rhythm in my soul the rest of the time I sit with him. The entire walk back to the tiny apartment I share with Kari, I feel those simple words pulse in my blood with every step I take. I hope she's not home because I want to sit alone on the couch, in the dark quiet, and savor the simple words.

Need. You.

I'm probably insane for thinking this way. Boys don't matter. Boys are bad. Look at my father. He's done nothing but hurt Mom their entire marriage. That she still supports him and remains married to him despite everything he's done makes me want to hit something.

Preferably my father.

I don't romanticize anything. I'm straightforward in how I think, what I do. Everything has a cause and an effect. A reason. And there is absolutely no reason for me to react this way when it comes to Owen. I hardly know him, and what I know of him doesn't impress me.

But I want him. I want to keep looking at him, get to know him. I want to know what it feels like to have him touch me. I want to touch his lips and see if they're as soft as they look. I want to feel his arm slide around me and hold me close. I want to . . .

My cell rings just as I approach the front door of my apartment. Pulling the phone from my pocket, I check who the caller is and answer. "Are you home?"

"Nope, and you won't be either when I come and pick you up in twenty minutes," Kari says cheerily, in this tone that tells me she's up to no good.

"What's going on?" I ask as I unlock the door and enter the apartment. It's quiet and dark, would have been the perfect scenario for me to sit and go over what happened with Owen earlier again and again, but . . .

Kari is totally ruining that option. And she's not even home.

"We're going out for drinks. I talked to these two cute guys in the library and they asked if we wanted to meet up with them later tonight."

"Kari. I'm not even old enough to *order* a drink." Uneasiness slips over me, settling low in my stomach. If they want to meet for drinks, they are most likely older. They'd probably run screaming the minute they met me. Kari's good at the flirtatious, carefree thing. Me, not so much. "Who are these guys?"

"I don't know, but they're pretty. And when I say pretty, I mean gorgeous. They're in a frat." At my hesitation she rattles on. She knows I'm going to say no or come up with some sort of excuse. She's got me all figured out. "Hey, we can just drink water and eat appetizers, Chelsea. We don't have to tell them we're not old enough for alcohol." Kari mutters something unintelligible. "I'm telling you, we need to get fake IDs, and soon."

The very last thing I want to do is get a fake ID. I'm not about to get into trouble with the law. "Where do they want to meet us?"

"The District." Kari's voice is practically vibrating. Her excitement is infectious. I can feel it bubble up inside of me despite my apprehension. "I've never been, and you know I've been dying to go there."

Kari wasn't exaggerating. The young, beautiful, and very trendy types hang out at The District. Kari would definitely fit in.

Me? Not really.

I set my backpack on the tiny kitchen table and go sit on the couch, heaving a big sigh. "I don't know. I have home—"

"If you say you have homework, I'm going to beat you." Kari's voice is so fierce I don't doubt her threat for a second. "You never, ever go out. Ever. You're going to shrivel up and die an old maid if you don't at least make an attempt at a social life. Despite what your mom says, and who is she to talk, boys are not the devil. They're actually a lot of fun if you'd just talk to one once in your life. Come on, Chelsea."

Her voice takes on that pleading sound that tends to work on me. "Do it for me. We'll have fun."

I want to believe her. I desperately want to fit in. It's been a struggle since I was nine and they accelerated me into the sixth grade when I should have been in the fourth. The older kids wanted nothing to do with me; the younger ones thought I'd ditched them and ignored me. I've been an outsider ever since.

Even now. Kari's the only one who stuck by me, even when we were in different grades. Look at her now, my room-mate, helping me out. Trying to get me dates.

"For once in your life you should ignore your responsibility and go hang out with a boy. Have some innocent fun and kiss him." I start to protest but she cuts me off. "I'm dead serious. There is nothing wrong with meeting a guy, flirting with him, have a little make-out session, and then move on. It's called being young."

My problem is I don't know how to be young. I've been saddled with all of this intense responsibility all my life. If it's not trying to keep up my grades, it's trying to take care of Mom when Dad's ditched her yet again.

I swear I'm a middle-aged woman trapped in a teenage body.

"Fine," I say, sounding all put out, feeling all put out, too. I don't want to do this. But I don't want Kari to hate me, ei-ther. I never go out with her. I'm always studying or working or avoiding real life so I don't get hurt. I'd rather lock myself up in my room and study when I don't really need to than go out and have fun.

Fun . . . scares me.

"Yay! You won't regret this, I promise. I'll be home in an hour. I told them we'd meet up around nine or so. We can hunt through my closet for something for you to wear and you're going to look smokin' hot. Trust me." Kari prattles on, talking about makeup and hair and whatever else. I'm really not paying attention. All I can think about is another boy. Someone else I'd rather impress, but he doesn't really see me like that.

I'm just the girl who's helping him out. Some nameless, faceless brain who'll get him where he wants to be. He'll forget all about me once he's finished.

Just like everyone else does.

CHAPTER 5

*Know then that the body is merely a garment. Go seek
the wearer, not the cloak.*
—Rumi

Chelsea

Their names are Tad and Brad.

I'm not kidding, though I wish I were. Why didn't Kari
warn me about this? I mean, really? Tad and Brad? They're
not twins, they look nothing alike, but they're fraternity
brothers, and they're both big and beefy, their arms bulging
with muscles. They almost seem to revel in the fact that their
names match. Like it's some sort of gimmick to meet people—
specifically girls.

So. Cheesy.

Kari acts like it's the cutest thing ever—like these two
shady dudes are the perfect matches for us. She attached herself to Brad's side the moment we arrived and found our dates
sitting in the lounge area of The District, which is just off
the bar. He's the better-looking of the two, with golden hair,
pale blue eyes, and an easy smile. Too easy of a smile, if you
ask me.

But she's not asking me, so I keep my opinions to myself.

I'm stuck with Tad. He's darker, as in darker hair, darker
mood, darker words. Whereas Brad is bright and sunny and
trying to put on the charm, Tad is rather serious, with somber

53

brown eyes, and only offering the rare smile. He's never without a full drink, even after we've been there for a couple of hours.

And the more he drinks, the handier he gets. I'm not referring to him as being helpful, either. He's constantly trying to touch me. Grazing my arm with his fingers, resting his hand on my knee. He even tried to place his hand on my thigh, which I immediately shoved off.

Bad enough I'm worried about getting caught sitting in the bar when I'm underage, though I'm not even drinking. It's even worse that I have to fight off Tad the Octopus every few minutes.

The night started off so promising, too. I'd actually had fun getting ready with Kari. She'd found a super-cute top for me to wear from her closet. Cream colored, with three-quarter sleeves, the front is cotton but the sleeves and almost the entire back are made of lace. With a tank underneath it, I felt sort of daring and free. Totally not myself at all.

I liked it.

All that confidence is gone now, though. I'm ready to bolt. And Kari is definitely not ready to leave. Brad has his arm around her shoulders and he's whispering something in her ear, nudging his nose against her cheek and making her giggle. He'd offered his beer to Kari multiple times and she never refused him, sipping greedily with his encouragement. I think she's a little drunk.

That's my cue to get us out of here.

"Sure you don't want something a little stronger?" Tad asks, leering at me as he holds out his glass. He's been drinking the harder stuff, no beer for him, and no way am I drinking anything from his glass.

Recoiling, I scoot away from him as discreetly as possible.

We're sitting on these low, very comfortable couches that are formed in a U-shape. Brad and Kari sit across from us, a glass-topped table in between. "No thanks," I say weakly, feeling bad about refusing him and irritated that I've been put in this spot in the first place.

Never again will I believe Kari when she says, "Oh, it'll be fun!"

"Shit," Tad mutters, taking a swig from his drink before turning his glare on me. "You need to loosen the hell up."

His remark has the opposite effect. I stiffen my spine, resting my hands on my knees like some sort of prim-and-proper schoolgirl—which I am. "I think maybe you should lay off the alcohol," I suggest timidly.

He sneers. "Jesus, what are you? Some sort of uptight little virgin?"

Flinching, I look away from him. His remark cuts too close to home and he yelled it loud enough for anyone to hear. Despite how noisy the bar and lounge are, filled with chatter and music, we receive more than a few stares in our direction.

I can't stand him.

Ignoring Tad, I turn my focus onto Kari, desperate to get her attention. Brad has his arm around her neck, pulling her in close so he can kiss her. If I lose her now, I'm done for, so I move quickly, grabbing a piece of ice out of my mostly empty water glass and tossing it at her.

My aim is perfect—the ice cube hits her right in the chest and she yelps, turning her attention on me. "What?" she asks, sounding totally put out.

Not that I can blame her. I'm the priss; she's the party girl. I'm the uptight virgin; she's the one who's letting some guy she barely knows maul her and kiss her in the middle of a public bar.

Somehow our friendship works most of the time, but tonight I need to end this. This is one part of our lives where we totally don't mesh.

"Can I talk to you for a minute?" I ask, keeping my voice low. "Privately?"

Rolling her eyes, she withdraws from underneath Brad's arm and murmurs something to him before she stands. I do the same, not acknowledging Tad whatsoever, and Kari and I head to the bathroom, neither of us talking until we've made our way inside.

Luckily enough, we're alone, which is like a small miracle, and I know I don't have much time before someone does come in here, so I just blurt out what I want to say.

"I'm leaving."

"No way." She shakes her head, irritation written all over her pretty face. Her hair is a deep, rich auburn, thick and wavy. She has hazel eyes that change color depending on her mood and what she's wearing. With her flawless skin and perfect figure, she's beautiful, both inside and out. She's my best friend.

I know she means well but I'm so uncomfortable with this situation, I can't get over it. I have to go.

"You're having fun, I get it. You really like Brad." I lower my voice, as if I'm afraid the two guys are going to bust into the ladies' room at any minute. Ridiculous. "But Tad . . . he's not my type."

Kari raises a brow. "Why not?"

"Well, for one thing, he called me an uptight virgin." I return the gesture, raising both of my brows back at her.

Kari sighs, shaking her head. "You know, he might have a point."

My jaw drops. *Say what?*

"Hear me out." She holds her hands up, like she knows

I'm about to tear into her. "You really do need to loosen up, Chelsea. I know you're kind of socially awkward, and that all has to do with the age difference and you graduating school and coming to college so early. But Tad is kind of right. You really *are* an uptight virgin."

Holy crap. I can't believe Kari is saying this to me. "Thanks a lot," I mutter, crossing my arms in front of my chest. My heart hurts, my mind tumbling over what they both said. Again and again.

Uptight virgin.

Am I really that uptight? Do people look at me and immediately think *virgin*? Probably. I guess that's better than thinking I'm a big nerd.

I slump my shoulders in defeat. It's not that much better. I am the quintessential nerdy virgin. They should make a movie about me. I even have the titillating angle of my dad being in prison for fraud. At the very least, I'm a Lifetime movie waiting to happen.

"Hey." She grabs hold of my shoulders and crushes me to her, giving me a hug. I don't uncross my arms, just stand there awkwardly while she holds me close. "I'm not trying to hurt your feelings. You've been at this college for the last two years and you haven't done anything wild or rebellious. But now I'm here to help you break out of your shell so you can have a little fun for once in your life. You deserve it, Chelsea. You've been pretending to live your life. Now you actually need to go out and do it. Find a hot guy and make out with him."

Not with a creeper named Tad who calls me rude names. "This isn't working out with Tad. I want to go home."

Kari withdraws from me, her expression forlorn. "You can't just leave me here alone."

Guilt swamps me. When Kari and I moved in together, we

made a vow never to leave the other alone at parties, on campus . . . anywhere. "I was kind of hoping you would go home with me."

Can't she see what she's doing? She broke up with her boyfriend from high school when they moved here and he realized there was more to this world than just him and Kari. And now she's running into the arms of another guy who's probably only going to use her? I don't get it.

Sometimes I feel like I'm the only logical person on this entire campus, I swear.

"Are you serious? It's barely midnight! God." She glances around the tiled bathroom, as if she'd rather look anywhere else but at me. "Come on, Chelsea. I really like Brad and I really think he likes me. I'm not going to call this night over so early when there's still so much that can—happen. I don't want to leave."

So she leaves me no choice. "Fine. I *am* leaving. I'll let you explain what happened to Tad." I storm out of the bathroom, not even bothering to look back when I hear Kari yelling after me. Pushing my way through the crowded bar area, I break free, moving down the short hall that spills out into the front lobby of the restaurant. The dining area is to my right and it's mostly empty, since it's a Monday night.

Doesn't matter what night it is in a college town, though. The bar is always in full swing.

I push open the front door, walking out into the cold fall night. I didn't bring a coat of any kind and the air seeps through the lace of my borrowed top with quick speed, chilling me to the bone. A shiver passes over me and I glance around, wondering how the heck I am going to get home.

Normally, Kari and I would walk even though we live kind of far. Stupid, I know, but hey, we're safer together than alone, right? Considering I *am* alone, no way am I walking tonight. Calling a cab would be pricey and I'd probably have to wait a while, but I don't really have a choice.

Pulling out my cell, I start scrolling online, looking for a taxi service, when I hear someone call my name. I glance over my shoulder to see it's Tad.

Great.

"Hey." He approaches me, his expression full of—worry? I must be seeing things. "Are you okay?"

I offer him a weak smile and a weaker excuse. "I'm fine, really. Just . . . tired."

"Um, sorry for what I said earlier." He shuffles his feet, dropping his head so he can stare at the ground. "It was a total jerk thing to do."

"Yeah. It's okay." I want to smack myself for saying it's okay when it so isn't.

"So you're leaving?"

I nod and glance down at my phone again. I really need to call a taxi so I can get away from Tad. He may be acting nice now, but I don't trust him.

I don't really trust anyone.

"I can take you home," he offers.

My head snaps up and I study him. He looks sincere, but there's something about his eyes . . . they're too dark, too hard. A little mean-looking. It would save me megabucks if I rode home with him so I didn't have to pay for a taxi, but I don't want to take any chances. Something about Tad makes me uneasy. This guy has ulterior motives written all over him.

"I appreciate the offer, but I'm going to have to pass." I try for the apologetic smile to ease my refusal, but all he does is frown at me.

"You won't even take a ride from me. First you treat me

like shit and will hardly talk to me and now you won't even get in my car? I mean, what the hell? Do you think you're too good for me or what?" Tad spits out at me.

I'm in shock. Too good for him? What is he talking about? "I'm not trying to offend you . . ."

"Too late," he interrupts, grabbing hold of my arm with so much force I yelp. "Though you'll make it up to me if you let me take you home."

There's no way I want this idiot to know where I live. "Let me go," I say, trying to jerk out of his grip, but he's holding on too tight. Any tighter and I'm afraid he'll bruise my skin.

"Come on, Chelsea. Loosen up, would you? This virginal act has got to go." Tad's whining now, which is almost as bad as angry Tad. "I'm just looking for a little fun."

So not the kind of fun I was talking about with Kari earlier. "Tad, please . . ."

"Let her go."

The familiar deep voice comes from behind us and I turn on a gasp to find Owen Maguire standing there, glaring at Tad like he wants to rip his head off. Relief floods me, heady and strong, as Tad loosens his grip, and I swear I sway a little when he lets me go.

"I don't want any trouble," Tad says, backing away from me with his hands up in front of him, his eyes never leaving Owen.

"Then keep moving and you won't have any," Owen practically growls as he stalks toward us so he's standing right next to me, his expression menacing as he stares Tad down.

Wow. No guy has ever come to my rescue quite like that before. Owen looks fierce, too, his hands clutched into fists at his side, his brows drawn down, eyes cold and mouth grim. Tad turns and breaks into a run, where to I'm not sure. I'm just glad he's gone.

Breathing deep, I turn to look at Owen, startled when I find him already looking right at me. "Thank you," I say, irritated when my voice comes out some breathy little whisper like I'm a dumbstruck girl.

Which I am. Not that I would ever admit it.

"What were you doing with that guy?" he asks, sounding irritated and looking mad. And hot.

Like, all sorts of hot. Those intense green eyes latch onto me like they're never going to let me go and he turns more fully toward me, his broad shoulders blocking my view. Gosh, he's tall! I tip my head back, trying to ignore the wave of yearning that washes over me at his nearness. He seems to make my brain short-circuit every time I get close to him.

"Um, my friend and I met up with him and his friend for a drink," I explain, wincing when I see his eyes widen.

"Aren't you underage?" he asks incredulously.

"Aren't *you*?" I toss back. God, he has some nerve. Who is he to talk?

"I *work* here. I'm not trying to sneak in and have a few drinks." He says the words as if he's passing judgment, but I see the waver in his gaze. I would bet big money he's done the very same thing, though probably not here since he claims he works here. "Where's your friend?"

"Inside." I wave my hand toward the door.

"And she didn't leave with you?" He shakes his head. "Some friend."

"Hey, don't knock her. Kari's my best friend." Practically the only friend I have.

"Could've fooled me. I thought best friends take care of each other."

Talk about cutting straight to the bone. "That was totally uncalled for." I tilt my head, lifting my nose to the air with a tiny sniff. My dad may have lost all our money and left us

61

broke while he languishes in prison, but I can still pull off that haughty rich-girl attitude when I need to.

Tad's words come back at me. Am I acting like I'm too good for Owen? I feel so defensive with him. Why does this guy affect me so much? It's unnerving how attracted I am to him. No guy does this to me and here I am, all hot and bothered and feeling a little feverish. All over a guy.

"Only speaking the truth," he says with a shrug. "Do you have a way home?"

"I do."

"How?" He looks skeptical, which he should. I can't pull anything on anyone, I swear.

"I'm calling a cab." I open up my phone again, once more searching for a taxi. "Thank you for helping me," I add, always polite, always so freaking good and never doing anything outrageous or wrong. Too afraid to get in trouble so I don't stray.

"Chelsea." He snags the phone from my hand and I lift my head on a gasp. Who does he think he is? I make a grab for my cell, but he's holding the phone above his head. Like a stupid little kid, I jump up and try to grab it from him. He laughs, but it's sorta grim-sounding, and I wonder what's wrong with me.

I feel . . . giddy. Did Tad spike my water or my Coke or something? I don't feel right. My head is spinning and goose bumps dot my skin when I brush against Owen. He's wearing a white button-down shirt that's rumpled from what I can only assume is a hard day's work and black pants. He looks cute.

Fine. He's more than cute. He's gorgeous. And sexy. I never think a guy is sexy. Owen sure is.

And maybe that's my problem.

Owen

I hold her phone over my head because I'm enjoying her hopping and try to get it. Her tits bounce with every jump and though they're not huge, I'm still checking them out. That lace top she's wearing is interesting, offering me a glimpse of skin that's not overtly sexy but still sorta hot.

And then there's that ass of hers, which is the stuff of dreams. I'm getting a sick thrill out of watching her jump up and down so I can see that tight little ass move with her every hop.

Yeah. Clearly I need to get laid if this chick's ass can get my blood pumping.

"Give me my phone." She sounds irritated as hell and her face is scrunched up adorably.

"Not until you agree to let me take you home." No way am I going to leave her alone so she can get a taxi when I can do the job.

And no way am I doing this to spend a little extra time with my tutor, either. She was the last person I expected to see standing out in front of my work, fighting off some jackass with grabby hands. I'd just ended my shift, totally exhausted and ready to go home and crawl into bed, when there she appeared, gorgeous in those jeans that fit her like a second skin, showing off those long legs and that . . .

Grimacing, I shake my head. I need to get over my fixation with her ass.

"Fine. Take me home, then." She sounds completely irritated. "Now give me my phone."

"Not until you thank me for the ride." I'm playing games with her and actually enjoying myself. I haven't enjoyed . . . anything for a while. I'm too stressed out. Everyone wants something from me and I keep fucking up. I can't seem to get my shit together.

She rests her hands on her hips, scowling at me. "You haven't even given me the ride yet."

"I know." I grin and her scowl deepens. I wonder if she hates me specifically, or does she hate all guys in general? "You're not going to like this, but we have to walk back to my place first, pick up my car, and then I can drive you home."

"Wait a minute. Your car's not here?"

"I live ridiculously close. I walk to work." I shrug. Everyone thinks I'm freaking crazy. They all know who I'm tied to at The District, especially since my sister used to work there. That I walk to work and try to keep everything low key when I could let everyone know the NFL's newest superstar, Drew Callahan, is my brother-in-law blows their minds.

I'm not about that kind of shit, though. Being obvious only causes trouble. I can just imagine how much greedier my mom would be if I got all flashy like that.

When Chelsea doesn't say anything, I take that to mean she's being agreeable. "Ready to go?" I start walking and she falls into step beside me, both of us quiet as we head toward my house. I live right downtown, among the older homes and the frat and sorority houses, not too far from campus. I like being so close, in the midst of everything. Fable thinks I'm crazy, but she got nothing but grief from all of those college types—specifically the type of guys I hang out with now.

Drew put a stop to all that. He's Fable's freaking hero. At times, he's been mine, too.

I glance down at Chelsea, who's taking about five steps to keep up with one of mine. Her head is bent against the wind that's blowing over us and she has her arms wrapped around herself like she's cold.

I'm tempted to slip my arm around her shoulders and pull her into me to warm her up, because I'm hot as hell after working a busy night, but I restrain myself. First, I probably smell, not that I'm trying to impress her or anything. Second, she'd probably punch me in the gonads if I tried to touch her. She's on edge and I can't blame her. That stupid loser was trying to manhandle her. What would have happened if I hadn't been there to stop it?

"Thank you for helping me get rid of Tad," she says, her voice soft.

She's a mind reader. "No problem."

"I didn't want to be there tonight. At The District," she goes on. "It was all Kari's idea. She set me up with Tad and he turned out to be a total jerk."

Weak statement. The guy was more like a total asshole. "Maybe you shouldn't let your friend set you up with guys you don't know."

"No kidding," she mutters. "Though it's really the only way I meet guys."

"What about the ones you tutor?" Hell, listen to me. I sound like a wimp trying to figure out how she meets guys. I shouldn't care. I shouldn't be attracted to her. I need to find some hot chick with an amazing ass and fuck her brains out. Fuck Chelsea right out of my head so I won't think about her anymore.

I don't know if that would work, though. The thought of finding some random chick and getting laid doesn't appeal whatsoever.

"The ones I tutor . . . I consider it—them—work." She looks up at me and our gazes meet. I don't look away. Neither does she. "Usually," she adds, sinking her teeth into her lower lip.

65

Okay. I need to pretend she never said that. Because my body is reacting all over the place as if she just whispered, *Fuck me, Owen.*

"What do you mean, 'usually'?" There I go, not pretending at all.

Shrugging, she tears her gaze away from mine, looking anywhere but at me. "I don't know."

I let it go, hoping that she's talking about me. Why, I'm not sure. I shove my hands in my pockets and slow my pace, contemplating her. I can see her skin through the lace of her shirt, though she's wearing a skimpy tank top that covers most of her. The jeans—I'm not even going to bother going on about her legs and ass yet again because, damn.

There's nothing else I can say about that.

Her long, dark hair tumbles down her back, straight as can be. It looks soft. I want to touch it. Wrap those silky strands around my fingers and give it a tug while I lock my lips with hers. Tilt her head back farther so I can lick my way down her throat and feel her pulse thrumming beneath my mouth . . .

"Do we go straight?"

Her sweet voice knocks me from my lusty thoughts and I blink, realizing that I've stopped at a cross street. "Turn left," I say gruffly. "My place is three houses down on the left side."

She doesn't say a word, merely does what I tell her to, and I let her take the lead, admiring her from behind. I need to face facts: I'm hot for the tutor. She's not my type. I hardly know her. But my body sure as hell wants to get to know her. And this is stupid because I'm asking for nothing but trouble, thinking like this.

As we draw closer to my house, dread sinks over me. Every window is lit up, and I can hear music and loud voices. Fucking Wade is having a party.

Just great.

"Um." Chelsea stops and turns to look at me. "Is that your place?" She points at my house, where I can see Des and some chick I don't know sitting on the couch on the front porch, passing a joint back and forth.

Shit.

"Yeah," I say, my jaw tight. "Looks like my roommate is having a get-together."

"Some get-together," Chelsea mumbles, bouncing from one foot to the other. She looks nervous.

"Come on." I flick my head toward my house. "I'll just grab my keys and we'll get out of here."

My car is parked in front of the house on the street. We don't have a garage, and the house is old and small, but I fixed it up inside pretty well when I first moved in and automatically had Wade move in with me. We've been friends forever. I couldn't ditch him. I don't even make him pay rent.

Drew takes care of it all—he bought the place. Paid cash for it and everything. Someday, I'd like to have that sort of power, that kind of comfort.

Smoking weed with Mom, drinking too much beer, and partying most of the week is not going to get me there anytime soon.

"Um, I'll wait outside," Chelsea says, shuffling her feet. She looks uncomfortable and I hate that.

"Are you sure?" I'm not going to push her into any sort of situation she doesn't want to be in. Bad enough what I saw earlier with that asshole grabbing her. I won't put myself in the same league.

She nods, lifting her head so she meets my gaze. "It'll probably be—"

"Yo, Maguire! Who's the hottie?" Des calls from his perch on the couch.

A sigh escapes me and I try my best to send her an apologetic look before I say, "Wouldn't *you* like to know?"

"Motherfucker, don't be all mysterious on me. Bring your new girl up here and introduce her to us properly," Des yells, a goofy-ass grin on his face.

"Hell." I run a hand through my hair, then let my arm drop. "Do you mind? Des is harmless, though I don't know the girl."

"Kinda like he doesn't know me, right?" She flashes me a tentative smile and shrugs. "How are you going to introduce me?"

"How do you want to be introduced?" I toss back at her.

She grimaces. "I don't know. Your friend?"

I stare at her for a long moment. "They're going to think I'm fucking you."

Chelsea gapes, her mouth dropping open. "Are you serious?"

"They think I fuck every girl I bring around the house." I give them good reason to think that, too.

She actually flinches. "Do you have to keep saying that?"

"Saying what? 'Fuck'?"

"Yes." Her expression is pained. "It's so . . ."

"Fucking vulgar? Yeah." I laugh when she glares. I can't help it. "Sorry. Come on, let's get this over with. And be prepared. Plug your ears or something, because Des curses like a motherfucker."

CHAPTER 6

The mind that opens to a new idea never returns to its original size.
—Albert Einstein

Chelsea

Funny how I was at a bar with my best friend yet still felt incredibly uncomfortable. Powerless. Out of control.

Here I stand with a guy I barely know at a house I've never been to, with a crowd of rowdy people, total and complete strangers who are partying inside and are either drunk or high or both. And I'm not scared at all.

It's because I'm with Owen. He makes me feel safe.

I follow him as he approaches the front porch, my gaze going to his friend Des. Owen's right. The guy looks perfectly harmless, with a stupid smile on his face and a can of beer clutched in his hand like it's his precious lifeline. The girl with him is plastered to his side as best as she can be, all voluptuous curves and bottle-blond hair, with blood-red lips and blinding white teeth. She gives me a withering stare, dismissing me on sight.

Great. She hates me. I'm not a fan either.

"Des, what the hell are all of these people doing here?" Owen asks as he stops right in front of the couch. I come up behind him, then step to the side so I don't look like I'm hiding. I refuse to let the girl with the scary red lips intimidate me.

"I don't know, but I'm drinking a fucking beer and smoking a J," Des says as if he has zero cares in the world—which is probably pretty close to the truth. I recognize him. He was with Owen the night I saw them at the diner. "You should join me, bro. You look a little tense. Wade invited me over earlier and we decided to call a few friends. Figured you wouldn't fucking mind. I mean, look—you brought a guest and everything." Des waves his beer can at me.

"Yeah. Great." Owen runs a hand through his hair, something I notice he does when he's irritated. It's all messy and sexy and I want to grab hold of it, yank his head down to mine, and kiss him.

Yikes. What in the world is wrong with me, thinking like this?

"So who's your guest to our fancy party? She's pretty." Des smiles brilliantly at me. He's cute. Dark hair cropped close to his head, warm brown eyes that are rimmed with red from the joint-smoking.

Probably that cloud of smoke that still hovers above him is why he doesn't recognize me.

"Uh, this is Chelsea." That's all Owen says. Waves a hand at me like I don't matter, which hurts a little, but I push past it. I guess he's trying to not make this a big deal and I can't blame him. I'm just his tutor. I'm not important to him.

"Hi." I smile at Des, then cast a more wary smile in the blonde's direction.

"This is Marcy." Des shoots the blonde a lusty gaze, which she returns with gusto. "We just met. But we're already old fucking friends, right, Marcy?" She doesn't respond.

"Awesome," Owen mutters with a jerky shake of his

head. "We just stopped by to get my keys. I need to take Chelsea home."

"Don't go home, not yet! The party just started. Have a beer, smoke a bowl, fucking relax. Or maybe get relaxed by fucking around for a little bit. Whatever." Des laughs when Owen shoots him a disgusted look. "Man, since when did you turn into such a downer?"

Owen doesn't reply. I feel like things are being said without words and I'm not catching on. Not that I would. I don't know anything about Owen beyond his school file and what little information I've gleaned since meeting him.

We leave the porch and head into the house, which is filled with smoke, lots of people, and loud music. The kitchen is especially packed as they all drink beer either from cans or the infamous red cups. There's a keg on the dining room table, and I wonder just how spontaneous this party was.

Considering I have zero experience with keggers, I have no idea how easy it is to obtain kegs of beer.

Everyone in the room seems to look at me like they wonder where I came from, not that I can blame them. They don't know me. I'm sure they all know Owen. They're in his house, after all. And I'm just some silly girl pretending that she knows what it's like to be young and easy and carefree.

The girls glare. The guys stare. I feel like I'm on display, that Owen is lord and master of the house and if they could, they'd all bow to him and thank him for finally coming home.

Heaving out a big sigh, I push past my dramatic thoughts and keep close to Owen, not wanting to lose him since the deeper we get into the house, the more crowded it becomes. When he grabs hold of my hand and yanks me close, I literally gasp, surprised that he's actually touching me. His fingers curl around mine and I try to ignore the reaction that pulses through me from his touch, but I can't. I swear my knees just went weak.

He pulls me closer and I feel as though I'm going to die. I can smell him, autumn and sweat and the slightly stale scent of working in a restaurant for hours on end. "My keys are in my room," he yells into my ear. The music in the house is deafening. "Just keep close—we'll grab them and then we're out of here."

I nod and give him a smile, which he returns. The sight of it makes my heart go pitter-patter and I try to ignore it. This crush I have on my freaking student is so not appropriate.

Owen entwines our fingers and leads me through the crowd and down the short, dark hall, stopping at the door at the very end. He pushes it open and glances around, probably checking to see if anyone's in there, and then he's walking inside, leaving me no choice but to follow him since he's still holding my hand.

Disentangling myself from his grip, I look around, trying to take it all in while Owen goes in search of his keys. His walls are blank. The furniture is nondescript though the bed is massive, covered in brick-red sheets and nothing else. I take a step back from it, suddenly nervous. How many girls has he brought to his bedroom before me?

Ugh. No way do I want to think about that number.

I'm all alone with Owen in his bedroom. If I were bolder, I'd try to make a move. It's the perfect opportunity to at least try and kiss him. Though I have no idea if he'd be responsive. I don't think he's that into me. He's just being nice. Probably felt sorry for his poor tutor when he saw her getting harassed out in front of his workplace.

"Shit," he grumbles as he kneels down and starts digging through a pile of clothes that sit on an overstuffed chair. "I always lose my keys."

"Want some help?" I offer, because I'm a nice girl and I always offer help to someone in need.

If I could roll my eyes at myself right now, I so would.

"I'm good. They're probably in a pocket in my jeans. That's where I usually find them."

I go to his dresser and check it out. There's a mirror, a jar full of quarters, and a shallow dish full of miscellaneous change. There's also a lighter, a discarded, faded dollar bill, and a picture in a frame. I pick it up and study it. It's a photo of a really pretty girl with blond hair and the same green eyes as Owen. She's wearing a wedding dress and smiling for the camera, her arm slung around Owen's shoulders. He's also looking at the camera, a big grin on his face that makes my breath catch. The guy who I can only assume is her groom is looking at the bride like she's the most beautiful thing he's ever seen.

It's a wonderful photo, full of love and joy. I can only assume the girl is Owen's sister, since they share a lot of the same features. And the guy is vaguely familiar.

"That's my sister and brother-in-law." Owen's right behind me; I didn't even hear him approach, and I carefully set the frame back on top of his dresser, a little embarrassed I just got caught snooping.

"He looks familiar," I say lamely, turning to face him. He's standing so close I can feel his body heat, and my body sways toward his as though I don't have any control.

Which I don't.

"He's Drew Callahan."

Oh. I blink up at Owen. A living legend around these parts, people still talk about Drew Callahan, especially now that he's gone on to play for the NFL. Which means . . .

"Seriously? Your brother-in-law is a professional football player?" My jaw drops.

"Yeah. I thought you knew. Everyone knows."

"I didn't." I tilt my head, studying him. "Is that why you play football?"

"He's been a big influence, yeah."

"How about your dad? Does he like football?"

Owen goes stiff all over, his expression eerily blank, as are his eyes. "I don't know what that asshole likes. I have no idea where he is."

"Oh." I should never have asked. My parents are a sensitive subject, too. I don't like talking about my father at all, so I get it. "I'm guessing you're close to your sister?"

"Fable? Yeah, she practically raised me." The blankness disappears, replaced with a warm fondness that shows just how much she matters to him. "She just had a baby."

"So you're an uncle." The thought warms my heart. The visual of Owen holding a baby in his arms makes me feel all shivery.

"Yeah. She's cute." He holds up his car keys. "Found them. Are you ready to go?"

Disappointment crashes over me. *No!* I want to shout. *I want to stay. I want to go back out there and have a couple of drinks. Get a little buzzed. Maybe even "smoke a J," which I've never done before in my life, though it sounds like it could be fun. And after I get a little high and get a little drunk, maybe I could drag you back in here and lock the door so I can kiss you. Fall into your arms, feel your hands press all over my skin . . .*

A rapid knock sounds before I can find my tongue to answer him and the door slams open, revealing a tall guy who's almost as broad as Owen standing in the doorway on wobbly feet. "You *do* have a girl in your room," he says, sounding shocked as he rocks back on his heels. "Shit, I owe that asshole Des twenty bucks."

"Get the fuck out of here," Owen says, though he doesn't sound that angry. "We were just leaving, so you can tell Des nothing happened. You don't owe him shit." He turns to look at me. "Ready to go, Chels?"

I like that he just called me Chels. No one does. I have no cutesy nicknames and I always wished I had.

"Don't tell me this is the tutor." The guy trips into the room, stumbling over his own feet until he's standing just in front of me. "You are, aren't you? The tutor? I remember you." He's pointing at my chest, his tone a mixture of accusations and laughter.

"Um . . ." I don't know if I should be honest or not. I'm not a liar like my dad, so I prefer to stick to the truth. And I remember him, too. He was at the diner with Owen along with Des. "Yes, I am."

"Well shit, Owen. You got her into your room this quick? Sly motherfucker." The guy grins. "I'm Wade. Owen's oldest, dearest friend."

"You're going to be my *deadest* friend if you don't shut your mouth and get out of my room," Owen says, his voice low and rumbly and sexy as can be. What sort of sick perv does that make me, that I like it when he sounds all angry and growly?

I should be mad. He talked about me to his friends—most likely in a lewd and inappropriate way. More than anything, I should be offended. This means he doesn't take me seriously.

Instead, I'm thrilled. That he actually talked about me beyond the "I have a tutor and I don't want to see her" realm fills me with hope.

As though maybe I do have a chance with him.

Grinning, Wade stumbles back out much the way he came, sloppy and a little drunk. The minute he's gone, I turn to Owen.

75

"How does he know about me?"

"Uh . . ." He looks vaguely uncomfortable, so I push for more.

"Did you talk about me to him?"

"He's my roommate. So yeah, I talked to him about having a tutor." He shrugs, going for nonchalance, but I don't believe him.

There's more to this story than what he's saying.

"So why would he say that you worked quick and that you're sly? What's that all about?" I feel like a dog with a bone, but I have to find out what he might have said.

"You don't want to know," he murmurs, keeping his gaze averted.

He has it all wrong. "I definitely want to know."

Anticipation thrums through me as I wait for what feels like forever. He remains quiet. Runs those long fingers through his hair again, rests his other hand on his hip. He looks frustrated. It's a good look on him.

Everything is a good look on him.

"You're going to be offended," he finally says.

"I've been offended since the moment I saw your house and your friend started cursing at you," I say, because it's true. Their . . . colorful language is horrible.

You're such a prude.

Fine. What can I say? People don't curse around me. They never really have. Kari drops the occasional bomb, but nothing major. The minute I find myself in Owen's stratosphere, all I hear is foul language.

He smiles at my remark. "I think I like that you find me and my friends offensive. Maybe I can corrupt you."

My entire body goes liquid at the promise in his voice. I wish he would corrupt me. Toss me on those red, red sheets and pull my clothes off until I lie there naked, pale against the

dark, scared and trembling and excited when his hands finally, finally skate across my body . . .

"You're avoiding the question," I say, my voice shaky, and
I lick my lips. When I glance up, I find him staring at my
mouth.

My lips tingle as if he actually physically touched them.

"They think I'm going to try and . . ." He huffs out a
breath, thrusts his hand in his hair, and tugs. Hard. "Let's get
out of here, Chels. You need to go home."

I let him drop the subject. Let him steer me out of his
room, down the hall, through the crowd in his house and
outside to his car. All the while his hand is at the small of my
back, his fingers branding me through the lace and the tank
top I'm wearing. He doesn't say much, though everyone calls
out to him. Yelling his name, begging him to stay, offering
him a drink, a smoke, a cup, a bottle, a bong.

This is not my scene. Owen is not my scene.

It doesn't matter. Despite it all, I still want him.

And I find that incredibly frustrating.

Owen

The second we get into my car, I breathe a sigh of relief. Fuck,
that had been an utter pain in the ass. All the people in my
house, all the questions from Des and Wade, and then the
finishing touch with the interrogation from Chelsea.

Shit. I barely survived it all.

It's past one in the morning and I'm fucking exhausted. I
have class later in the morning and for the first time in a while,
I plan on going. Only to please the girl sitting next to me and
to help get my grades up—but if I don't get some sleep and
soon, I'm gonna skip.

And that's gonna suck.

She gives me directions to her apartment in this subdued voice that makes me nervous. Why, I'm not sure, but she's scarily quiet, keeping her head bent, her fingers busy as they scrape across the tops of her thighs. Back and forth, back and forth in this rhythm I can fucking hear since she's dragging her nails along the denim.

I check out her legs when I hit the brakes at a stoplight. She has slender thighs. Thighs I wouldn't mind grasping hold of and spreading. Just for me. Just for her. I bet no guy has ever stepped between her thighs before. Placed his hands on them and pushed her wide open. I have a feeling I'd be her first.

For whatever strange reason, I like that. Makes me feel all possessive and shit.

The light turns green and I hit the gas extra hard, making the car jerk as it lurches forward. I can feel Chelsea's eyes on me. She's probably wondering what the fuck is wrong with me and I can't give her an answer. I have no freaking clue what's wrong with me.

Yeah, you do. She's what's wrong with you.

Within minutes I'm driving into the parking lot of her apartment building, pulling into an empty spot. She climbs out of the car without a word and I do the same, following her as she walks down the sidewalk, then cuts across the grass.

"I got this," she calls over her shoulder. "Thanks for the ride."

Now she's dismissing me? Screw that noise. "I'm not going to let you walk into the darkness and disappear without at least making sure you get to your front door."

She stops and turns on me, her expression downright ferocious. "So, what? You're a gentleman now? Give me a break.

Like you care. You won't even answer me when I ask you a question."

Jesus. So we've circled back to that again? I know exactly which question she's talking about, too. "You don't want the answer. Trust me." I already told her what they thought she was to me.

An easy lay. A quick fuck. She's not, though. Not at all.

"Actually, I do. I'd *love* the answer." She marches toward me, her eyes blazing with indignation. She's furious and beautiful and when she reaches out to shove at my chest, my entire body reacts at her touch.

"I already told you. They think I'm going to try and get into your panties," I say, wincing the moment I blurt out the words. I'm putting it mildly. Wade's been on me since he realized I didn't fuck one of the tramps he brought over last weekend. I woke up Sunday to his endless shit. He thinks I'm hot for Chelsea.

His thinking would be correct.

She stills, her eyes going wide. "Are you?"

"No." I'm halfway lying, shaking my head. I don't know what I want from Chelsea exactly, but I do know one thing. "I don't want to fuck this up."

"Do you always have to use that word?"

"Yeah." I grin. Fable still gets on me about my mouth. She's actually cleaned hers up. Sort of. "I fucking love that word. Always have."

A ghost of a smile appears, curving Chelsea's delectable lips. "I think you say it just to irritate me."

"I probably fucking do." I glance around, the chill of the night air biting into my skin. She's gotta be cold, too. "Where's your apartment?"

"Are you avoiding our conversation again?"

79

"What's to avoid? I told you what you wanted to know."

"So they think you want to get in my panties." She stumbles over the word *panties*, which is cute. She contemplates me for a minute, her gaze intense. "What if I told you I don't wear any?"

Her words startle me so much I cough. Like, start hacking so hard I have to bend over to try and catch my breath, my hands on my knees as I stare at the dew-covered lawn before me. The image of my pretty little tutor not wearing any panties beneath those jeans that look painted on her body almost pains me. Makes my fingers itch to touch her. Undo the snap and slide the zipper down and see if she's telling me the truth or not.

"So." I clear my throat. "Are you wearing any? Panties?" I ask when I finally find my voice again. I stand up straight, hands on hips, my lungs still burning.

She smiles. *Fuck*, she's cute. "Yes. I am. Sorry. I tricked you."

Well, hell. That's a disappointment. "Come on." I go to her, grab her by the crook of her arm, and start walking with her. "Which building is yours?"

Chelsea points it out and I take her there, following her up the stairs as I check out her butt. Again. My mind is now filled with images of her with no panties on. Picturing that perfect ass of hers naked makes my cock twitch.

"So I'll see you Wednesday?" I ask as she unlocks her door. I'm leaning against the rough stucco of the building, noticing that her fingers shake the slightest bit as she tries to turn the key. It takes her a couple of attempts before she flips the lock and opens the door.

I wonder if I make her nervous.

"Yes." She flashes me a quick look. "Thanks for helping me out tonight."

"No problem. Maybe we could . . . meet again sometime."
What the fuck do I mean by that?

Don't go there, Maguire.

"To work on your assignments?" She turns to face me
fully, her hand clutching the door handle. She could just slip
inside if she wanted to. There's no need to finish this conversation.

But here she is. Talking to me. Showing interest. There's
more going on between us than I want to admit. She feels it,
too. I know she does.

"Yeah," I say, lying through my teeth. I want to see her
again but not to work on assignments. "I usually have practice tomorrow night but since I'm suspended from the team,
I'm free. But only if you can get together, of course."

"Of course." She offers me a grim smile. "But I have to
work."

"What time?"

"I go in at eight and work till two."

That shift sucks. It's not safe for a girl to be out that late,
especially a sweet, innocent one like Chelsea. "How about
earlier? We can . . . have pizza. Or whatever you like."

This sounds like a fucking study date. And I don't do
study dates. I don't date period. I wonder if she's caught on to
what's happening yet.

"And I'll help you catch up. Before I go to work." She
sounds wary, like she doesn't trust me.

"Yeah. That sounds good. What do you say?" I feel hopeful. I *sound* hopeful.

"How about I come to your place around five?" she suggests.

She can come all she wants, whenever she wants. As long
as she's coming with me.

Shit.

"Sounds good." I go for my usual, casual tone. I wonder if she's falling for it.

I wonder if she thinks I'm a complete dick. I would if I were her.

She smiles, her eyes soft. "Yes. Sounds good," she repeats. Chelsea's looking at me like she doesn't think I'm a dick at all. More like she's looking at me as if she could actually . . . like me.

That thought carries me all the way home.

CHAPTER 7

A flower cannot blossom without sunshine, and man cannot live without love.
—Max Müller

Study Date #1

Owen

Wade is gone. The house is kind of clean. As clean as it can get the day after a spontaneous party and with three dirty guys living there. Well, two live here and the other crashes on our couch all the time. I made those two assholes I call friends clean it, then I went behind them and picked up, wiped down, or threw away what they missed.

Des left hours ago. The guy has his own place, but he's always with us. It used to not bother me, but lately I've been getting sick of it. He's dealing out of my house and that sucks. Fable would flip the fuck out if she knew.

So I don't tell her.

Wade's at work—he's an associate at your local discount mega-store, ringing up customers and wishing he were any-where else. Poor Wade. Poor Des.

Lucky me.

Tonight, it's just gonna be me and Chelsea and my home-work assignments. Oh, and a pizza I'll order when she gets here and a six-pack of Coke I picked up at the liquor store on the corner. I probably should have got diet, since that's what girls usually prefer. Empty calories and all that bullshit—I've heard Fable say it before.

I really wanted some beer, but that shit is all gone from the house. Not a drop of liquor survived last night's so-called get-together. Besides, I know Chelsea wouldn't like that. She doesn't approve of my extracurricular activities. I don't have to ask her to know that's the case. Not that she judges. She's just not comfortable with it.

She's innocent. Sort of naïve. I get this feeling she's been pretty sheltered so far, and I think back on what I said to her last night.

Maybe I can corrupt you.

I want to corrupt her so bad it's killing me. I saw the way her eyes darkened when I said it. Her lips parted, her tongue darting out for a quick lick. I'd remained neutral, but deep inside I'd gone all hot and sweaty and lusted for her. It would be my absolute fucking pleasure to corrupt her. Show her what she's been missing. Touch her here, there, and everywhere. Kiss her until we both can't breathe.

I'm getting hard just thinking about it.

So I stop thinking about it. At least, I try. Glancing around the house, I check out the overstuffed dark brown leather couch and notice a new, jagged scratch on one of the cushions, the coffee table with fresh scratches on the surface, and the missing lamp on the end table since some jackass broke it last night.

Hell. Despite all the cleaning, this place still looks like a dump.

There's a knock at the door and I go answer it, trying my best not to look too eager. Chelsea must be early and I'm excited, like a little kid about to go on his first play date. Wiping my sweaty palms on the front of my jeans, I take a deep breath and throw open the door.

To find my mom standing on my front porch with an expectant look on her haggard face.

Fuck. Fuck. *Fuck*.

"What do you want?" I ask, pissed that she's here, pissed that I'm rude to her.

She rolls her eyes and barges inside, pushing past me so I have no choice but to step back and let her in. "I need money."

No hi, how are you—none of that shit anymore. She at least used to play at acting as if she cared. "You already spent what I gave you?" I glance outside, hoping I'll spot Chelsea, but I don't see her. Besides, it's too early. She still has at least fifteen minutes, and I have a feeling she'll show up right on the dot. She's punctual like that.

"Yeah, I did. It wasn't enough," Mom answers, her voice shaky, a little loud.

It's never enough, what I give her. Money, attention, weed, whatever—it's never, ever enough. She's greedy as hell and doesn't care who knows it.

"I don't have any more to give you," I lie, because I flat-out don't want to dip into the secret stash hidden away in my closet. That's for emergencies only. Definitely not for my mom's drug and booze habit.

"You're a goddamn liar." She rounds on me, her mouth like a thin slash across her face, her dull green eyes narrowed slits. "Call your sister. Get some money from her and that rich shit she married."

"I'm not calling Fable," I say, my voice tight, my blood boiling. "If you want something from her, *you* call her."

"You don't think I've tried? Little bitch won't talk to me. I go straight to voice mail every single time. I'm sick of it. Sick of all of you." Mom waves her hand, stumbling around like

85

she's going to fall, and I go to her, catching her by the elbows before she drops to the floor.

I look into her face, see that her eyes are dilated and her breaths are coming fast. She's high.

And not from smoking a little weed, either.

"Stay right here." I give her a little shove, so she settles on the couch with a grunt and I make my escape to my room. Glancing over my shoulder to make sure she didn't follow me, I go into my closet and head for my old varsity jacket from high school. A jacket I rarely wore but Fable insisted I get. She was so damn proud of me for being on the football team, especially when we won the regional championships. The smile on her face that night was unforgettable.

The look in my mom's wacked-out eyes just now was unforgettable, too. I need to get her the hell out of here. Before Chelsea sees her. Before Mom starts bad-mouthing Fable again. I want to scream at her. Ask her why the fuck she's so selfish. Doesn't she realize how much she's hurt Fable? How much she's hurt me? Mom is a freaking grandma now. Autumn is her first grandchild, her blood flows through the baby's veins, and it's like she doesn't even give a shit.

I'm not sure if she's aware that Autumn even exists.

I find the wad of cash in my jacket pocket and pull a couple of twenties and a fifty-dollar bill from it. I shouldn't give her this. I told myself not even five minutes ago I wouldn't. I'm funding her drug habit and that is such bullshit, but when it comes to my mom, I can't stop myself.

She's my bad habit. The one I just can't seem to quit.

Frustrated with myself, feeling weak and stupid, I go back out into the living room to find Mom pacing around like she can't keep still. She keeps rubbing her bare arms as though something's crawling on her skin and she's trying to brush it away. She doesn't see me yet, and I stare at her in dawning horror.

There's something going on here I don't want to face. I don't have time to deal with it right now. I'd rather shove money in her hand and send her away. But I can't keep on doing that forever. Avoiding my mom isn't going to fix this. Fix her.

Can she ever be fixed?

"Here." I rush toward her and grab her wrist, making her splay out her hand. I slap the cash into her palm and her fingers curl around it, crushing it so hard it turns into a crumpled wad of green. "Don't come back for at least two weeks. I'm not your personal bank."

"Fuck you," she spits at me just before she turns on her heel and runs out the door.

Shock renders me frozen as I stare out the still open front door. She came and left, just like that. No thank you, no "you're the greatest son alive," none of that. Just a demand and a curse—that's all I get for my troubles.

I'm the world's biggest fucking idiot.

Anger streams through my blood, makes me stalk around the house with clenched fists and a broken heart. Why the hell does she do this to me? Why do I let her get to me every single time? I wish I were more like Fable. She's pushed Mom right out of her life, and with no regret. Moved on with someone she loves, someone who takes care of her. Created a family out of nothing. And though I'm a part of that family and I know it, it's still hard. The distance between us makes it harder.

I'm here and the three of them are there. Drew and Fable and Autumn. It used to be Drew and Fable and Owen.

Now I'm just Owen.

Sometimes, I hate that. Growing up, moving on. Being alone. Finding my footing, when all I do is stumble around in the dark. *Fuck*.

I need a hit.

Glancing at the clock on the microwave, I see I have less than five minutes before Chelsea's supposed to show up. Just enough time to take a drag off a joint, maybe even a couple of hits if I'm fast. I have one I rolled a few nights ago stashed in the top drawer of my dresser and I go to it as if in a daze. Pull the drawer open, pull the joint out, grab the lighter, and flick it again and again until there's a flame.

Then I'm lighting it. Sucking up the smoke and the seed, inhaling until it fills my throat, slips into my lungs, and I feel the familiar, pleasurable burn. I exhale, thin tendrils of smoke escaping from my mouth, and I close my eyes briefly. Let it take me away to another place. A simpler time when I didn't have all this goddamn pressure weighing on me.

I take another puff and then stub out the joint against the side of my dresser, not giving a shit if I'm messing up the wood. Stash everything away quick, my buzz already washing over me, zipping through my veins, settling in my still pissed-off brain and making all my troubles slowly melt into nothing. The haze comes, warm and comfortable and just enough to leave me numb. I want to forget. Forget Mom and Fable and my grades and my job and football. Focus on the here and now and a girl named Chelsea who thinks she's coming over here to help me with my homework assignments.

That's the last thing I want to do with her. But I'm afraid that's all I'm ever going to get.

"Hello? Anyone home?"

Her sweet voice calls to me and I leave my room to find Chelsea standing in the middle of the living room, a hesitant look on her face as she looks around. When she spots me, I see the relief wash over her and I smile. Feeling cocky, feeling good, feeling like nothing can get me down now.

Not with Chelsea here, lighting up the room like sunshine and flowers and pure, unadulterated beauty.

"Hey," I say, letting my gaze roam over her unabashedly. She's wearing jeans and a long-sleeved white top that clings to her breasts and makes me wanna cling to them, too. Her backpack is slung over her shoulder, her smile tentative as she sets the bulky, heavy-looking object down on the floor beside the couch.

"Hi. Um, your front door was wide open, so I hope you don't mind that I just walked in," she says, waving toward the now closed door.

"No problem. Glad you made it." I'm sincere as hell about that. I am so damn glad she made it. I'd be climbing the walls if she weren't here.

"Are you ready to get to work?" She kicks at her backpack. "I brought some stuff that I printed up, but I'm hoping you know what you need to do."

"Yeah, I totally know what to do." I wave a hand, dismissing her worry as I approach her. She takes a step back and I brush by her, wishing I could reach out and grab her. Kiss her.

This is the weed talking. It has to be.

She squints at me, watching as I go to the dining table and grab the folder I keep with my missing assignments in it. "Are you all right?"

"I'm feeling pretty fucking amazing." I turn to face her once more, noticing how she's looking at me as if I've lost my head. She might be right. Mom coming over, the weed, having Chelsea standing here in front of me looking cute as hell—it's all sending my head spinning out of control.

She makes a face at my choice of words, then leans over

89

and unzips her backpack, digging inside for all the work she wants me to do, I'm sure. I stare at her ass, tilting my head to the side so I can get a better view, and when she turns she catches me.

Her gaze narrows. She is such a suspicious little thing. "Are you checking me out?"

I decide to be straightforward. No bullshit games from me tonight. "Yep." I lift my head slowly, since it feels like it weighs a ton. For whatever reason, the weed has loosened my tongue, which is not a usual side effect. "You have a really great . . ."

"A great what?" She stands to her full height, hands on her hips as she waits for my answer.

"A really great everything," I finish, not wanting to focus on her butt and nothing else. There's more to this girl than just her figure. "I'm fucking starving. Want me to order a pizza?"

She does that face again. It's cute, makes me want to keep saying things she doesn't like just to see her do it again. "There's a really good Chinese place that delivers. I love it. You like Chinese?"

"Sure." I shrug, ignoring my rumbling stomach. Right about now I'd eat a piece of cardboard, I'm so hungry. "Sounds good. You have the number?"

"Will you let me order?" She shoots me a questioning look, nibbling on her full lower lip in that innocently sexy way she has. Watching her makes me want to be the one nibbling on that lush lip. Tugging and pulling with my teeth, making her gasp just before I soothe the hurt with my tongue . . .

"Be my guest," I say, sounding like I'm in a daze. I sorta am.

This girl works some sort of magic over me. And I can't quite figure out how. Or why.

She smiles and grabs her backpack, hauling it over to the dining table and setting it down with a loud thump before she starts rummaging through it. "Their food is pretty cheap and I know just what to order. I'll even pay."

"Hell no." I grab her wrist when she pulls out her cell from the depths of her backpack, stopping her. "You are definitely not paying for it. I will."

"But I don't mind." She glances down at where I'm touching her. I wonder if she's as aware of me as I am of her. "I'm the one who wants Chinese."

"I want it, too." I circle my fingers around her slender wrist, feel her wildly beating pulse beneath my touch. I want more than just Chinese food, that's for damn sure. I feel like we're talking in secret code. Saying one thing and really meaning another.

At least, I am.

"Fine. I order, you pay." She doesn't try to tug out of my grip and I take advantage, sweeping my thumb slowly over the inside of her wrist in the lightest of caresses. I swear I feel her shiver, and when I look at her, I find her staring at me like she's so fucking hungry she just might gobble me up.

"Sounds good." I let my hand drop from her arm, disappointment clanging through me like a living, breathing thing. The tension between us is fucking ridiculous. If nothing happens tonight, I'm afraid I might burst. At the very least, I'll have to go whack off after she leaves, like some sort of deranged pervert in need of constant relief.

I want her but I don't. I'm attracted to her though I shouldn't be. I'm high, and it's not just from the weed.

I'm also high on Chelsea.

Chelsea

He's pushing through his assignments way quicker than I thought he would. I knew Owen was smart. I'd studied his student file well enough to see he just lacked focus or flat-out didn't apply himself. His past grades reflected that. Going to college does that to a person. It's all so much, sometimes too much, and students either thrive or they fail.

I'd thrived. The structure, the complexity of the courses, all of it had given me such a rush I'd dived right into my classes headfirst and never looked back. No one cared how old I was here; none of my past mattered. I could blend in, become someone new, someone free.

But I'm *not* free. I'm still tied to the guilt of my mother and the anger with my father. Deep down inside, I'm still a scared, too-smart-for-her-own-good little girl who's afraid to really live for fear she'll get hurt.

Boys are trouble, my mom would say. *Then they grow up to be men and become even more trouble. Stick with yourself, sweetie. Count on only you. Everyone else will just disappoint you.*

Mom had whispered those words of so-called wisdom to me when I was fifteen. The year before I graduated high school. I'd known there was trouble in my parents' marriage. From the time I was eleven, when I became privy to a secret phone call between my dad and one of his mistresses, I knew he was unfaithful to Mom.

He didn't love her. And if he didn't love her, he didn't love me. That's what I believed at fifteen. I would listen to Mom talk about how awful men were, how bad they treated women. She would talk that way when she was mad at him, when she knew he was cheating on her.

Then he'd sweet-talk her, convince her she was the only

one for him, and she'd change her tune. Her reaction to him, the constant push and pull between them, left me a confused mess most of the time, especially over boys and relationships.

I don't really talk to my dad. He's tried. He's called me a few times, but I always hang up when I hear the recorded message from the jail. He has to know I don't want to have contact with him.

When Mom was in one of her moods, working me over, she told me I needed to do right by my father and stand by him. So right before he was convicted for his crime last year, I'd gone to visit him in jail. He'd promised me he would get out. He'd be acquitted. He'd been so sure, so convincing, I believed him.

I'd gone home and begged my mom to let me go to court. I wanted to watch. Wanted to be there when he was set free and we could celebrate together. She told me no. Her excuse? I was too young and might not be able to handle it.

I'd been so confused, so devastated, I hid away in my room, crying into my pillow, believing that my mom didn't understand. Why would she ask me to stand by him and then tell me I couldn't go to court? It made no sense.

Now I'm glad I wasn't there. He'd been found guilty. I heard they carted him back to jail and he'd been in a state of utter shock, Mom wailing the entire time.

Men can't be trusted, Mom said before I left for college this last summer. *But you already know this. You're doing such a good job, sweetheart. Keep focusing on your school-work. Get your degree, find a career that is fulfilling. Then you can worry about a husband and babies, if that's what you really want.*

She'd said the last bit with such resignation, I wondered if Mom would prefer I become a lesbian rather than find a good man to settle down with. That had been during her down-with-men stage. The one she still clung to. It's sort of funny, considering she hadn't believed me when I came to her with my lesbian declaration.

Sitting next to Owen, I wonder what Mom would think if I became involved with him. What would she say if I brought him home and introduced him as my boyfriend? She'd probably tell me to run. *I* would tell me to run. His home life sounds chaotic. He has drug issues. Drinking issues. School issues. All sorts of issues.

He *is* an issue . . . for me. I'm drawn to him despite all the arguments that war inside my too busy, overthinking brain. All the danger signs that I usually bow to, I'm ignoring. Instead I'm just blazing on, fascinated by every little thing he does and says. He's sitting next to me at the table, concentrating on whatever assignment he's completing while he stares at his laptop, and I'm preparing a lesson plan for one of the students I'll meet with tomorrow.

We consumed the Chinese food as soon as it arrived, and I was inordinately pleased by how much he liked it. He raved on, eating enthusiastically while my appetite slowly vanished, replaced with a battlement of butterflies fluttering in my stomach. He makes me nervous in the most delicious, oh-my-God-I-want-him kind of way.

And I've never wanted any guy. Never felt that instant connection with one, either. I always figured I'd want someone like . . . me. Steady and patient and smart. Quiet and shy and kind of nerdy.

Owen is seemingly none of those things. He's gorgeous and sexy and charismatic. Tall and broad and athletic. Says what he wants and does what he wants—goes after what he wants. He acts like he can do anything.

Is it wrong that I wish he wanted to do me? God, I can feel

my cheeks heat just thinking it, let alone I could never say something like that out loud, especially to his face.

I'm a complete weenie. I've coasted my entire life in this sort of subexistence. Not really noticed for anything beyond my brain and even then, I hide behind it. My father becomes the biggest scandal in my hometown—heck, in all of California—and still I hide. No one knows Chelsea Simmons.

I never wanted anyone to know me . . . until Owen.

Mom would think I'd completely lost my mind for even thinking something like this.

"Are you okay?"

His deep voice washes over me and I lift my head to find him watching me, his brows furrowed in concern though his mouth is quirked up on one side. Almost like he's . . . laughing at me.

Wariness settles over me like deflective armor and I flick my gaze away from his, focusing on the textbook open in front of me but not really seeing the words. "I'm fine. Why do you ask?"

"You've been staring off into space for, like, the last five minutes at least." When I look back at him, shock and horror rushing through my veins, he shrugs those impossibly broad shoulders, a sheepish expression on his face. "I was watching you."

Now I'm gaping at him. He watched me? And just admitted it? "I was . . ."

"Lost in thought? You looked worried." He reaches out toward me and I go completely still, my breath lodged in my lungs as he brushes his finger across my lower lip. "I was afraid you'd chew a hole through your lip."

I want to die. Both at him touching me and at the fact that he called me out on my bad habit.

"I used to chew it so bad I'd make it bleed." Okay, why did I just go and admit that?

He frowns. "You have that much to worry about?"

I want to laugh. He has no idea. "Kind of." I need to play this off. "I've never really . . . fit in." Seriously? Now I'm pointing out my lack of social skills? What is wrong with me?

"I find that hard to believe." He looks surprised as he leans back in his chair. His T-shirt rides up, revealing a sliver of flat stomach, and my gaze automatically drops to that spot. "Why?"

I'm completely transfixed. There's a trail of dark hair that starts just below his navel and disappears beneath his jeans. My mouth goes dry and I'm filled with the urge to trace it with my finger. "I've always been kind of a nerd. I kept getting tested and the schools kept moving me up a bunch of grades. I graduated high school when I was barely sixteen."

"Really? So you're like a genius? How old are you?"

"Almost nineteen. I'm a junior," I say, knowing that's going to be his next question.

"Wow. No wonder you're a tutor." He laughs and shakes his head. "You make me feel like a complete dumbass."

I should never have told him. I make everyone feel dumb when they realize what I'm capable of. And really? I'm not capable of much. I'm great at memorization. I have a photographic memory. I'm a fast reader. Big deal. "You're not a dumbass," I tell him, my voice gentle.

He settles his chair back onto all four legs, a giant grin on his face. "Did you just say what I think you said?"

"What do you mean?" Then I realize what he's referring to and I roll my eyes. "Okay, fine, yes. I said a bad word."

"I don't think I've ever heard you say a bad word." His grin widens and it's downright irresistible. I can feel my mouth tremble at the corners, ready to break out into a smile. "I'll have you saying *fuck* in no time."

"No way." I shake my head, my smile blooming despite what he's saying. "That is like the worst word ever."

"Not even. It's more like the most versatile word ever. You can use it in so many ways." He stretches his arms out, then curls them behind his head, elbows bent, hands linked at his nape. His biceps bulge against the sleeves of his T-shirt and my body goes all fluttery and weak.

"What do you mean?" I ask.

"Well, it can be an adjective, a verb, a noun. It's fucking magical." He laughs when I glare at him. "I'm dead serious."

"Prove to me all its uses, then." I may as well turn this into a lesson. I have to go soon and clearly I'm not going to get any more work done, with the way he's looking at me, talking to me. My concentration is shot.

For once, I don't really care.

"Well, it can be used as a noun. 'Chelsea is smart as fuck.' "

Oh my God.

Is he really using it as a noun, though? Even if he's not, I'm not going to argue with him.

"And then it can be used as an adverb. As in, 'Chelsea is so fucking smart.' "

I want to laugh but I clamp my lips shut. He knows it, too. The look in his eyes is telling. He's totally trying to get a reaction out of me but I refuse to give him one.

"Or it can be a verb. Like, 'Owen really wants to fuck . . .' " His grin fades, his expression going from amused to sexy in a millisecond. He drops his arms to his sides and shrugs. "You know what I mean."

Everything inside of me goes loose and damp. I do know what he means. But is he referring to me?

No way.

"Um, yeah," I finally say, slamming my textbook shut. "I should, uh, really get going. I have to be at the diner soon." I stand and start gathering all of my stuff, keeping my gaze averted from his. He gets up, too, grabbing our dirty plates and stacking them before he takes them into the kitchen. I watch his retreating back, my breaths coming fast, my heart racing.

There is no way he was talking about me being someone he really wants to . . . I can't even *think* the word. I press my hands against my cheeks, can feel the heat emanating off my skin, and I wonder if he saw me blush.

I hope not.

He comes back toward the table, stopping right in front of me. Reaching out, he grips the top of the chair next to him with one hand, his fingers curled around the metal so tight his knuckles go white. "Did I offend you?"

"What?" I zip up my backpack and sling it over my shoulder before I turn to face him fully.

"With all my 'fuck' talk. Did that bother you? I was just teasing. I didn't mean anything by it." He looks remorseful, a little worried, as he flicks his gaze downward at the floor. His eyelashes are long and thick, and golden-brown stubble highlights all the places on his face where I want to touch him. When he lifts his lids to meet my gaze once more, I'm dazzled by the look in his gorgeous green eyes.

Then I remember what he said. What he's trying to tell me without coming right out and saying it.

He didn't mean anything by implying he wanted to . . . *me*. Heaven forbid he misled me in any way.

"I get it. Really." I smile, but it feels forced. Like I'm baring my teeth or something. "Don't forget to turn in your assignments tomorrow."

I turn away from him and hurry toward the door, ready to make my escape. My heart pounds with my every quick step and I need to get out of here quickly. I can't take this any longer.

Being in Owen's presence messes with my head. He's too much.

And I am definitely not enough.

"I won't forget." He's right behind me, lightning quick, and he reaches out around me, grabbing hold of the handle so he can open the door for me. "I'm sorry, Chelsea, if I embarrassed you. I didn't mean to."

I stand there in the middle of the open doorway, closing my eyes for the briefest second as the sound of his voice saying my name washes over me. I really love it when he says my name. I shouldn't. I shouldn't like anything about Owen Maguire. "You didn't. I'm fine. I just . . . I need to go and get ready for work. Thanks for the Chinese food."

And with those last, extremely lame words, I escape from his house as if the very devil were chasing me.

CHAPTER 8

*Life without love is like a tree without blossoms
or fruit.*
—Khalil Gibran

Owen

"How's the tutoring going? Are your grades picking up?"
Fable asks, sounding distracted. I hear the baby coo in the
background and I know she's holding Autumn. Fable can't
seem to concentrate on just me anymore. She's always multi-
tasking and juggling a million things at once.

Sometimes, when I have these thoughts, I yearn for the old
days. When it felt like it was just me and Fable against the
world, doing whatever we had to do in order to survive.
When I could take off and claim I was with Wade at his house
when really the two of us were out fucking around. My biggest responsibility back then had been homework.

Oh, and taking care of Fable and my mom. That had always weighed heavily on my shoulders.

It still does.

"They are. I turned in a bunch of assignments at the end
of last week." I'd even been allowed to come to Saturday's
game, though they hadn't let me play. I sat on the bench the
entire time, suited up and ready to go out onto the field, but
the coach wouldn't let me.

I think he had me sit there to prove a point.

See what you can't have?

It worked. I slaved away on the portfolio for my Creative Writing class most of Sunday. Begged my boss at The District to start giving me more hours again when I went in to work my lame-ass four-hour shift that evening. And I plan on going to practice later tonight after I meet with Chelsea and hopefully present my coaches with my new grades so they'll allow me to play.

My life is coming together again. I'm getting back on track, and this is a good thing.

So why do I feel this nagging, incessant buzz just beneath my skin, as if I'm forgetting something or someone?

Chelsea.

Yeah. She's pissed at me. I went in to see her after that semi-disastrous night with her at my house and she'd been distant. Not cold or bitchy, but . . . preoccupied. All business, no friendliness, and she'd shot out of her chair and exited the room the minute our hour was over. Didn't even bother to say goodbye.

It sucked.

"Your coach called Drew," Fable says nonchalantly.

I collapse in the overstuffed chair in my room, sitting on top of the pile of clothes I always leave there as I lean my head back and close my eyes. This could be either really good or really bad. "What did he say?"

"That he's impressed with the way you're playing and wishes he could have you back on the team. Drew said he's eager to work with you again. He can't wait for you to pick up your grades." She pauses. "Sounds like you've done that. I'm proud of you, Owen."

"My English teacher said she talked to my tutor and that my grades are going to be updated within the next couple of days," I say.

"That's awesome. So you like the tutor, then? You two get along and it's working out?"

Wish she were working out *beneath* me, but that's definitely not going to happen. I screwed all that up by being a crude asshole and offending her. "She's nice. Super smart."

"Cute?"

"Gimme a break, Fabes." I crack open my eyes and stare at the ceiling. Chelsea is more than cute. She's beautiful. Intelligent. Sweet. And she hates me. Because I'm a foul-mouthed idiot who acts like a little boy every time I get near her.

"That means you think she's cute."

"She's out of my league." The words leave me before I can stop myself. No way did I want to admit that to my sister.

"Please. No one is out of your league. You're good-looking, smart, and you're on the freaking football team. What girl wouldn't want you?" She bursts into laughter. "What am I saying? I ran from Drew as fast and far as I could when I first met him. Maybe you intimidate her."

"No, that's not it." *She* intimidates *me*. Chelsea has her shit together. I'm just some jackass still out fucking around, smoking too much weed, trying to please someone who's only using me for money—and just so happens to be my mother—and I can't keep my life together unless someone is right there beside me with a checklist, asking if I've done everything I'm supposed to do. "Why am I even having this conversation with you? There's nothing going on between me and Chelsea."

"Oooh, *Chelsea*. Your voice changed when you said her name. Got all soft and stuff. I think you like her." Fable's teasing me, just giving me shit, but it cuts too close to the bone.

Because I do like her. In more than a *hey, let's bang* kind of way, too. I like talking to her. Looking at her, just basking in her presence. She offers up these little tidbits about herself that are never enough for me. I want to know more, more, more, but I don't push. I'm afraid she'll push back. I have enough secrets—she'd go running if she discovered them.

But Chelsea? She's a mystery. And I desperately want to figure her out.

"My voice did not change." Jesus, she may be a wife and mother, but Fable is still my pain-in-the-ass sister sometimes.

"It so did. Say her name again."

"No." I push out of the chair and go to the mirror that hangs on the back of my bedroom door. I need to get a shirt on and get to school soon. Probably should take a shower before I do all that because . . .

Yeah. Because I'm seeing Chelsea today.

Sucker.

"Oh come on, Owen. Say it. I dare you to."

Hell. She knows that's my weakness. "Fine." I heave an exaggerated sigh. I think Fable's enjoying this.

Correction: I *know* Fable's enjoying this. I miss her. I think she misses me, too. I hate that she's so far away, but I guess I shouldn't complain. Drew could be playing for a team clear across the country. I'd never see them then.

"Okay. Repeat after me." She pauses and I can hear the baby coo again, a soft, sweet little sound that strikes me right in my heart. Damn it, I wish we were all in the same room together. " 'I'm in love with Chelsea.' "

Now it's my turn to burst out laughing. "I am definitely not saying that."

"Spoilsport." She laughs, too, but it's tinged with sadness. I need to go see her. I don't know when I can find the time, but I want to see Fable and the baby and Drew. I want to watch Drew play live. It's been too long.

I miss my family.

"I don't ever plan on falling in love," I say, turning away from the mirror so I don't have to see myself when I say something like that. It's such a macho, assholish remark and I know Fable's going to give me shit.

Maybe I said it on purpose so I can get her to stop talking about Chelsea.

"You can't make such a broad statement like that. It's guys like you who are the ones that fall hard and fast. Just ask Drew," she says, ever my wise and level-headed sister.

"Whatever. Love is for sissies." I flop onto my unmade bed and stare up at the ceiling, cradling the phone between my shoulder and ear. "I should go, Fabes. I need to get to class soon."

"Be good, okay? Have fun with your tutor. What's her name again?" She asks the question innocently, trying to get a rise out of me, but I don't take the bait.

"Chelsea." I say her name again because I want to. I like how it rolls off my tongue. And yeah, my voice did soften when I said it, but I'm not going to examine that too closely.

I might not like what I discover.

"Yes. Chelsea." Her voice softens, too. It's taking everything within her not to make total fun of me. She's a total brat. "Don't do anything I wouldn't do with your precious Chelsea."

"Ha, that leaves it wide open." I laugh.

"Jerk," she says good-naturedly. "Love you."

"Love you, too, Fabes." I hang up and toss the phone onto the mattress beside me, my gaze locked on the ceiling fan circling lazily above my head. Inhaling deep, I recognize the pungent smell of weed and I wrinkle my nose.

No way can I bring a girl into my room with it smelling like this.

You're not thinking of just any girl. You're thinking of . . .

I close my eyes and fight my thoughts about Chelsea. I don't know her that well. There's really nothing to know. Within the next few weeks, everything will be over between us and I'll never see her again. We definitely don't run in the same social circles.

Resting my hand on my chest, I feel my heartbeat beneath my palm. The steady thud, thud, thud letting me know I'm alive. But I don't feel alive. Not really. Everything just . . . happens. I work hard and it's the same old thing. I work not as hard and it's still the same thing.

Nothing changes. I go to school, I play football, I work, I get high, sometimes I get drunk, I want to knock Wade and Des's heads together. Lather. Rinse. Repeat.

Then Chelsea walks into my life and I'm thinking differently. I think . . . I want to ask her out. On a bona fide date. And I never want to date anyone. I fuck around and that's it. Something lasting isn't what I want. A quick lay? That's always worked.

But it's not working when it comes to Chelsea. I want more. And I doubt she wants to give it to me.

Chelsea

I'm nervous. Owen should be here any minute for our weekly meeting and I don't know what to do, what to say. The last time we saw each other, I'd been so stiff and uncomfortable I hardly said anything to him. Then I bolted out of the room like a frightened chicken without saying goodbye.

He probably hates me.

I pace the classroom, too agitated to sit. Back and forth in front of the whiteboard, my gaze constantly straying to the door no matter how much I tell myself I don't care when he shows up. I'd prefer he never show up.

I am also a complete liar.

Yet again I dressed with care, wanting to impress him despite myself. Another good pair of jeans; these are old and worn, a little faded and comfortable, yet they make my legs look long. Not that I care about what my legs look like. Or any part of me. I just want to look nice. Not because I'm trying to catch Owen's eye or whatever.

God, I sound like such a failure even in my own mind. I stop pacing and hang my head, staring at my feet. I'm wearing fake Ugg boots—it was cold this morning—and I have my jeans tucked into them. And a big, slouchy cream-colored sweater that keeps slipping off my shoulder and revealing my pale pink, lacy bra strap.

I withhold the groan that wants to escape. My entire outfit looks calculated. Even Kari asked me earlier this morning when we were both getting ready for class who I was dressing for, and I lied. Told her no one. She doesn't know about Owen. She never seemed to care what happened that night at The District when I left her with Brad. I told her I found a ride home when she asked. That I saw someone I knew and he offered.

She never questioned me beyond that. Kari's too wrapped up in her own thing lately. I know she's been seeing Brad casually but he's not giving her the attention she wants.

What a surprise.

The door creaks open and my gaze jerks to the door. There he stands, looking like complete male perfection, wearing a blue-and-red plaid flannel unbuttoned shirt over a white T-shirt and dark jeans with boots that are for whatever reason unlaced. His hair is a haphazard mess and that sexy golden-brown scruff still shadows his face.

My God, he's just . . . devastating.

"Hey." He pulls the door shut behind him with a quiet click, then leans against it. "How's it going?"

Swallowing hard, I flip my hair back, exposing my bare shoulder and the pink bra strap. His gaze drops immediately to it and my skin warms as if he actually touched me. "It's . . . going well." I tug my neckline up but it immediately falls off my shoulder again. I should have worn a tank top.

"You look good," he says as he pushes away from the door and slowly saunters toward me.

Oh. I hadn't expected such a quick compliment. Or any sort of compliment. "Thank you." I clear my throat, pray for strength. Just like that, it comes to me. "You look good, too."

He smiles crookedly, without revealing any teeth, as he approaches the table I'm standing next to. "So you're talking to me."

I have to tilt my head back when he stands so close so I can meet his gaze. "Why wouldn't I be talking to you?"

"Last time we met here, I think you might've said fifteen words to me, tops. And every one of them you had to force out."

"You were counting?" And am I flirting? This is . . . so unlike me.

"I figured I pissed you—" He presses his lips together, his eyes dancing with amusement. "Made you mad."

Really? When was I supposedly mad at him? Freaked out? Yes. Embarrassed? Oh yeah.

"You know, when I kept saying that one particular word to you." It's as though he can read my mind. Freaky. "You ran out of my house like your shoes were on fire, and then we met here the next day and you hardly talked to me." His eyes seem to bore into mine. "I figured you might not show up today."

"Oh, now I *am* offended. I never, *ever* ditch my tutoring appointments unless I'm sick. Like on-my-deathbed sick." And even then, I've missed only one session since I started working. I take all of my jobs pretty seriously.

"You're really offended?" He raises a brow and my heart trips.

I roll my eyes. "No. I think . . . we might've had a misunderstanding."

"I think so, too." His voice lowers and he shuffles closer to me. So close I can see tiny golden flecks in his green, green eyes. "So you're not mad at me?"

"I'm not." I shake my head. "Actually, I'm proud of you. You've completed all the assignments you needed to do so you could catch up in your English class. Right now, you have a solid B minus."

He smirks, looking pretty proud of himself. "I have one more test to take. I bet I can bring that grade up to a B."

"I bet you can, too. I also hear you're going to get back on the football team within the next few days."

Pulling out the chair he was holding onto, he indicates for me to sit with a wave of his fingers. I do so, consciously aware of his hands at the top of the chair, pushing it closer to the table. When he pulls them away, his fingers brush against the skin of my bare shoulder and a shiver moves through me.

If he can make me all shivery with an innocent touch, I'm in huge trouble. Imagine what might happen if we decide to take it further?

Keep dreaming, Chelsea.

"Where'd you hear that?" He pulls out the chair next to mine and settles in, just like he did that first day we met and he set me on edge by being so close.

I'm having a total repeat performance. Just like that, I'm on edge. If he nudges that thigh of his any closer, it'll be brushing next to mine. Anticipation curls through me at the thought. "I had a meeting with your counselor this morning. She's actually the counselor for a few of my students."

"Are you talking about good ol' Dolores?" He grins and shakes his head. "How old do you think she is, anyway?"

Poor Dolores. She's a former chain smoker; her face is covered in wrinkles and her voice is so raspy I almost mistake her for a man when I talk to her on the phone. She's sweet, but she probably should have retired about five years ago. "I don't know. Fifty?"

He laughs and shakes his head. "I really hope that was a joke."

"Definitely." I smile and zip open my backpack, reaching in to pull out his file so I can flip it open. "I hear she's seventy-plus."

"I wouldn't doubt it if she was ninety-plus." He flicks his chin toward the open file. "Why do you have that?"

"Just because you're off the hook with English doesn't mean you don't still have work to do." I tap the edge of the file with my index finger. "You have your creative writing portfolio to work on."

"Yeah." He shakes his head. "About that. Can't I just drop the class? Isn't it an elective?"

"Well, you could, but it's already kind of late. You pull out now, you'll have a big, ugly W on your schedule and that'll mess up your grade point average." I pull the file closer to me and look over the list of assignments he still needs to complete for his portfolio. I decide to push him. "I thought you were a decent writer. A lot of this stuff you need to do isn't too hard."

He puffs out his chest. "I'm better than just a decent writer."

"Prove it." I push the assignment sheet toward him so he

can read it over. "Write something. Like a poem or what-ever."

He glances at the list, then looks up at me. "Do you like to write poems?"

I wrinkle my nose. I'm not a flowery kind of girl. I prefer facts and figures. Math and history. Though I am strong at composition when I set my mind to it. Truly, I shouldn't have been assigned to Owen. I'm not the perfect match for his tutoring needs, but I was one of the few people available and they chose me. "Not really."

"I thought all girls liked to write about love and sadness."

Is that what he writes about? I doubt it, but who knows? "I'm not like most girls."

"I know." His smile softens as his gaze roves over my face. "That's what I like most about you."

Oh. I am so. Done for.

CHAPTER 9

At the touch of love everyone becomes a poet.
—Plato

Owen

I'm racking my brain for a subject. I don't normally write poems. Well, I used to, when I wanted to be just like Drew Callahan when I grew up, but nothing—and no one—inspired the supposed poet inside of me, so I gave it up near the end of my freshman year in high school.

I still can't believe what I said to her. It's as if I took some sort of truth serum before I showed up and I can't help but be honest with her. Not that I mind. It's kind of nice, saying what I want and not playing any games. What's going on between Chelsea and me isn't all about sex or a one-time thing. It's almost like we're friends.

Right. I'm becoming friends with a girl I'd also really like to get naked with. That sweater she's wearing is sexy as hell. It keeps slipping off her shoulder, revealing creamy pale skin and a lacy bra strap that just begs for my fingers to push it off. Kiss her there . . .

Shit.

"There must be something you want to write a poem about," Chelsea says.

Glancing up, I find her watching me expectantly, her eyes sparkling, her smile infectious, and I smile back, feeling at a loss for words. I need a topic, and quick. And I'm thinking maybe she can provide it. "Tell me. What's your middle name?"

She frowns. "What's that got to do with anything?"

"Come on. Humor me."

"Fine. It's Rose." She rolls her eyes. "I was named after my grandma."

"Chelsea Rose." The name rolls off my tongue easily. I like it.

"It's lame, right?" She laughs, sounding uncomfortable, and I hate that. I don't want her to feel that way around me. I wonder how many guys she's gone out with.

I have a feeling the number is pretty small. That fact would normally send me running far, far away.

Instead, I'm sitting here thinking of all the things I could teach Chelsea. While we're naked. In my bed.

"No, not at all," I say. "I think it's pretty."

Her laughter dies. "Really?"

"Really," I say firmly. Has no one ever showed her any sort of attention? She acts sort of starved for it sometimes. Not in a psycho-chick way, not even close. More like she's a slowly blooming flower that grows brighter and even more beautiful the more you water it and talk to it . . .

Hmm. My brain is churning.

I think of Drew's tattoo for Fable. How he always wrote her little poems, spelling out words with the first letter of the first line. Crazy, sappy shit that used to drive Fable wild. Like make her cry and kiss Drew and tell him how wonderful he was.

Memories flood me . . . the time I punched Drew in the mouth, one of my favorite memories ever. Not because I punched Drew, but because I became this angry, almost inhuman thing who could think of nothing but defending his sister. That I knew I could jump to her defense without thinking twice and be her hero pumped me up. Made me feel strong.

Made me feel like a man.

Plus, I mean, come on—it was pretty damn epic, flattening Drew Callahan to the ground with one punch. I know I had the advantage since he hadn't expected it, but still. I told everyone at school I knocked him out. Maybe 15 percent of them believed it happened, and I'm being generous with that figure. Everyone was skeptical.

But I know the truth.

"You should probably get to work," she says, not sounding too thrilled by the prospect. I'm starting to think we might be on the same page more than I first realized. She points at my backpack, which I set by my feet. "Did you bring your laptop?"

"Well, yeah." I reach down and unzip my backpack, pulling out my laptop and opening it. I bring up a Word doc and stare at the blank screen, at that damn blinking cursor I always want to sock in the face since it feels like it's taunting me, and I start to type. I come up with something totally stupid.

Real
Open
Sexy
Extra pretty

Frowning, I delete it all. That's Drew's specialty, not mine. Besides, Chelsea's not that open with me. Not yet.

So I try a different approach.

Prickly with thorns, pretty little rose.
She's shy. She's pink. She belongs to no one.

I win her over with my touch.
Slow at first, my fingers gentle, searching as she
    opens . . .
Caressing her, I bring her close.
So close.
Until I've completely destroyed her.
Petals scattered everywhere, her beauty wrecked.
All by my hand.
And now she's become everything.
To me.

"So? What did you write?"

Her voice breaks into my thoughts and I glance up, startled to find her watching me, her expression open and hopeful. She's got her elbow propped on the edge of the table, her chin resting on her fist, and she looks freaking gorgeous. Her pretty blue eyes sparkle like a clear summer sky and . . . yep, I see a sprinkle of freckles across the bridge of her nose. I wonder how many there are. I wonder if she'd let me get close enough to count them.

"I really hope you came up with something good. You've been working on it for almost a half hour," she says.

"I have?" I'm shocked as I glance down at the clock on my computer screen to see that she's right. "Uh . . . yeah, I came up with something. It's sort of rough, though. Like, it still needs a lot of work." More like I need to change the entire thing.

The poem is about sex. As in, I'm talking about fingering Chelsea and making her come.

Jesus. What is wrong with me?

You want her. That's what's wrong with you.

"Can I read it?" She scoots her chair closer to mine, trying to catch a glimpse of the poem. I immediately slam the laptop shut and she rears back, her tempting mouth turned down in a frown. "Guess that's a no."

"It's super rough." I smile weakly and she stares at me, as if she's attempting to penetrate my brain or something, and I hold her gaze. Trying my best to look completely neutral. "And sort of personal."

"Oh." She blinks and leans back. "Sorry."

"Don't apologize." I try to soften my rudeness by reaching out and grasping her hand in mine. Her fingers are slender and cold and I squeeze them, hoping I can warm them up. "I'm the one who should say sorry. It's just . . . it's a mess. I need to work on it some more." Like trash it and start completely over.

"I bet it's fine. Just add it to your portfolio. Don't worry about it." She tries to pull out of my grip but I won't let her. "You have a printer, right?"

"Yeah, I have one." This conversation has taken a strange turn. I just wrote about making Chelsea come and now we're talking about printers and shit. I have to get this back on track. "Chelsea. Go out with me."

"What?" Her jaw drops open and this time she does tug her hand out of mine, almost recoiling. Reminding me of that flower I described at the beginning of my poem. The one I had to gently coax open. "What do you mean?"

"Are you doing anything after this? Do you have to work later tonight?" I hate that stupid job she has at the diner. It makes me worry about her.

She slowly shakes her head. "No. I'm off tonight. Though I do have a paper I should start on."

"When's it due?" If she turns me down, I'm not asking her out again. A guy can take only so much humiliation, and I hadn't been lying to Fable when I told her I thought I was beneath Chelsea. Her refusal would only prove my point.

"Right before Thanksgiving break," she admits, and I chuckle.

"Chels. That's weeks away," I point out.

"I know. I just like to think ahead and be prepared." Her voice drifts and she glances down, lifting that one bare shoulder, the one I'm dying to touch. Trace the pale pink lace of her bra, slip my finger beneath it and slowly tug the strap down her arm. "You think I'm a freak."

"No, I think you're kind of mean." She lifts her head, her eyes so wide they look like they're going to pop out of her head. "You're leaving me hanging here, Chels. You want to do something with me tonight or what?"

"Oh." She blinks at me again and leans back against her chair. "Are you asking me out on a date?"

"Yeah. I am." My schedule is going straight to hell within the next few days. I'll be back at work, back at practice, and back in action. I won't have time for girls. For Chelsea.

Meaning I shouldn't string her along and get her hopes up. But hell, sitting here, breathing in her scent, seeing her pretty face tell me everything she's feeling and thinking, I know I have to do this. I want to do this.

I want to be with her. Even if it's only for tonight, for a few hours. We don't have to do anything. I have zero expectations. She's not the type of girl who'll put out. She has more respect for herself than that. I respect her, too.

But nothing says I can't kiss her. I'm going to try my damnedest to taste those soft, pink lips of hers before the night is through. That's a fucking promise.

"All right," she says, her voice so soft I almost don't hear her. "I'll go out with you tonight."

Relief floods me, and it takes everything within me not to

reach out and tug her into my lap. "Want to go out to dinner?"

"Okay."

"A movie?"

She shrugs. "Not really. I can hardly sit still through
them." When I don't say anything she makes a funny little
face. "I don't like wasting time."

"So going to a movie with me is wasting time?" I'm almost offended.

"Yes, when I could be spending those two-plus hours
talking to you instead." She smiles dreamily and fuck, that's
it. I'm done for.

"Hey, Chels?"

"Yes?"

"What you're wearing right now? Wear it tonight."
Reaching out, I give in to my urge and draw my finger across
her shoulder, trace the lacy bra strap. Her skin is so fucking
soft. I wonder if she's that soft all over. "I like it. A lot."

A shiver moves through her. I feel it beneath my finger,
and that little hint that my touch affects her kick-starts my
heart. Makes it pump wildly in my chest.

Damn. I have got it so bad for this girl it's scary.

Chelsea

"You're going on a date," Kari says, her voice flat, her expression full of utter disbelief.

"Yes. I am." I tug a brush through my bone-straight hair,
then toss it onto the counter, where it lands with a loud clatter. "And I totally hate my hair."

"Why? It's so pretty. Such a rich color and so thick." Kari
stands just behind me, that stunned, I-can't-believe-you're-
going-out-with-someone look still on her face. "So you wear

117

this sexy little sweater, show off some skin, and now you're going on a date? With whom?"

I smile, wishing I could keep my secret to myself for as long as possible, but I know Kari is going to keep at me incessantly until I have no choice but to confess. She could convince just about anyone to reveal all their secrets. She should go work for the CIA or something, she's that good. "It had nothing to do with the sweater."

Okay, it probably did, though I don't necessarily want to give the sweater that much credit in Owen asking me out on a date. Yeah, he liked it. And *I* liked it when he traced my bra strap, his finger moving beneath the lace to actually touch my skin.

I'd wanted to die, all over a too brief touch that had somehow set fire to my skin. I can still feel his finger on my shoulder, and it happened over an hour ago.

Which means I need to get a move on, because Owen will be here soon to pick me up for our date.

I'm so excited, I feel like I'm going to burst.

"Don't act all mysterious, you little bitch." Kari starts to laugh when I shoot her a dirty look. She loves getting a rise out of me, too. "Tell me who you're going out with. And please don't say it's Tad."

Grimacing, I shake my head. "No way. I haven't seen him since that night at The District."

"Lucky you! I've seen him a few times when I've been with Brad. He's just as moody as ever," Kari mutters.

I don't even bother asking her for any more details. I really don't care. The very last person I want to talk about is stupid, mean Tad. "Will you curl my hair for me, Kari? I want it to look pretty."

"I told you, it already looks pretty," she says as she moves around me so she can grab the curling iron that's sitting on the counter, plug it in, and flick the switch on. "Stop holding out, Chelsea. I need to know who this mystery date is with."

"You probably don't know him."

"You're probably right."

I give her a look in the mirror. "Don't be mean." I bet she thinks my date is a big, studious loser like me.

"I'm not. Just stating fact." She shrugs, then grabs the brush I threw onto the counter and starts running it through my hair. "You sure you want me to curl it?"

"Yes." Pressing my lips together, I grip the edge of the bathroom counter and count to three before I start my confession. "He's one of the students I tutor."

"Ooh, scandalous, babe! I thought you swore some oath or something. Like you had to sign in blood that you wouldn't date your students."

"Nothing like that." It's definitely frowned upon, though. Not that I'll tell anyone beyond Kari that I'm going on a date with Owen. I mean, who else would care? "He's a football player."

Kari lifts a delicate brow. "Now we're talking. What's his name?"

"Um." I squeeze the edge of the tile counter, the words sticking in my throat. He's mine to savor and hold onto and keep quiet. Once I confess to Kari, it becomes public and real and . . . kind of weird. "His name is Owen Maguire."

"*What?*" Kari's screech hurts my ears and I wince, thankful she hadn't started curling my hair yet. She probably would have burned me. "Are you freaking serious?"

I nod, my heart in my throat. I dread hearing what she'll say next. It can't be good.

"Everyone knows who Owen Maguire is. And he's a total

player, Chelsea." The worry on Kari's face is clear. "He's got a horrible reputation."

"Like what kind of reputation?" So dumb to ask that, but I have to know. I don't want to, but it's like a bad car wreck. You don't want to stare but you can't help yourself.

"He goes through a ton of girls; he likes to party and drink and smoke pot. Like, all the time." Kari winces. "He's so not the type of guy I picture you with, that's for sure."

"Why, because he's good-looking and I'm not?" I know I'm on the defensive, but I can't help myself.

"I never said that." She reaches out to test the curling iron and finds it hot enough to her liking. "Turn around."

I do as she asks, trying to calm the bubble of anger threatening to grow inside of me. "What did you mean, then?"

"You're sweet and nice and he's . . . not. At least from what I've heard." She takes a chunk of hair from the back of my head and winds it around the curling iron, waiting a few beats before she slowly undoes it, showing me the result in a hand mirror. It falls in a perfect curl. "He is super hot, though, you lucky girl. His body is amazing."

My cheeks heat. It is. Everything about Owen is amazing. "He's really nice."

"Oh, I'm sure." She curls another piece, then another, and we both remain quiet for a few minutes, me chewing over what Kari said. I shouldn't think anything could come out of this between Owen and me. Kari is right. We have nothing in common, and he's definitely not my type . . . not that I have a type.

But I want a type.

"When he looks at me it's like he wants to—do stuff to me," I admit, my voice low.

"Ha, I'm definitely sure about that." Kari slowly shakes

her head, releasing another perfect curl. I could never make my hair look this good. I always screw up the back. "Watch out, Chelsea. I know you don't have a lot of experience with guys. I just don't want him to take advantage of you."

"He won't. I trust him." I do, surprisingly enough. I only started working with him a couple of weeks ago, but I do trust him.

Men can never be trusted. They all want only one thing. Your body. And once they possess that, they toss you aside like yesterday's trash.

Mom's words ring through my head and I try to banish them, but it's no use. The familiar anxiety fills me and I try to focus on anything else but the hatred my mom has toward all males in this universe.

No wonder I thought I wanted to become a lesbian. My man-hating, turn-around-and-forgive-my-dad-for-anything mom would make any girl consider turning.

"Just . . . keep your clothes on. This is your first date with him, after all." Kari's gaze meets mine in the mirror. "Right?"

My first real date *ever*, not that I'm going to confess that. "Yes. Definitely. We haven't done anything beyond the tutoring lesson stuff." Well, I've been at his house. And in his bedroom. I've actually spent a lot of time with him but never like this, on an official date and all.

"Call me if you need anything. And I mean *anything*. I'll be home all night." She moves to my right side, curling my hair with quick precision, like she's a pro. "Your hair looks awesome."

"And you didn't want to curl it," I remind her, keeping my gaze on my reflection in the mirror. Kari's right. My hair looks pretty fabulous. "It does look good."

"I have skills, what can I say? Plus, I have sisters. Lots of practice." She sets the curling iron on the counter and turns it off. "Turn and face me."

I do as she asks, letting her fluff out my hair so it falls past my shoulders in luxurious, perfect waves. "He'd better not drive you anywhere on a motorcycle or anything. Losing these curls would be a tragedy," Kari says. She grabs a can of hair spray and takes the cap off. "Close your eyes."

She sprays my hair for what feels like five minutes but was really only about ten seconds. "Not too much," I warn her. What if Owen wants to touch my hair and it's all sticky and stiff? Talk about ruining the mood.

"What? You want lover boy to run his fingers through your pretty hair?" I open my eyes to see her set the hair spray on the counter. She pulls open her makeup drawer, contemplating the contents within. "Can I do your makeup?"

"I have a little bit on already. Some mascara," I answer. "And my lip gloss is in my purse."

She gives me a look. One that says "you've got to be kidding." "That you say 'my lip gloss' like it's the only one you own scares me."

"It *is* the only one I own. You know this." I don't wear a lot of makeup and I don't have the money to buy a bunch of stuff, so I don't waste it. I have one great L'Oréal lip gloss I bought at Target a year ago and I use it sparingly.

"You're a travesty to all women, especially ones who would die to go on a date with Owen Maguire. He's, like, the hottest man alive. And he's only a sophomore. We have many years of him on campus still." She digs through her drawer, pulling out all sorts of mysterious stuff. "I'm doing your makeup. I'll do a really smoky eye and then keep the rest of your face relatively clean. We'll slick your lips with that special singular lip gloss you own, and then he'll want to kiss it all off when he sees you."

My cheeks grow so hot they must be blazing pink. Kari laughs when she sees my face and shakes her head. "You won't need any blush if you keep that up."

I could punch her for giving me grief. Instead, I let her work her magic. Applying what feels like layer after layer of way-too-dark shadow on my eyes, then nearly poking my eyes out with the mascara wand. She won't let me look at my reflection until she's done and I wait in fidgety anticipation, both excited to see the result and afraid I'll look absolutely ridiculous.

It's a chance I don't mind taking. I want to look beautiful for Owen. Like a sophisticated woman who knows exactly what she's doing versus the naïve, silly girl I really am.

He already pretty much knows the real you and despite it all, he still asked you out.

I'm totally ignoring the naggy voice inside my head.

"Okay. I'm done." Kari steps back from me, assessing her work with a shrewd eye. "Wow, you look gorgeous if I do say so myself."

"Can I see?" She grabs my shoulders and turns me this way and that, totally checking me over. "Please?"

"Yes." She turns me toward the mirror slowly. "See what the makeup master did."

I stare at my reflection, shocked that I'm staring back at myself. I look so different. Not overly made up or crazy-looking but definitely . . . older. My skin is flawless. The eye shadow I feared was too dark actually accentuates my blue eyes, making them look brighter and giving them a smoky, sexy glow.

"Wow," I whisper.

She nudges my shoulder with hers. "I know, right? Your eyes really pop."

"They do." I turn to the right, then to the left. I wonder

what Owen will think. Will he like it? Some guys don't like makeup. "Thank you, Kari. You did a great job."

"You're welcome. Are you going to change?"

I shake my head, embarrassment making my cheeks redden again. "He asked that I keep the sweater on."

She laughs, sweeping all the cosmetics she used back into the drawer before she slams it shut. "Why am I not surprised? I'm sure the sweater distracted him. Well, more like your bra did."

I roll my eyes but laugh with her. She's right. I know the bra distracted him.

And I'm hopeful I can distract him some more.

CHAPTER 10

Love is the flower you've got to let grow.
—John Lennon

Chelsea

His eyes nearly bugged out of his head when he came to my apartment to pick me up. The look on Owen's face alone was worth the drill Kari had put me through as she remade my face. Not that she'd asked too many outrageous questions or anything like that. I just . . . it's hard talking about Owen and me and what we share.

First, there's not much to tell. Second, whatever is going on between us feels so fresh and special and new, I really don't want to talk about it.

I'm still trying to figure it all out.

We're quiet on the ride over to the restaurant, the air within the confines of his relatively new and surprisingly clean car filled with some sort of foreign tension that I'm pretty sure is sexual. I may be a virgin and horribly inexperienced with guys, but I'm no idiot.

I'm ultra aware of him and how he looks, what he smells like, how he moves. The subtlest shift of his body as he settles in the driver's seat, the tension in his arms, how his big hands grip the steering wheel. The thick muscles in his thighs draw my attention and I can easily imagine reaching out and resting my hand there. Slowly curling it around so that my fingers rest on the inside of his thigh . . .

Yeah. Being with him makes me want to be bold. Makes me want to do things I've never, ever considered doing before. It's exhilarating.

It's also really scary.

He didn't change clothes. He's still in the same outfit he wore to our earlier session and I'm glad. I like the way he looks in the plaid flannel, the stretch of white cotton across his broad chest. I like even more how he casts the occasional glance in my direction, smiling in that self-assured way of his. That smile says everything is going to be just fine. That I'm in more-than-capable hands.

I believe him.

"I think you'll like the food here," he tells me as we enter the restaurant.

"Oh, I've been here before," I say, glancing around the Mongolian barbeque place. The décor is simple, the dining room big, and usually it's packed wall to wall with people. But it's a Monday night, so it's not as busy as usual.

"You have?" He shakes his head. "Why am I not surprised? I can't impress you no matter how hard I try."

He's trying to impress me? "I like to come here with my roommate. It's cheap and the food is delicious."

"Do you make your own sauce or do you follow the menu?"

Huh? Sometimes Owen asks really weird questions. "Um, I always follow the menu."

"Of course you do." He smiles down at me and I tilt my head back, offering him a tiny smile in return. He's so ridiculously good-looking that I tend to get a little lost when I'm with him. So lost that we stare at each other for a while, until the guy standing behind us clears his throat to indicate we should get moving.

"Sorry," I mumble at the middle-aged man as we step forward, my apology making Owen chuckle.

We both grab our bowls and go down the buffet line, preparing our meals until we stop in front of the sauce station, my shoulder bumping against his arm. It's like falling into a wall of muscle, he's so solid.

I study the menu of various sauces, my gaze snagging on the recipe I always stick with. A few scoops of soy, another couple of teriyaki . . . and I always bypass the spicy stuff since I'm a total wimp.

I'm also totally boring. I never venture out of the familiar. Ever. I keep to myself. I read, I study, I do my homework, I hang with Kari when I can, and I work, work, work.

"Live a little," he says, bending down so his voice is right at my ear. A shiver moves down my spine. He's so close I can almost imagine his lips grazing my skin. "Don't follow the recipe. Just throw in a bunch of different ingredients and see what happens."

I wrinkle my nose. "What if I hate it?"

"Trust me. You won't hate it." He reaches past me and grabs the ladle that's in the garlic oil, scooping it up and dumping it in my bowl.

"But—that wasn't on the menu," I say, a little shocked that he'd take such liberties with my food.

He laughs and then dumps two scoops of the garlic oil on top of the ingredients overflowing his bowl. "I know. We're gonna get a little crazy tonight, Chels. I gotta warn you."

"What if I'm allergic to garlic?"

Owen turns to look at me, his green eyes open wide. "You aren't . . . are you?"

127

Slowly I shake my head, smiling a little. "No, I'm not."

He blows out a harsh breath. "You scared me for a second."

I doubt anything scares him. "But now I'm going to have garlic breath."

"No big deal. So will I." He grabs the ladle in the soy sauce and adds it to his bowl. "When I kiss you later, it won't really matter, right? We'll both have garlic breath."

My heart skips three beats, I swear. He says he's going to kiss me so casually. Like it's no big deal. It might not be for him, but for me . . .

It's a *huge* deal. Like major. When I'm comparing a kiss from Owen Maguire to the measly few boys I've kissed in my life, I know without a doubt this is going to be different. The way I feel about Owen is different. Cody Curtis attacked me and it had been awful.

A kiss from Owen is going to be the complete opposite of awful. As long as I'm not awful either . . .

I start tossing a variety of ingredients into my bowl just like he does, my mind going over what he said again and again. Worry dances in my stomach. Anticipation is such a killer. "So you plan on . . . kissing me tonight?"

He lavishes on the homemade teriyaki sauce, scoop after scoop, until all the vegetables and meat and noodles are swimming in it. "I have lots of plans for you tonight."

His voice is full of so much rich promise I feel slightly dizzy. I follow Owen to the giant barbeque griddle, where the cook takes each of our bowls and tosses them on the round surface, separating my ingredients from Owen's with a large metal cooking utensil that looks like a sword.

This is usually my favorite part of the process, but I can't focus tonight. I'm too aware of the boy standing next to me. The things he just said. It's as if he's purposely trying to unnerve me, keep me on edge, and I wish I knew what he was thinking. I'm a logical person. I like facts and figures. Yet what's happening between us is completely illogical.

And I can hardly wrap my brain around it.

He turns toward me, dipping his head and lowering his voice. "Can I confess something to you?"

I brace myself. "Um, sure."

Glancing up, he looks around, like he's making sure no one's listening. Considering there's no one near us at the moment and the cook can probably only hear the sizzle of the food on the gas grill, it's kind of funny. "I used to like coming here when I was high as hell. The food always tasted a lot better."

Ah, a drug reference. I almost forgot the rumors I've heard that Owen Maguire was once a major pothead. I'm pretty positive that the one night I went to his house to help him study he was high, but I can't be sure. As if I'd know. I have no experience with drugs whatsoever. Mom and Dad both completely sheltered me. "Do you still get high?"

"Sometimes." He shrugs, avoiding my gaze.

Disappointment settles over me and I try my best not to judge. "Don't they drug test you to be on the football team?"

He sends me a look. "There are ways to get around that, Chels. Trust me."

I'm incredulous. I can't believe he would admit such a thing. "I'm surprised you would risk it. Here you are working so hard to get your grades up to get back onto the team and then you admit you still spark up the occasional joint?"

"I never said I was perfect, you know?" He stares off into the distance, his jaw hard, his gaze dark. "I have my issues. Sometimes getting high helps me forget."

"Temporarily," I add. "You can't run away from your

problems, you know." Listen to me, offering advice when I love running away from my own problems.

Well, it's more like I avoid them. Pretend they don't exist. Problems like my father.

He doesn't say anything and I'm afraid I've made Owen mad. *Whatever*, since I'm not too happy with him at the moment anyway. His admission reminds me how different we really are. I'm the good girl, the straight arrow who never does anything wrong. The girl that learned it's best to remain good after witnessing the demise of her very, very bad father.

Owen is a bad boy. I've turned into the total cliché. The innocent, naïve girl who's fallen for the guy who smokes pot and plays football and can barely keep up his grades.

"Here you go." The cook hands over our bowls and we go to the register to pay, Owen taking care of everything. I stand behind him, declining when he asks if I want a soda.

I want to run and hide. My appetite has left me, and that never, ever happens when I come here.

When we finally sit at a small table near the back of the restaurant, Owen leans toward me, his expression earnest and full of regret. "Hey, I'm sorry about what I said earlier. I just . . . I'm trying to be better. It's hard, you know?"

No, not really, but I'm not going to hold it against him. "Apology accepted," I say, grabbing my fork and stabbing it into the steaming-hot bowl of food. "I have no business judging. I'm only . . . watching out for you."

"I know." He sighs. "You sound like my sister."

"Is that a good thing or a bad thing?"

"A good thing." His gaze meets mine, warm and green, and I forget everything else. He's all I can focus on. "You'd like her."

"Tell me about her." I'd rather direct the conversation so he does all the talking and I do all the listening.

I don't want him to ask personal questions. The last person I want to talk about is Dad. Or Mom, for that matter.

"Fable is five years older than me. She's married and she just had a baby."

Such an unusual name, Fable. Makes me wish I knew the story behind it. Because you know there's a story. "Right. I saw the picture and you told me about the baby. Is it a girl or a boy?"

"A girl. Her name is Autumn."

"Ah, that's so sweet."

We talk as we devour our food, my appetite back in full force once I caught a whiff of the delicious, mouth-watering scent wafting up from my bowl. Owen tells me about growing up here, that his sister means everything to him, and the influence her husband had on his early teen years.

He doesn't mention his parents once. He doesn't seem to even know who his dad is, but what about his mom? Where is she in this picture? Did she ditch her children? Was she always working? She's a mystery, and I find it weird that he never talks about her.

Of course, I never talk about my father, so who am I to question him? Our first date isn't the place for me to divulge to Owen all about the convicted felon who just so happens to be the man who raised me.

"What about you?" he asks, knocking me out of my thoughts. "Do you have any brothers or sisters?"

Uh-oh. Here come the personal questions. "No," I say, shaking my head.

"You're an only child?"

"Yes."

He studies me, his gaze narrow, trying to figure me out, I'm sure. "You don't like talking about your family?"

I shrug. "There's not much to tell."

"Hey. I get it," he says softly, then takes a sip of his soda.

And that's it. He doesn't press, doesn't ask for more. I almost want to collapse with relief. He makes me feel so wonderfully *normal*.

"So you never did tell me how it was," Owen says as he pushes his empty bowl away from him. For someone who's as fit as he is, he can certainly pack it away.

"How what was?" I'm stuffed. I did my best to finish everything but as usual, my eyes were bigger than my stomach and my bowl is still practically half full.

"Your dinner. With the magical, crazy I've-never-tried-this-before sauce." He smiles.

"Oh." *Crap*. I almost hate admitting how delicious it was. "It was all right."

"Uh-huh. You didn't finish it." He nods toward my bowl.

"I'm full. I guess I don't have a big appetite like you do." I wave my hand toward his very empty bowl.

"Hmm." He snatches up my bowl and takes a bite that consists mostly of noodles. The look of pleasure that crosses his face is unmistakable. "Damn, this is good. Better than mine."

"Give me a break. I pretty much copied you." I roll my eyes.

He laughs and continues to eat my dinner. Where does it all go? "Maybe you have the special touch. Because this shit is amazing."

I watch, enraptured with everything about him. He laughs and talks and eats like he doesn't have a care in the world, but

I know that's somewhat of a façade. What Owen wants all of the world to see. There's more beneath the surface. I can sense it, have seen glimmers of it, though he's pretty secretive.

But then again, so am I.

My gaze drops to his lips, and I see the tiny bit of mushroom clinging to the corner. "You have something right there. On the corner of your mouth." I point right at his face and he smirks, a sexy glow lighting his eyes as he studies me.

"Yeah? Maybe you should lick it off, then," he suggests.

Now I'm really shocked. "Are you serious?"

He tilts his head. Doesn't bother removing the bit of vegetable hanging off his lip and I swear it's taunting me. Just begging me to lean over the small table and lick the corner of his mouth. "What do you think?" he asks.

"No. You're definitely not serious." There's just . . . no way.

"What if I told you yes, I was?"

"I wouldn't believe you."

Owen

Well, she *should* believe me because I'm dead-ass serious. We've been going in circles all night. Dinner was good, though it got tense at one point with the pot talk. But that quickly became a non-issue and I actually talked to her. Told her a little about my private life, and I never do that. I'm not one to open up, especially with girls.

She hardly said anything. I'd try to ask her a question and she'd deflect it with another. Or she'd give me those bogus one-word answers. I thought *I* was secretive. This girl won't give an inch, no matter how subtle my questions, or how blatant. No information about her family, where she's from, nothing. I figured out she's from the Bay Area and that's about it.

I want to know more.

We've been flirting, having fun. I like giving her shit for going out on a limb and breaking a rule here and there. She's so damn orderly and in control, she needs to learn how to let loose. Be free. I might be a little too free sometimes, but that's better than being so rigid you don't know how to enjoy life.

I think Chelsea's been on such a tight schedule of studying, working, then studying some more, she doesn't know how to relax. And I want to help her. I want her to relax.

With me.

Since I know there's no way in hell Chelsea's going to lick my freaking face in the middle of a restaurant, I'm ready to go. Take her for a drive and kiss her in the quiet confines of my car. Wade's home tonight and has a few friends with him. I bet Des is there, too. They're probably drunk as fuck or worse, high as kites.

Forget that shit. I need to avoid it.

I grab a napkin and wipe the mushroom off my face, ending that little discussion. I'm over it. It's time to kick this date into the next level. "You ready to go?"

Chelsea nods and tosses her napkin on the table before she stands, her purse slung over her bare shoulder since that sexy-as-hell sweater slipped again. She did something to her hair between the time I saw her at school and picking her up at her place. Gorgeous waves that fall past her shoulders tempt me to run my fingers through her silky hair. Cup the back of her neck and draw her in close. So close our lips are almost touching but not quite. I want to breathe her breath, anticipate the kiss for long, trembling seconds before I finally move in and close the deal.

I have never been patient. If I'm interested in a girl, I go for it. There's no holding back. But with Chelsea, I'm taking it slow. I'm afraid I'll scare her.

More than anything, I'm scared I'll somehow fuck it up. I . . . like her. A lot. I actually want to spend time with her, and that's not normal for me.

At all.

I follow her out of the restaurant, resting my hand on her lower back when we walk outside. She's warm, even through the thick fabric of her sweater, and I slip my hand down slightly, wishing I could slide it over her backside.

But I wait.

The night air is cold and misty; a high, thin fog has settled in, and little sparkles of moisture dot her hair by the time we end up at my car. I open the door for her, feeling all gentlemanly for once in my life, but then all thoughts of being a gentleman fade as I study her ass when she slides into the passenger seat.

Get it together, Maguire, I tell myself as I round the front of my car and open the driver's door, slipping inside.

"Where to now?" she asks, chewing on her lip in that nervous way she has as she reaches for the seat belt.

"Can't go to my place unless you want to deal with Wade, and most likely Des." I start the car and let the engine idle. "They're both there, and I'm sure other people are over, too." They can't ever be alone. Always got to turn everything into a party.

"Oh." More chewing of the lip. Poor thing. I should probably kiss it and make it better. "My roommate's home and I think she was having her new so-called boyfriend over, so that probably won't work."

"So-called boyfriend?"

She rolls her eyes. "It's a casual thing that I think she wants to make serious."

"Ah." Sounds familiar. I've been that guy not willing to make it serious.

I've never been in a real relationship, ever. Mom screwed me up in that regard. Though seeing Drew and Fable through the years made me realize that a solid love can last, I'm still full of doubt.

Insecurities. I'm a mess. What girl would really want to deal with me? What with my mommy issues and minor drug problem, I'm no prize.

"Since we can't go home, want to go for a drive?" I ask her.

She turns her body toward mine, her scent wafting in the air, making me inhale as discreetly as possible. "Where to?"

Damn, she smells good. I could breathe her in all night. "I know a place that has a great view of the city. No one will bother us up there." I might have parked in that very spot a few times in high school. Always taking a girl with me, it was somewhere private where we could make out and I could possibly get my hand up her shirt or in her panties. No worries about the cops coming by unless we happened to be up there past midnight.

I haven't been to that spot in a couple of years. Once I graduated high school and got my own place, there was no need to sneak around. Why fool around in the backseat of a car when you can get busy and naked in the comfort of your own bed?

But I'm not getting busy and naked with Chelsea tonight. So I'm looking forward to this.

"Okay." She runs her tongue over her lower lip, then smiles. "Let's do it."

I can read all sorts of things in her "let's do it" statement but I ignore the urge. Instead I smile, reach out, and give her knee a gentle squeeze. "Let's do it," I murmur, making her cheeks flush as she turns away from me and stares out the passenger-side window.

I see the mysterious little smile that curves her lips, though. And I know without a doubt I am definitely kissing Chelsea before the night is through.

CHAPTER 11

You should be kissed and often, and by someone who knows how.
—Rhett Butler

Chelsea

Owen drives us out of the city limits and heads up the Skyway, a road I've traveled maybe twice since I moved here. But he's a local, he's grown up in the area and he knows his way around, all the little-known roads and spots with the best views.

I'm not stupid. We're not driving to this spot with the awesome view to check out the twinkling lights of the city. I might not have much experience, but even I know that a girl and guy going to park in an isolated spot to check out the view are going to end up making out.

I both can't wait and am quietly freaking out.

Neither of us really talks during the drive. We listen to the radio. Owen has it on one of those specialty satellite stations that only plays nineties rock. One song comes on in particular and he turns it up, a little wisp of a smile curling his lips.

"Candlebox. This song reminds me of being a little kid," he says wistfully. "My mom loved this band."

I've never heard of them, but Mom always preferred listening to top-forty-type stuff. Grunge rock was not a part of my growing-up playlist whatsoever. "I like his voice," I say sincerely. It's a pretty good song, and I've come to realize my tastes have changed over the years. I've come into my own, found things I like versus what my parents had me listening to, reading, watching . . . whatever.

"The words remind me of you," he says softly.

I turn to look at him, shock washing over me. "How?"

"The song is called 'Blossom.' Since you told me your middle name is Rose, every time I hear the words *rose* or *flower, blossom,* or *bloom,* I think of you." His smile grows, but he's not looking at me. Just tapping the edge of the steering wheel to the beat of the music, his smile growing as he drives in the dark, cold night.

There's nothing dark or cold about his admission, though. My heart is thumping so hard I'm afraid he can hear it, and I wish I could say something as sweetly poetic as he just did.

Instead I remain quiet and listen to the words of the song. It's sad, about love and loss, and I wonder what he means by the song making him think of me. Is it only because of the title? Or does he really think we'll be over before we've even begun?

As usual, I read too much into it and worry.

When we finally arrive at our destination, I'm a bundle of nerves. Owen shuts off the car and puts it in park, then turns to look at me. "You cold?"

"I'm okay." My breaths are coming quick, and I swear I need to get it together before I hyperventilate.

"Want to go outside? I know it's kind of cold but if we sit on the hood of the car, it'll warm us up." He glances in the backseat. "I have a hoodie back there if you want to borrow it."

"Why do you want to get out?" I keep my gaze locked on

the windshield, impressed with the view before us. We're above the fog line and we can still see the city since the fog is thin and seems to float like a lacy, see-through curtain over town.

"We can see the view even better outside." I turn to look at him and he's got that charming, you'll-do-anything-I-ask look on his face. "Come on, Chels. Live a little, remember?"

"All right."

"You won't regret it," he says, reaching between the seats to grab the hoodie he promised from the backseat. His shoulder brushes against me with the movement and his head is so close to mine, I could reach out and touch his hair.

Instead, I clutch my hands together in my lap.

"You want to use this?" He holds the black hoodie out toward me and I take it, my fingers curling into the cool cotton. It smells like him, fresh and tangy sweet with that hint of spice. I wish I could hold it to my face and inhale.

He'd think I was a total freak.

"Maybe," I say, holding the sweatshirt close. "Thanks."

He flashes me a smile, then climbs out of the car and I do the same, meeting him in the front. I stare at the car's hood, wondering how in the world I'm going to get on there without looking like a complete fool, and I sink my teeth into my lower lip, wincing when I hit a particularly sensitive spot.

I've been chewing on my lip a lot lately, I guess.

"Never crawl onto the hood of a car before?" he asks.

I turn to look at him, feeling like a dope. "Not really."

"Need some help?"

"Uh . . ." I turn back to face the car, contemplating my choices. "I'm not—"

Owen grabs hold of my waist before I can even finish the sentence and I squeal, shocked that he's lifting me off my feet

140

and setting me on top of the car as if I weigh nothing. He settles me on the hood and I scramble backward, my feet slipping on the slick painted surface, but I'm careful, not wanting to put a dent in his nice car. Thankfully I don't slide right off and I plant my hands on either side of me, bracing my body as best I can.

He climbs on top of the car like it's no big deal, all long, strong limbs and graceful ease. Grinning down at me, he swipes his hair out of his eyes. "Want to sit on the roof?"

I glance back at it. "How am I going to get up there?"

"Come on." He offers his hand and I take it, emitting another squeal when he hauls me to my feet and grabs my waist again, basically tossing me onto the roof. I spread his hoodie onto the very cold metal and settle in, laughing when he scrambles up the glass windshield and sits besides me with a goofy smile on his face, a little out of breath.

"You promised me a warm hood and instead all I get is cold metal under my butt," I chastise him, leaning in to nudge his arm with my shoulder.

"Come here, then." Without warning he slips his arm around my shoulders, pulling me in close to him, and my entire side is pressed against his. "Well, I guess that worked."

"You act like you planned this." I shove lightly at his chest, my voice sounding breathless, my heart tripping over itself, and I glance down, noticing how perfectly we fit next to each other.

"It wasn't premeditated. More like a spontaneous thing." He stretches out his long legs before him, his firm thigh against mine, his body warmth seeping into me. We remain quiet for long, peaceful minutes, the only sound the chirping of a few random insects and the roar of the cars speeding by on the Skyway in the near distance.

Before us, the city lights twinkle and sparkle, the fog a misty veil. There's nothing but darkness surrounding us, only the silvery light of the quarter-sized moon above us casting its gentle glow.

"It's beautiful," I finally say. "I've never been up here or seen this view before."

"Yeah. Not many people have. Us locals know about the location but we don't like telling you foreigners about it." He chuckles and the deep sound reverberates through me, making me tingle.

"I don't blame you," I whisper, and he doesn't reply. He doesn't need to. Our silence is comfortable, soothing. I could so get used to this. Sitting on top of Owen's car, his arm around me, the top of my head hitting at his chin. He's so warm and solid, his arm curved around my shoulders a heavy, comfortable weight, and when he starts lightly stroking my bared shoulder with his fingertips, I want to melt.

"Comfortable?" he asks, his voice a low, sexy murmur that sets my insides trembling.

I nod, unable to form words.

"Still cold?"

"No," I whisper, leaning my forehead against his chin. His stubble is prickly against my skin and I close my eyes, savoring this new intimacy between us. He holds me closer and shifts, his finger sliding beneath my chin so he's lifting my face to his.

Oh. God. This is it. He's going to kiss me. I crack open my eyes to find him studying me, his gaze roving over my face, and I release a shuddery breath.

"Nervous?"

He must think I'm a complete novice. He's pretty much right if he does. "Yes."

"Why?" He trails his finger along my jawline, across my

142

chin, leaving a wake of tingles with his touch. "You had to know this was going to happen."

"Um . . ." I start but he presses his finger against my lips, silencing me.

"You still going to tutor me after I kiss you? We're not breaking any sort of code or rule, are we?" I shake my head and he traces my lips, first the top one, then the bottom, pressing gently against the sore spot my teeth have worn. "I hate that you get so nervous that you hurt yourself."

"I've had the habit since I was a kid," I admit.

"It's a bad one." Leaning in, he brushes my mouth with his, the kiss so brief I could almost believe it didn't happen. "Shit, Chels. Did you feel that?"

"Feel what?" My eyes are still open, staring into his beautiful green, glittering gaze, and then he's cupping my cheek, tilting my head back for his kiss. His eyes shutter closed right before mine do and I see his thick, long eyelashes in my mind just before he whispers, "This," and then his mouth settles on mine.

I'm lost. Completely and totally lost to the drugging, delicious feeling of his mouth connecting with mine. One gentle, sweet kiss after another, our lips parting with each press and glide, until he slips his tongue inside my mouth, just as he slips his hands into my hair. His fingers tug, his tongue tangles with mine, and I've never, ever had a more perfect kiss in all my life.

Sitting on the roof of his car, the faint chirping of the crickets in the tall, dry grass, the even fainter whoosh of the cars rushing by, I'll never forget this moment. His fingers in my hair, the sound of our lips connecting again and again, the soft whispers and our accelerated breaths.

It's sensory overload.

He leans more into me, his arm braced around my shoulders, fingers slipping beneath my bared bra strap and caressing my shoulder. I reach out and rest my hands on his chest, feel his rapidly beating heart beneath my palm, and a thrill runs through me.

Owen seems as affected by this kiss as I am. The realization is heady, powerful.

Exciting.

He breaks the kiss first, pressing his forehead to mine, then nuzzling my nose. "This is really uncomfortable, sitting on top of my car, trying to kiss you," he admits.

I laugh, opening my eyes to see him smiling at me. "Wasn't this your suggestion?"

"Yeah . . ." His expression is pained, and I wonder why.

"Let's go back inside the car, then."

"You want to go home?" He almost looks devastated.

Slowly shaking my head, feeling bold, I lean in and press my lips to his, letting them linger for a long, warm moment before I pull away. "No," I whisper.

His eyes light with a hunger I've never seen before and then we're scrambling off the top of the car, Owen jumping down first before he reaches out, his big hands slipping beneath my sweater and grasping hold of my waist as he helps me get onto solid ground. He goes for the back door on the driver's side and throws it open, indicating he wants me to get in first. I do so, giggling when he slides in behind me, his hands reaching for me, curling around my waist again before he brings me to him, over him, until I'm straddling him with my knees on either side of his hips, sitting on top of him in the most wicked, delicious way.

I can feel him, everywhere. Hovering above him, I stare down at his beautiful face, drink him in, touch him however I want. Wherever I want. I smooth his hair away from his forehead, letting the soft strands sift through my fingers, and he closes his eyes, a low, masculine sound of pleasure escaping him.

I feel that sound pulse throughout my body, settling between my legs, and I press into him, my mouth meeting his, our kiss becoming deep. Deeper. Our tongues slide against each other, our bodies rock, and he grips my waist, stilling me, keeping me in place.

But I don't want to be kept in place. I feel restless, needy. I want more. More Owen, more of his mouth, more of his hands, more of his tongue. He breaks our kiss to feather his lips across my jaw, down my throat, his tongue darting out to lick, and I clutch him close. My arms wrap around his neck, and I close my eyes as I tilt my head back.

We're taking it from zero to one hundred between us and I don't even care. I've already thrown caution out the window.

All I want is Owen.

Owen

It's getting out of control and quick between us. I'd wanted to keep it outside on purpose, for fear I'd get in over my head and want to get Chelsea naked. I had a sense it would be good between us the moment our lips first touched. But I had no idea she would be so incredibly responsive, so eager, feel so fucking right in my arms. I hold her close but not too close, my fingers pressing into the soft skin just above her hips, trying my best to keep her still as I map a path of fire down her neck with my lips.

I lick, I nibble, I taste. My cock is painfully hard beneath the button fly of my jeans and it would be so easy. Easy to strip her of her clothes, touch her in all the right places, show her how to touch me in all the right places and then fuck her right here in the backseat of my car.

So. Freaking. Easy.

But I don't do any of that. I'm not going to push. She's totally inexperienced—I can tell just by her at first tentative kiss, how nervous she got, how nervous she's always been with me. I gotta take it slow for her sake. Gotta remember that before I let myself lose complete control and I get busy corrupting her for the rest of the night.

Breaking our kiss, I lean my head back against the seat, staring up at her. She's beautiful, her lips swollen from our kisses, her wavy hair in complete sexy disarray around her face, all from my fingers. Her chest rises and falls at a rapid pace and it would be so easy to slip my hands beneath her loose sweater and feel her. Cup her. Thumb her nipples, make them hard before I draw one into my mouth . . .

Inhaling sharply, I push those thoughts out of my head. My overly vivid imagination is definitely not helping matters.

"Owen." Her voice sounds needy, edgy, and I know what she wants. I want it, too. "What are you doing?"

But I'm not going to give it to her. Not tonight.

"I should get you home." I thread my fingers through her hair, brushing them through the long, dark strands again and again. She slowly closes her eyes, her lush mouth parted, a shuddery little breath escaping her that I feel all the way down to my dick.

"Maybe I don't want to go home," she admits.

"We need to get you home." The disappointment on her face is clear and I decide to be honest with her. "I'm not going to fuck you in the backseat of my car, Chels. You deserve better than that." *For your first time,* I want to say but don't.

What if I'm wrong that she's a virgin? I don't think I am. She acts like a girl who has zero experience and for once, I'm okay with that. The mere idea of Chelsea being with another guy fills me with pure, white-hot rage. I can't stand the thought.

Since when did I turn into such a possessive caveman? Ready to beat my chest with my fists and declare Chelsea as mine. She belongs to no one else.

And I never feel that way about any girl.

Her gaze softens and she leans down, kissing me once. Twice, her lips lingering. Like she never wants this to end. I feel the same way. "Okay." She sounds sad. Defeated. And I hate that.

"Hey." I catch her chin, keeping her face close to mine. Her breath flutters across my lips, smelling wintergreen fresh from the mints we grabbed before we left the restaurant. I close my eyes for a brief moment, searching for the strength I'm gonna need to be able to resist her.

Because really, I'd rather do nothing but fuck her in the backseat of my car. I have no problem with that whatsoever.

I open my eyes to find her studying me as she licks her lips, her expression hopeful, frustrated . . . beautiful.

Fuck, I like this girl. A lot. How am I going to keep her in my life? Will she be able to stand me once everything gets all crazy again? I barely have time for myself, let alone someone else.

"I'm going to be busy," I say, letting my thumb drift across her chin. "Once I get back on the football team, my schedule is gonna go to hell. And with work and school, it'll be crazy."

She exhales softly, sadness etched all over her face. "Okay. I get it. You don't have time to see me."

"That is definitely not what I'm saying." I kiss her because

147

I can't help it. Her lips are pure temptation. Soft and pink and fucking delicious. "I'm asking you to be patient with me," I whisper after I end the kiss. "I know you're busy, too."

"Right." She nods, her brow wrinkling. "I am."

"You work a lot. School." I smile, trying to ease the wariness I see in her gaze. "I'm trying to say I want to see you again but I'm kind of fucking it up, aren't I?"

A soft huff of laughter escapes her and she nods. "Yeah, you sort of are."

"We still on for Wednesday?" I'm referring to our next tutoring appointment.

"Yes. Of course."

"Do you work after?"

"I do. My usual eight-to-two shift." She shifts on my lap. I can feel the heat between her legs brush against my erection and I want to lift up and press against her, right there. Let her know exactly what she does to me.

But if I do that once, I'll end up doing it again. And again. And then I'll be kissing her, my hands reaching beneath her sweater, her hands beneath my shirt, and then we're done for.

"You need to quit that job. The hours suck." I slide my hand that still grips her waist a little higher, touching her ribs, just below her bra. I must have the control of a saint tonight because normally, I'd be tearing into that within seconds.

"I can't. I need the money."

"Why?" I want information. I want to know why she works so hard yet sometimes acts like a haughty little rich girl. Is she broke? Cut off from mommy and daddy for doing something awful? I can't imagine her doing anything to make her parents cut her off. That's a pretty damn drastic move. She's a fucking genius; she wouldn't be that stupid.

"I just . . . it's only my mom and me, and I need to work both jobs to afford living here," she admits, dropping her gaze. "I got a scholarship for school but my apartment, utilities—all that stuff is expensive."

Finally she's sharing something personal about her family. I savor it as though she handed over her entire life story. "What happened to your dad?"

"I don't want to talk about him," she mumbles, her gaze still locked on my chest.

Frustration fills me and I shove it aside. I can't push. I got pissed at her when she asked about *my* dad, so I need to respect her wishes. Clearly she doesn't want to talk about hers.

But that only makes me want to know even more what happened between them.

"We should go, then," I say reluctantly, letting her slide off my lap. She falls to the side of me, landing on the seat with a soft plop. Reaching out, I grab the handle and open the door, climbing out of the car with Chelsea right behind me. But before I can open the driver's-side door, she's grabbing me, pulling me to her so she can kiss me.

I drown in her, grab hold of her so I can press her against the car, holding her in my arms as we kiss, our tongues busy, our hands roaming. Just like that, I feel out of control again. I fucking need to get it together, and quick.

It's her turn to break the kiss first and she gazes up at me, her eyes wide and fathomless as they drink me in. "I . . . want you to know that it means a lot to me, you taking me out tonight. Bringing me up here." She pushes up on tiptoe and presses her face against my neck, kissing me there. "Thank you," she breathes against my skin, making me shiver.

I tighten my arm around her waist and hold her close, burying my face in her hair so I can breathe in her scent, absorb her heat. "So Chels?"

"Yes?" Her voice is muffled against my neck and another shiver moves through me.

"Was tonight enough of an adventure for you?"

She laughs and pulls away from me so our gazes meet. "Most definitely."

"Good." I drop a kiss to the tip of her nose. "Because it's only just begun."

CHAPTER 12

Life is the flower for which love is the honey.
—Victor Hugo

Owen

"Autumn and I want to come see you."

Fable's words surprise me and I sit up straight, run my hand over my head as I glance around my bedroom, squinting into the darkness since the blinds are closed tight and my door is shut. It's Sunday, and I always sleep in since if I'm not working Saturday night, I'm usually at a game. Or I'll play in the afternoon and sometimes if my schedule's real intense, I'll end up working that night, too.

Exactly what I did last night—and those are the worst days. I'm fucking beat.

"Autumn wants to come visit me, huh?" Yawning, I stretch my neck, my entire body sore. I almost felt out of shape out there on the field. Taking a few weeks off from practice threw me.

"Absolutely. She misses her Uncle Owen terribly. I miss you, too," Fable adds.

"So when do you two want to come?" I ask, scrubbing a hand along my jaw, the rasp of my beard poking at my palm. I need to shave, and soon. Chelsea would probably complain if I kissed her with a face like this.

Thinking of kissing Chelsea makes my skin tingle and I fight it. I'm talking to my sister, for the love of God.

"Well, you're playing a big game this next weekend, right? Archrival team, getting closer to playoff season and all that homecoming crap?" I love her sarcastic enthusiasm for college life. She always felt like an outsider looking in.

"Yeah, it's a pretty big game next weekend. Starts in the late afternoon, though I don't remember the exact time," I say. "I'd love to have you here. It would be just you and Autumn, right?"

"Yeah. Drew will be out of state next weekend. Green Bay."

Freaking cold and a hell of a team. I don't envy him that. "You . . . don't want to stay at my house, do you?" I'd probably have to fumigate if that were the case.

"Hell no. Are you kidding? That place scares me. I'll get a hotel room," she says with a soft laugh.

"Okay, cool. Yeah, if you want to come for the weekend, I'd love it."

"Awesome. I'll talk more with Drew about it and figure out the schedule." She breathes a relieved little sigh. "It's so nice talking to you on the phone with no baby in my arms. She's always wiggling around, crying or reaching for things."

"Where is Autumn, anyway?"

"Taking a nap. I have a sitter coming later. I'm going to Drew's game tonight."

"Wish I could go," I say, like always missing my sister. And Drew. Even the baby, because I bet she's changed a ton since the last time I got to hold her. Thank God Fable always sends me pictures. Probably too many, considering all the ones I have on my phone and the baby isn't even six months old yet, but I enjoy every single one she sends my way.

"You should! What do you have going on tonight? Are you working?"

"I'm not, actually." The drive to San Francisco would be almost four hours. Considering it's barely nine o'clock—damn, my sister's mean, calling so early on a Sunday—I could be there in plenty of time.

But do I want to make the drive? This is my one day off. The rest of the week is packed. What with school, practice, work, and Chelsea, I can hardly keep my schedule straight.

I think of Chelsea again and smile. It's been a week since the night I took her up the Skyway and kissed her on the roof of my car. We've seen each other a couple of times since, though never long enough for my liking. And we sort of ruined last Wednesday's tutoring lesson. More like it turned into me teaching Chelsea the art of slow, hour-long kisses.

She'd been so worried about getting caught, which only made it that much more intense, that much more exciting. I sat on a table, my legs spread, Chelsea standing in between them, her hands in my hair, our mouths fused. Kissing, whispering, her trying to pull out of my arms only for me to drag her back in.

Fuck, it had been hot. Knowing I couldn't do anything with her beyond kissing. As if I'd get her naked on campus. I want her, but I'm not that stupid.

Besides, I really am still working on my portfolio and need to keep up with my English assignments. Though truthfully, I hardly need Chelsea for any of that anymore. Not that we've cancelled our arrangement yet.

Hell, I'm starting to believe it's the only time I can get to see her.

"I could get you skybox tickets. I usually like to sit on the field, but the skybox is so much fun and the weather is crappy today, so we should definitely sit in the box," she says, sounding excited. "Though I totally understand if you can't make it, Owen. You're busy—you need some time to relax rather than drive all the way here only to turn around and go back."

An idea forms in my brain, one that would make going to San Francisco to see my family even more worth it. "I want to go. I'd love to see Drew play." I pause, trying my best to sound nonchalant. "So hey. Can you get me two tickets?"

"Absolutely. Who do you want to bring with you? Wade?" I'd brought him to a couple of games in the past, so her assumption made sense.

"No . . . I want to bring, uh . . . Chelsea." I wince, waiting for the barrage of questions and teasing.

"Owen. Really? You want to bring a girl?" Fable sounds shocked. "The girl who's your tutor?"

"Well, yeah. I do on occasion hang out with girls, you know." I'm irritated and I don't really have a reason to be.

"Right, I do know. But I figured that was all you were doing. Hanging out with them and that's it. You sound sort of serious about this Chelsea girl."

"I'm not. Not really." I grimace at my lie. I don't know how I feel about Chelsea. We're having fun. We're taking it slow. Does she really fit into my life?

No.

But I'm working on somehow making that happen anyway.

"So she's a friend?" Fable asks.

"Yeah. That's exactly what she is." I'm not too far off the mark with that. We *are* friends.

Friends who like to sit on my couch when Wade's gone and make out for hours. Until we're both so worked up I have to practically shove her out the door for fear I'll strip her naked and jump her bones right there in the middle of the living room. And no way can I take her back to my bedroom. I do that and we're done for. Naked and me buried deep inside her within seconds, I have no doubt about that.

"Come on. Friends? Really?"

"Really," I say firmly. "Let me ask Chelsea if she's able to go and I'll text you. Is that cool?"

"As long as you tell me as soon as possible. I need to ask for those tickets as soon as you know."

I hang up and immediately text Chelsea, hoping she's not sleeping in.

But hey, it's Chelsea. I'm sure she's already been working on her homework for the last two hours, knowing her.

Wanna go to a professional football game?

I barely have to wait two minutes before she's responding.

When?

Today, I type.

Are you serious?!?!

Smiling, I answer her, giving her the details, then asking:

Do you have to work tonight?

No. It's my day off.

I couldn't make this work out any more perfect if I tried.

Then you should take your day off and come with me
to San Francisco.

You really want to take me? What about Wade or Des?

They'll kill me if they find out I'm going to a game and I didn't invite either of their asses to go.

Tough shit.

I'd definitely rather take you.

I wait for her reply, nerves eating at my gut. This girl has me all twisted up inside and I don't quite get it. Still.

My phone rings and I answer it without even looking to see who it is. I already know.

"I know absolutely nothing about football," she says when I say hello.

"I can teach you." I lie back on my bed, scratching my chest. I wish Chelsea were in bed with me. That would be a most excellent way to spend a Sunday morning.

"I'm boring. You'll probably wish you had one of your friends with you the minute the game starts," she says. "I'll probably play on my phone or whatever. Or be so completely lost I won't know what's happening on the field."

"You are definitely not boring. And hey, if you're going to spend more time with me, you gotta learn about football sometime, right?"

She pauses. I can practically hear the cogs turning in her brain as she processes what I just said. "I guess you're right," she say, her voice soft.

That soft voice of hers gets me every single time. "I want you there with me, Chels. It'll be fun. You could meet my sister and after the game's done, I bet you could meet Drew, too. Come on, say yes."

"I'd get to meet your sister?" she squeaks, sounding nervous. "Oh wow. I didn't realize that, though it does make sense." She pauses again, and I swear I can feel her nervousness come over the phone loud and clear. "Okay. Yes. I'll go."

"Good," I say, relief sweeping through me. I'd truly been afraid she'd say no.

We make arrangements for me to come pick her up within the hour and then I hang up, immediately texting Fable that I need two tickets for Drew's game.

I can't wait to meet your Chelsea, Fable answers.

Yeah. I can't wait for Fable to meet her either. Though she's definitely not *my* Chelsea. Despite the occasional possessive wave that comes over me when I'm with her, we are really just friends. Friends who make out. Friends who wish for more, but neither of us is doing anything about it.

I'm almost afraid to push for fear I'll ruin it all. She's afraid because . . . I don't know why. But taking it slow isn't so bad.

Most of the time, it's pretty damn good. Except when I'm walking around with blue balls.

Climbing out of bed, I exit my room and go to the kitchen, on the hunt for something quick to eat before I make my way to taking a shower and getting out of here to go pick up Chelsea.

"What are you doing up so early, asshole?"

I stop short to find Des in my kitchen, eating a bowl of Cheerios and way too much milk. It's practically sloshing out of the bowl and onto the table. "Good morning to you, too," I mutter, irritated.

The guy acts like he lives here. It's annoying as hell, especially since he doesn't pay rent. Of course, neither does Wade, but that's the arrangement we made before Wade moved in.

I've known Wade since I was a kid. His mom bailed me out multiple times and let me stay at their house way more than she ever had to. She understood Fable was always working and Mom was never around. Wade's mother always welcomed me with open arms.

It was the least I could do, offering Wade a free place to live while we went to college. His mom may live in the same town but he wanted to be on his own, just like I did.

But Des? The guy is loaded, one of those rich kids from the Bay Area who come to the university looking to party now that they're free from their parents. He'd been the drug-dealing high school kid in the suburbs and now he's the drug-dealing college student on campus. I like him, but not just because he's my dealer. He's my friend.

He's also a user.

Aren't we all?

"Why you up so early?" Des pushes more cereal into his mouth, munching loudly on his Cheerios. "I usually have the house all to myself on a Sunday morning."

"You act like you live here," I say, leaning against the counter. I need some fucking coffee, stat.

"I practically do."

"So why aren't you paying any rent?"

"Because I sleep on the fucking couch. Why should I have to pay rent to sleep on a come-stained couch?"

"Jesus, Des." I reach for the coffeemaker, thankful Des actually made some. Grabbing a mug from the cabinet, I pour myself a cup, then dump sugar and creamer into it before I take a sip.

And grimace as I swallow. Damn it's strong, even with all the cream and sugar added to it.

"You know it's true. How many girls have we all banged at one point or another on that couch? Too many to count." Des chuckles and shakes his head, sounding proud of the fact that my couch has hosted an endless list of chicks sprawled naked across it.

The image disgusts me. Not even a few weeks ago I probably would have high-fived him.

Now all I can think about is Chelsea. And how grossed out she'd be if she really knew all the dirty shit I'd been up to in my not-so-distant past.

"I just feel like if you're going to stay here all the time, you should at least contribute something," I mutter.

"I do contribute. Plenty of beer and weed to keep y'all on a continuous buzz," he says matter-of-factly.

"Yeah, but I always pay for the weed, bro." I do. I never expect a handout.

"I'm getting real sick of your poor-ol'-me act. You act all hard up and like you always need money, but gimme a break. Wade lives here rent-free. Why can't I hang around here on occasion?" Des pushes the now only filled-with-milk bowl away from him and leans back in his chair, running a hand through his longish brown hair. He always has a shaggy, slightly unkempt look about him. Thin, worn T-shirts, old, holey and torn jeans, scuffed shoes. His hair is a mess, his face covered in four-day-old beard. It's like he's cultivated this drug dealer image, but I know he's full of shit.

"I've been thinking about it and I don't know if it's smart that you're always here," I say, sipping from my coffee. My appetite has left me. I don't want to have this conversation with Des. Not now, not really ever. He's a friend, even if he irritates the shit out of me. I'm not in the mood for a confrontation.

"Why the hell not?" Des sounds indignant, looks shocked. "What does it matter?"

I set the mug on the counter beside me, meeting his gaze. "You're a drug dealer."

"So what? I've supplied you with enough joints to last you a lifetime."

Chelsea would die if she knew Des was a dealer. "Maybe I'm trying to clean up my image."

Des glares, his gaze narrowed, his jaw tight. "It's the girl, right?"

I never said Des was stupid. "Maybe. What does it matter? Doesn't look good that I'm on the football team and like to get high. They could kick me off."

"That's never bothered you before."

"Yeah, well it should've," I mutter.

Des studies me. "You know you're fucking around with a chick who is nothing like you, Owen. She's too goody-goody for your ass. You get in her panties yet?"

"That's none of your goddamn business," I spit out.

"Meaning you haven't." Des sighs and shakes his head. "Stick with what you know, buddy. Find some girl who's looking for a good time and that's it. Chelsea is just some smart, sorta plain girl who's slumming. You're exciting, you're nothing like any guy she's ever known, if she's even known any guys, because if you want my opinion, she has virgin written all over her."

"You need to watch what you say about her," I warn, fury eating me up, ready to burst out and unleash all over Des's skinny ass. "Show her some respect."

Des laughs. "You got it bad, don't you? I don't think I've ever seen you like this over a girl. You usually just fuck 'em and leave 'em. Hell, Wade and I both have slobbered after your leftovers and you've never protested. What would you say if I told you I'd pick up where you left off when you're done with the tutor?"

"I'd say I'd beat your fucking face in until you couldn't speak," I say, my voice low as I stare at him.

The motherfucker actually smiles. "Well, well. Look at you. All worked up over a girl. It's kind of cute, Maguire. But you're wasting your time with that one. She's going to be the one who leaves first and damn, is it going to hurt. You'll need me and what I supply more than anything once she's gone."

Does everyone think I'm a weak asshole who can't function without a joint dangling from my fingers or what? "Trust me, I don't need you."

"You will. Once your precious little tutor is gone." He

grins, gets up from the kitchen table, and saunters out of the room. Leaving his dirty bowl on the table for me to pick up.

So I do. I pick it up and throw it in the fucking sink, so hard the ceramic smashes everywhere, but I'm not satisfied.

I'm pissed. And a little scared. What if what he says comes true and Chelsea does leave first? I've never even thought about it. I'm always the one who walks away.

If the tables were turned, I don't know if I could stand it.

Chelsea

I always thought I hated football, but this has turned out to be one of the best days of my life. Despite the dark, gloomy skies, the rain somehow decided not to fall once we arrived at the game. We're watching from high above in a humongous skybox in the new stadium that opened a few years ago.

I'm not even paying attention to what's happening. How can I? I'm too consumed with Owen as he watches the game with rapt attention, his expression tense, his gaze locked on the field for every play, especially when the 49ers have the ball, specifically his brother-in-law. Every once in a while he says something to either Fable or me, or he leans over to give my hand a quick squeeze. He even drops the occasional kiss on my lips.

All the while his sister sits there, watching us in obvious shock though she's trying her best to fake it.

She's nice, his sister. When he introduced us, she actually hugged me, her pleasure at meeting me genuine. I was a little overwhelmed at first because Owen had warned me on the drive here that she could be pretty standoffish when she first meets someone. Says she has a hard time trusting people.

I could relate. Maybe she saw that, too; I don't know.

Fable's definitely beautiful, petite yet busty, with long, sunny blond hair and those same flashing green eyes as Owen's. The affection between the two of them is palpable, and it makes me happy to see such obvious sibling love.

It almost makes me a little jealous, which is so stupid and pointless. Would I ever matter as much to Owen as his sister does? Totally not fair of me to think that way, but I can't help it.

The drive to the stadium in Santa Clara had been long but fun. He'd come and picked me up in a sullen, agitated mood, but then he'd seemed to brighten a little when he saw me. And when he kissed me, his lips had lingered, and he'd held me extra close. Told me he missed me, his gaze roving over my face as if he couldn't get enough of me, and for whatever reason, he seemed to calm down.

Had something happened before he came to pick me up? The thought nagged at the back of my mind the entire drive. I tried not to distract him too much since it rained on us most of the way and the roads were slick, so I kept my worry to myself.

And I am a total worrier. I inherited that trait from Mom and I hate it. Though she always claimed all the worry made me that much better of a student, since I feared missing an assignment or getting a bad grade. Worrying kept me on track, she told me more than once.

Whatever.

"So how is Owen doing in school?" Fable asks, her expression curious.

It's halftime and Owen has taken off. Probably going to the bathroom, leaving me and Fable alone together.

"He's doing a lot better," I say, my voice a little shaky. I wish I weren't so intimidated but oh my God, this is Owen's sister. The one person he seems to love more than anyone else.

She pretty much raised him and he respects her so much. I just want her to like me. "When I first started seeing him, he wasn't applying himself, you know? And he also wasn't going to class, which is obviously a problem."

Fable sighs. "He can be so irritating. And stubborn. If I keep telling him to do something, I swear sometimes he'll flat-out not do it just because I want him to. You know what I mean?"

I shrug. Not really, because that's not how I am whatsoever. And somehow I convinced Owen to do his schoolwork. Of course, he had so much on the line at that point I don't think he was willing to risk it.

"It's always been hard to keep him focused," Fable continues. "He'd much rather be doing something else. I think he gets bored easily in class. He's very smart. He just tends to get . . . distracted."

"Well, he's back on the team, he's working, and he's going to school but somehow maintaining his heavy schedule pretty smoothly. I'm trying to help keep him on track. He's still playing catch-up with his portfolio for the Creative Writing class but I think he's almost there," I explain.

"So it sounds like he doesn't really need to see you anymore, does he?" Fable asks, her voice gentle.

I shrug, unease slipping down my spine. "I guess not."

She smiles. "He likes you."

My cheeks heat with embarrassment. "I like him, too."

"Owen has never introduced me to a girl before."

Now I'm shocked. "Really?"

Fable slowly shakes her head. "He's always been very . . . independent. We both have. We've had to be."

I have no idea what she's alluding to and I wish I did. But it's not my place to grill Owen's sister. He should just tell me about his life on his own. Of course, I hold my own secrets close to my chest and I'm still not ready to admit anything to him.

Such as how guilty I feel for being here, in Santa Clara, when really Mom's place isn't that far away. I should have gone by to see her. She misses me terribly. I just talked to her on the phone yesterday and she'd sounded so sad, so desolate. She has no one, she likes to constantly tell me. No one but me. She can't wait for me to come home and go to graduate school. She truly thinks I'm just going to move in and it'll be the two of us against the world again.

I hate to break it to her, but that's the last thing I want to do. And who knows what my life will be like two years from now? Things could change. Dramatically.

"He admires you a lot," I say, wanting Fable to know just how much she means to Owen. I assume she realizes it but it must feel good to hear it, too. "You and your husband. He says the two of you pretty much raised him."

"We did—well, mostly during his teen years, but those are the worst, right?" Fable smiles. "Owen and Drew became super close despite Owen's initial distrust of him. But Owen hardly trusts anyone, so that's normal. Now they're so close; it's sweet. Drew's like the big brother Owen never had."

"Don't tell me you're talking about me."

At the sound of his deep voice, I turn to find Owen standing above us, a smile on his face and a shopping bag clutched in his hand. I return his smile, my heart flipping over itself when he settles into the empty seat beside me, his shoulder brushing against mine.

"You know it," Fable says, a wicked grin on her face. "I'm telling Chelsea all about your bad habits."

"Gimme a break." He rolls his eyes. "I'm perfect." Grinning, he sets the bag in my lap. "I got you a present."

"What?" I'm shocked yet pleased. "You didn't have to do that."

"I wanted to," he says simply, nodding toward the bag. "Open it."

I peek inside and then pull out a thick, white hooded pull-over sweatshirt with the 49ers emblem on the front. It's soft and warm, a little oversized, and I clutch it close, my gaze snagging on the price tag, eyes widening when I see the price.

Holy crap, it was expensive.

"I love it," I tell him, touched that he would think of me and want to buy me a gift. "Thank you."

"Put it on. Show your 49er spirit." He takes the sweatshirt from me and tears off the price tag with a firm tug.

I shrug off the pale gray cardigan I'm wearing and take the new sweatshirt from Owen, then slip it on. It's bulky and thick, cozy and soft, and I slip my hands into the front pocket, practically hugging myself. "How does it look?"

"Good. Real good." The heat in Owen's gaze momentarily steals my breath and I give him a stern look, tipping my head to the side toward his sister.

The last thing I need is him wanting to attack me in front of Fable. How embarrassing.

"You two are so cute." Fable sighs and shakes her head. "Just friends, my ass."

Owen says nothing and neither do I. Where did she hear we were just friends? Is that what Owen told her? We've not declared ourselves in any sort of relationship, but I did figure we were headed that way.

I definitely wouldn't describe us as "just friends."

The words bother me the rest of the game. Through the entire second half, though I put on a brave and happy face when the 49ers win. I chat with Fable but I can feel myself withdrawing, folding into myself. She knows a lot of people in the skybox—it's filled with other players' wives and girl-friends, and they all want to talk to the star quarterback's wife. She matters; she's important.

I don't matter. I'm not important. I'm just Owen's friend.

Trying my best to muster up being in a good mood, I meet Drew after the game and he's just . . . dazzling. Gorgeous and friendly and so incredibly sweet to his wife; clearly he loves her madly. I can see his respect and affection for Owen; the three of them are close.

But not me. I'm not close to Owen. I'm just his friend.

So stupid, how I can't let this go, but . . . it devastates me. What did I expect, though? We've only known each other for a few weeks. I've never been a believer in insta-love, though Kari certainly has been. She's still chasing after that stupid Brad, yet he acts like he doesn't want to give her the time of day.

Owen always acts like he wants to give me the time of day, yet we're just friends.

Argh. If I could smack myself in the face and knock some sense into my head, I so would. I'm like a broken record. The iTunes playlist put on repeat. Again and again the words rat-tle around in my brain, pulse through my blood.

Just friends. Just. Friends.

Maybe I need to embrace those words. Remember them. Maybe that's all we really are. At least, according to Owen. I need to prepare myself. He'll leave me eventually. Move on, because that's what he does. He's never had a steady girl-friend; he's admitted that to me more than once. So what am I doing, setting myself up to fail with Owen?

I need to harden my heart. Not let him in.

But I'm afraid it's too late. He's already so in, there's no way I can get him out anytime soon.

And I don't want to, either.

CHAPTER 13

I'm not sure I even know how to love.
—Owen Maguire

Owen

Something happened. And somehow, I ruined everything.

The weather is shit. It's like the skies closed up special for the game and the minute it was over, the clouds parted, opened up and dumped enough water to flood the entire stadium. Getting out of the parking lot was less of a nightmare for us than for the regular folks, since we got to park in the special team lot, but still, it took awhile. And I flat-out couldn't resist when Drew asked us to go out to dinner with them.

Chelsea had agreed readily, but she was quiet the entire meal. I have no idea if I pissed her off and I wasn't about to ask her in front of Fable and Drew, so I tried my best to include her in the conversation. But she wasn't having it. Not that she was rude, but she'd sort of withdrawn into herself, remaining quiet as she sat by my side. Fable noticed. She asked Chelsea if she was feeling all right, and Chels confessed she had a headache and that she was tired, but she'd be fine.

That was Fable's cue to give me a sharp look that told me point blank I needed to take care of her. I promised I would, sending her an equally pointed look back that she should stay out of my business, but I think it went undetected.

Typical.

We'd already finished dinner and Drew looked exhausted, his arm slung along the back of Fable's chair, his fingers twirling the ends of her hair. I watched them, trying to see them from Chelsea's perspective, wondering what she might think as she spent time with them. Seeing them with fresh eyes, especially with a girl I'd like to make mine sitting next to me, I'd never been so aware of the easy, affectionate way between them until now.

The love between them is like a living, breathing thing. They look at each other and you feel it. They touch each other and you see it. When I was younger—hell, six months ago—I always thought the two of them were ridiculously sappy together. Like, over-the-top in love. When we'd first all moved in together, I'd been embarrassed to catch them in each other's arms, kissing. They'd never done anything inappropriate around me, but I guess their open affection for each other just never felt that comfortable for me to see.

Of course, I'd been a teenage boy full of hormones, and not a big believer in love and all that shit. Checking out hot chicks and wanting to get my hands on their bodies in any way possible, yeah—that's what motivated me at that age.

Now, though, I'm starting to realize I want what Fable and Drew have. I know I'm young, but shit, they were young, too, when they first met and fell in love. And look at them. Years later, they still act like they're totally gone over each other. They're married, they have a baby, he's beyond busy with his career, she's busy taking care of Autumn, and they still look at each other as if they've only just met and they can't believe they have each other.

Yeah. I want that sort of thing. And I think I want it with Chelsea.

She doesn't seem to want it with me, though. I don't know what happened, what turned her mood. Maybe she hadn't enjoyed herself at the game after all. I know sports aren't her thing and she's not a football fan whatsoever, but shit, we were sitting in the skybox, getting the deluxe treatment. Wade will shit himself when he finds out I went and didn't take him. At least he would have appreciated the game.

Maybe Fable told her something that freaked her out. I know they talked about me when I took off and bought the sweatshirt for her, but what could Fable have said that would have made Chelsea become so damn quiet?

I haven't a clue, but she's completely withdrawn from me and I fucking hate it.

We leave the restaurant right after Drew pays the bill, and we're all standing under the awning waiting for the valet guy to bring both cars around.

When you go out to dinner now with Drew Callahan, you always go out in style. The guy is a fucking celebrity.

Chelsea makes her escape back inside, claiming she needs to go to the bathroom before we start our long drive, and Fable turns to me, her mouth cast in a stern line, her gaze narrowed as she pulls me aside, away from Drew.

"Be careful driving home," Fable says, motherly concern lacing her voice. "It's raining pretty bad and I'm sure the roads are terrible."

"I'll be careful, I promise," I reassure her, pulling her into a quick hug. "Don't worry."

"And it's so late." She withdraws from me, her mouth pulling into a frown. "Maybe you should stay the night with us."

That's a long-ass drive back to San Francisco in this kind of weather. No thanks. "I think Chelsea has class in the morning. I know I do."

Fable sighs. "I just hate thinking of you out driving for hours in this rain."

"We'll be fine, don't worry. Seriously." I ruffle her hair, something she used to do to me when I was younger but since I tower over her by about a foot, I've got the upper hand now. "I'll text you when we get home, okay?"

"You'd better. I'll be lying awake until I hear from you," she says.

"Please. You'll be passed out with Autumn cradled in your arms," I tell her. She's admitted to me already that when she's feeding the baby in the middle of the night, they end up asleep in bed together. She's up all hours of the night taking care of Autumn, though I guess they've found more of a schedule. I don't know. I start glazing over when Fable starts talking endless baby shit.

But I know I don't want to be the other one who's keeping her awake.

"You're probably not too far from the truth." Fable smiles, her gaze going to Drew when he calls her name. "Our cars are here. We should go."

Chelsea exits the restaurant at that very moment, heading toward me. Her gaze is dim, her skin pale, but she offers a real smile to Fable when she pulls Chelsea into her arms and gives her a big hug.

"So great meeting you. Keep Owen in line, okay?" Fable says.

Chelsea laughs as Fable releases her. "Great meeting you, too. And I'll try."

Drew envelops Chelsea in his arms and when he lets go, she looks a little starstruck. I guess I can't blame her, but I'm also a little jealous. I don't know if I've ever seen that particular look in her eyes after I touched her.

But I've seen other looks. Eyes glazed with lust. Happiness. Affection.

I want to see those looks in her eyes again. I want to kiss

her, hold her close. Taste her, touch her, slip my hand inside her jeans, touch her between her legs and show her I know exactly how to make her feel good.

Shit. I'm breaking out in a fucking sweat just thinking about it. Maybe Fable's right. Maybe we should stay the night, but instead of staying at their house, we should find a hotel. Then I could drag Chelsea into bed and get her naked. Finally do what I've been dying to pretty much since I met her.

I know I've been all about taking things slow with her, but I've never been patient. I've never had to be, not when it comes to girls. I've always gotten what I wanted. Who I wanted. When I wanted.

So why do I want this girl when she runs so completely hot and cold? Is it more of a case of wanting what I can't have? Or do I really like her?

Oh, you like her, asshole. More than you ever want to admit.

"Are you mad at me? Did I do something to offend you?" I finally ask once we're on the freeway headed home. Traffic is heavy, it's still raining, and I've got both hands on the steering wheel, my gaze locked on the windshield, the glow of red lights indicating that everyone's hitting their brakes constantly. I don't want to be distracted, but . . .

Chelsea's low, distant mood is totally making me lose focus.

"No, I'm not mad at you." I flick a quick glance in her direction and she offers me a pitiful little smile. "Not really."

Not really.

What the hell does she mean by that?

"What did I do?" I ask, my voice grim. "I'm not in the mood to play guessing games, Chels. So just give it to me straight." I hate games. Mom is a total game player. Most females are . . . at least, the ones I know. Fable is an exception.

I'd hoped Chelsea was the same. But maybe she's not . . .

"It's stupid." She waves a hand, smiling at me, but her smile is brittle. Doesn't light up her eyes and I can tell it's fake. "I have a headache and it's been such a long day. A long weekend, really."

"You had fun, though, right? And you liked my sister? And Drew?" I sound like an insecure little kid wanting to make sure she's happy, desperate to ensure that she's pleased. God, does she even realize how easy it would be for her to completely wreck me? I never hand that sort of power over to anyone. Okay, I do so with Fable, but she's my sister and she would never hurt me. We've proven our trust in each other again and again. And Mom's wrecked me over and over, but I can't help but hand her that power.

As I've come to realize time and again, it's natural. She's my mom. I want to please her and she shits on me every chance she gets. Yet I keep taking it.

"Yeah. I had fun." There is absolutely no emotion in her voice and it scares me. "Except when I found out you told your sister we're just friends."

I have no idea what she's talking about. "Wait a minute. What did you say?"

"You told Fable—I don't know when—that we were just friends. Is that how you really think of us? Am I just a friend, Owen? Do you always stick your tongue in your friends' mouths? Or am I a *special* friend?"

Shit. She's pissed. She's practically yelling at me. "I never told Fable that . . ." My voice trails off.

I so did. When we were on the phone and Fable was giving me shit. I didn't want to hear it from her anymore so I said it to shut her up. I never thought Fable would ever say anything and I hadn't meant a word of it. Well, I guess.

Hell. I don't know. Chelsea confuses me so completely, I don't know how or what to think anymore.

Not that Chelsea would ever believe that.

"I thought I—meant something to you, but I guess not. Just wishful thinking on my part," she says, her voice soft and full of sadness. "I'm being ridiculous."

I chance a glance at her and see how she's staring out the window, her expression devastated.

My heart aches. *Fuck it*, I just did that to her. And I don't know how to explain myself. Not sure I really want to. I mean, what the hell are we doing, Chelsea and I? I like her, but I can't take this too seriously.

Fuck. I'm a liar. I hardly know Chelsea but I want to know more. So much more, my heart aches in anticipation of it. Yet she gives me such mixed signals, I never know whether she's coming or going. Whether she really likes me or not, and that freaking kills me. I was just feeling confident, too. So damn confident, I was letting my guard down. Kissing her in front of Fable, for Christ's sake, and I don't do that sort of thing ever.

Never, ever, never.

"Chelsea . . ." I start, but she shakes her head.

"I don't want to hear your excuses," she tells me, cutting me off before I can say anything to explain myself. "I don't want to talk about it anymore."

She's completely pulled away from me again and I hate it. I refuse to let this go. I need to make this better between us, before she pulls away from me even further.

More than anything, I need to apologize for being such a thoughtless asshole.

I drive for almost an hour, still not fully out of the city, what with traffic slowing constantly until the freeway is feeling almost like a parking lot. I look at Chelsea and see she's curled up in the passenger seat, her head leaning against the side of the door, her eyes closed tight, her forehead wrinkled with worry, pain—God, I don't know what.

Determination fills me. That's it. We should definitely stay the night. She'll probably be mad but I'm doing it. So what if we miss class in the morning? It won't kill us. It might kill her, but shit. I'm tired and she's not feeling well. I'm irritated and she's trying to sleep.

Not bothering with waking her up, I take the next exit, where I see a few hotel signs flashing in the night sky, and pull into a hotel parking lot. She stirs in her seat, lifting her head when I park the car beneath the overhang and in front of the hotel entrance. Frowning, she turns to meet my gaze.

"Where are we? What's going on?"

"We're staying overnight here." I incline my head toward the front doors.

Her mouth drops open. "Are you serious?"

"Definitely, I'm serious. The weather is for shit, Chels. The freeway is barely moving and I'm exhausted." Reaching out, I touch her cheek and she flinches—literally flinches—away from my fingers. I let my hand drop, frustration raining through me. My heart hurts. Has she ever rejected my touch before? I can only blame it on her headache.

Oh, and me telling Fable she's just a friend.

Man, I really fucked this up.

"You don't feel well," I tell her, trying to forget what I said, how much it hurt her. "You need a good night's rest."

"But I'll miss my morning classes," she protests. "I have an important paper to turn in, too."

"Is it already finished?" If this were me, I'd be working on that stupid paper at this very minute. I'm the king of procrastination, especially with homework.

"Well, yeah. Of course it is." She shrugs, chewing on her lower lip.

Why am I not surprised? "Then turn it in later tomorrow afternoon. I'm sure your professor will understand when you explain what happened. It's not like you ever turn anything in late. They'll let you off the hook." I pause, studying her. "We'll leave first thing in the morning. We're out of the city somewhat, so it probably should be about a three-hour drive. And everyone will be traveling in the opposite direction, so we should be good. The minute you get home you can go to school and turn in everything you need to."

"I don't know . . ." Her voice drifts and she glances down at her lap. "I have nothing to change into for tomorrow. Nothing to sleep in. No toothbrush."

I'm still stuck on her nothing-to-sleep-in statement. Sounds good to me. We could crawl into bed naked. I'm totally game. Not that there's any chance of that happening. "We can pick up a toothbrush and whatever else we need in the hotel, I bet. And we can take a quick shower, go to bed, throw our clothes back on, and head home in the morning. What do you think?"

Does she even hear the order I put that all in? And do I really think I have a chance with her tonight, with the way she's been acting? How pissed she is with me?

An idiot can hope, I guess.

"Can we get separate beds?" Her cheeks color and she keeps her gaze averted. "I just—I'll feel more comfortable that way."

My hopes are smashed into a million pieces with five simple words. *Damn.* I want to scream at her, what did I do wrong? But I keep my lips clamped shut, trying to control the overflow of emotions that want to escape. I know what I did wrong. It's just hard to face. God knows, I never want to face anything. "Whatever you want, Chels, I'll make it happen if I can. Depends on what the hotel has available."

"Okay." She nods. "Thanks for being so understanding, Owen."

Even her voice sounds different. I hate this. I should apologize. But how?

Hey, sorry I told my sister we were just friends but I wanted to get her off my back after she gave me an endless amount of shit. I didn't mean it.

But I might have meant it. I mean . . . if she's confused and giving me mixed signals, maybe I'm just as bad. I want her. I don't. I want more than just sex. I'd rather run.

I'm contradicting myself in my own brain. I'm a mess.

"I'm gonna go inside and get a room," I tell her. "You want to come with me?"

She slowly shakes her head, keeping her gaze locked on the passenger-side window, staring at the front of the hotel. "If you don't mind, I'll sit out here and wait for you."

I exit the car and head toward the hotel's entrance, swearing I can feel her gaze on me as I walk. If she's watching me, I know we still have a chance. This is just a blip in the road or whatever.

But if she's not looking at me, then forget it. I can almost guarantee it won't work out.

Fuck. I'm afraid to turn around and look, but finally, after taking a deep breath and counting to five, I slowly glance over my shoulder, my gaze falling on the passenger-side door's window.

Chelsea's watching me, her fingers resting on the glass, her expression full of sadness. I smile at her, give her a little wave, and she waves back.

Glad to know there's some hope between us after all.

Chelsea

The hotel room is nice and clean, but there's one king-sized bed. It was the only type of room available, Owen had said apologetically when he'd come back to the car so he could park it. I'd sat there, quietly stewing, wondering if he was lying to me. I was going to confront him about it once we got to the hotel room but changed my mind when we stood in front of the door, where I watched Owen slide the card into the lock and open it.

I don't need to start any fights. He already knows how I feel and I should be mad that he hasn't apologized, but what do I expect? Owen begging for my forgiveness?

He's been very quiet, almost somber, I'm sure in reaction to my mood. It's hard for me to pretend everything's okay when deep inside, I'm sad. Disappointed. And I know Fable hadn't meant to make me sad or ruin the mood. Truly, I should be ecstatic by what she said because clearly, Owen and I don't give off a just-friends vibe.

I just hate that he said it in the first place.

He'd glanced around the hotel room, asking if I thought everything looked okay, and when I said yes, he said he was going to go pick up a few things for us, toothbrushes and toothpaste and whatever else we might need. He asked if I wanted to go with him, but I told him I was going to hop in the shower instead. His eyes had gone all dark in that sexy way of his and he hardened his jaw, gave me a quick "all right, I'll be back," and then he took off, closing the door with a firm slam behind him.

I go into the bathroom and flick on the lights, impressed with what I find. The room is huge, the fixtures new, and everything's so clean. I wish I had something different to change

177

into after I take a shower, but I do find a hotel robe hanging on the back of the door and decide that will have to do. And when I push back the shower curtain and turn on the faucet, I notice the water pressure is amazing.

The shower at my apartment is lackluster at best, so I'm going to soak under this for as long as I can.

A sigh of relief escapes me when I step beneath the spray and I tilt my head back, letting the water wash over my hair and face, consciously trying to relax my forehead since it's still super tense. I wasn't lying about the headache. It came on just before we left the stadium, and I can only assume it formed because of a combination of things.

Travel can set me off. That time of the month does, too, though I'm not due for my period for a few more days at least. The tension between Owen and me has added to it, too, of course.

I wish I had asked him to pick up some ibuprofen for me. I should text him, but by the time I get out of the shower, he could be on his way back to the room . . .

I decide not to bother.

The water seems to help ease the tension keeping me rigid. My bones and muscles melt under the heat and pressure of the water, and the soothing scent of the shampoo and body wash that I found on the bathroom counter relaxes me. Steam fills the bathroom, making everything feel hazy, almost dreamlike, and when I finally shut the water off, I breathe a heavy sigh of relief.

My mind is deliciously blank and my eyelids are heavy, my head drowsy. I towel myself off, my skin pink from the hot water, and I don't bother putting back on my panties or bra, deciding to save them for tomorrow. The thought of wearing them two days in a row is kind of gross, but what can I do? I don't have a choice.

I finger-comb my hair as best I can, wiping the steam from the mirror so I can see my reflection. My cheeks are rosy, my eyes sleepy, my lids heavy. The look is almost . . . sexy, and I never think of myself that way. If Owen sees me looking like this, I can almost imagine him trying to jump me. Even if we are in the just-friends zone, he'd at least notice me because I'm naked, right?

I mean, what nineteen-year-old guy can resist a naked girl with a decent body? I'm no sexy bombshell porn star, but I'm not bad. I don't have huge boobs or anything, but I'm sufficiently curvy, and Kari's always ragging on me to show it off a bit. Wear a top that reveals a little cleavage or a short skirt, but that's so not my style. I'd never feel comfortable wearing something like that.

Taking a step back, I assess my figure, something I definitely don't do on a regular basis. I never have time to stand around and check myself out in the mirror and besides, I never really thought of myself as a sexual being, until I met Owen. Was never really aware of myself, or the power of my body.

But now I look at my breasts and wonder if he likes them. He's never tried to touch them, not really. He'll skim his hands along my sides, make me crazy with wanting him to boldly touch me, but he hasn't done it yet. I cup one breast, feel its weight in my palm, and my nipple prickles with awareness, hardening just like that. I flick my thumb across it, gasping a little when the sensation seems to travel through my body and lands between my legs, a gentle throb that makes me momentarily breathless.

Just like I feel when Owen kisses me. Holding me close, his mouth fused with mine, his tongue doing all of these wickedly delicious things . . .

I drop my hand away from my breast and cover my cheeks

with my hands, exhaling loudly. This back and forth, push and pull I'm feeling for Owen is slowly starting to drive me crazy. I need to not get so hung up on statements and words, especially when I don't know what was really said. It's dumb. And I pride myself on being logical and thorough, exploring all the factors, all the benefits and all the negatives.

But there's nothing logical about relationships. I've learned that quickly, seen it my entire life. Actions speak way louder than words, right? I definitely learned that by watching my father, especially these last few years, before he ended up in jail.

He made so many promises. Ridiculous, unbelievable promises that I always, always wanted to believe. He told Mom again and again how much he loved her, needed her, wanted her, always with a smile and a reassuring hug, a gentle kiss. She believed every word he said, ever the faithful, devoted wife while he was off running around stealing money, having affairs, being the awful, immoral liar he truly was.

He said one thing and did another. All the flowery words in the world can't hide a black, emotionless heart.

Whereas Mom loves to pretend she's the one with the black, emotionless heart that feels nothing. That she hates men. It's all a lie. She's in denial. She always believes every single word Dad tells her.

It's pathetic. She's pathetic. He is, too.

So I need to watch Owen's actions, not his words. We say things as a way of pretending we feel something else. Maybe that's what he meant when he told Fable we were just friends.

Maybe he wants us to be something more.

Either that or I'm completely reaching.

Grabbing the sample of body lotion on the counter, I slather it on, using practically the entire bottle. The subtle, lemony scent is delicious, and a little smile curves my lips.

When I finally wrap the hotel robe around my body, I'm cozy and warm. More than ready to slide beneath the sheets and go to bed.

With Owen.

Hmm. The idea of doing that has me suddenly wondering. It's not going to be so easy to go to bed and fall asleep, with him lying beside me all night long. What was I thinking? I may be all sleepy and content at this very moment, but the second he comes back into the hotel room, my heart rate will pick right back up and I'll be extremely aware of the fact that I have nothing on under this robe.

Alone. In a hotel room with Owen. He could grab hold of the robe belt, slowly untie it, and peel the fabric away from my body. Find me naked and warm, my skin soft and lemony, my body languid and ready for him to take me . . .

Oh God, what am I thinking? No way can I give up my body to him yet. It's too soon. I want to, though. Despite my worry, I definitely, definitely want to explore more with Owen.

Exhaling slowly for courage, I open the bathroom door, the steam billowing out into the room. I peek my head around the corner of the door frame but I'm greeted with complete and utter silence, the only sound the low murmuring of the room's heater.

I'm hot enough. I don't need that thing running to make me hotter.

I walk into the room and flick off the heater, then grab my purse from the tiny desk. Pulling my cell phone out, I send Kari a quick text, letting her know I'm safe and we're staying the night in the city and that I would be home in the morning. She immediately replies:

Gonna get some with the sex bomb huh? Don't forget to use protection!!!

I roll my eyes and reply. Of course she'd think Owen and I got a hotel room for a night of illicit, out-of-control sex.

My body aches at the thought.

I don't think so. I'm exhausted and don't feel very good. Have a terrible headache.

I bet he could cure whatever ails you. With his big ol . . .

Don't say it! I type back.

A giggle escapes me. God, Kari can be so crude sometimes. I know she does it to freak me out. She texts back a few minutes later, when I'm curled up on top of the giant bed, leaning against the fluffy pillows and anxiously awaiting Owen's return.

Have fun. Get naked. Live a little.

I smile. Maybe I should take Kari's advice.

Though I doubt I will. I'm too chicken.

And deep down inside? I'm still too hurt.

CHAPTER 14

I want to crawl into her chest and kiss everything that she'd thought I'd hate.
—Unknown

Owen

I am such a complete asshole. I snuck back outside to my car after I left the hotel room and dug around in the trunk until I found half a joint. No way can I go back into the car and light it up. The smell of weed will permeate the interior and Chelsea will figure out quick that I did this. She's not stupid.

So I'm standing out in the rain, getting pelted with tiny, stinging droplets of water, my hoodie doing a crap job of keeping me dry as I cup my hand around the lit joint to protect it from going out. I take a couple of puffs, trying to clear my mind and ease the tension because I am so tight inside, I feel like I'm going to burst.

It does the trick. Within minutes, I'm high as fuck, my body and brain numb, not caring in the least that I'm soaking wet as I run back through the parking lot and enter the hotel.

My mind is clear. Blank. That's all that matters.

Hanging out in the lobby, I quickly text Fable and let her know we're okay and spending the night at a hotel about an hour out from where we left them. I then go in search of and eventually find the tiny gift shop in the hotel, lucking out since they're just about to close. I grab a couple of toothbrushes and a toothpaste, a travel-sized brush for Chelsea since she has all that hair, and a small bottle of pain reliever for her headache.

Yeah, see? I can be a good guy when I want to. Thoughtful. Nice. So why in the hell is Chelsea so mad at me? What did I *do*?

You said you were just friends.

Big fucking deal. Chicks can be so sensitive.

After I pay for the supplies, I head back up to our room, dread making my footsteps feel heavy despite my still blissfully blank mind. I should just confront her. Demand to know why what I said in some offhand way was enough to flip her mood like a switch from totally on to completely off. I stand outside the door, staring at the card key clasped in my fingers, zoning out so hard I nearly fall against the door.

Fuck. Whatever was in that joint was some extra-good shit. Maybe it would be best if I didn't confront her. I might say something infinitely awful.

I open the door after about the fifth try and stride inside, setting the gift shop bag on the bathroom counter. I notice that it's still warm and steamy from Chelsea's shower and the faint scent of lemon lingers in the air.

My imagination runs wild. A naked Chelsea beneath the water, her skin all slick and wet and tempting me to touch her.

Yeah. Fuck. That sounds just about perfect. Wish I'd come back sooner. Maybe I could have found her like that.

Instead I find Chelsea lying in the middle of the bed on her side wearing a thick white robe, her legs tucked up, her body curled into a ball. Her long, wet hair is spread out on the pillow, her eyes are closed, and her rosebud lips are parted in sleep.

I stumble against the wall and brace my hand against it, my heart thumping about a million miles a second. Seeing her like this, vulnerable and beautiful and sexy as hell, makes me wanna do something crazy. Like grab her, undo the belt, and spread the robe wide open. Feast my gaze on her skin and pray she begs me to fuck her.

No, dude, you can't fuck her. Not like this. You're high. She's a virgin. You can't be high her first time.

The longer I stare at her, the more my entire body tightens, my cock twitches, and . . . *fuck.*

I want her despite my altered state. I always want her.

Fuck it. I'm taking a shower and I'll jerk off to thoughts of her. How she tastes, the sweet, hot sounds she makes when I kiss her, when I let my hands wander all over her body, never lingering too long. I'm patient with Chelsea. Always, always patient.

For once, I'm dying to linger. Dying to get her naked and have her writhing beneath my hands. I want to be the one to slide deep inside her body, staring into her eyes when I enter her the first time. Have that connection with a girl that I've never really had before.

Closing the bathroom door, I strip out of my wet clothes and get in the shower, letting the hot, pulsating water wash over me, cleanse my chilled skin and my dirty thoughts. My cock is so damn hard it hurts and I wrap my fingers around it, grip it tight, slowly stroke. Close my eyes and think of Chelsea.

But I don't want to waste it. She's out there. Sleeping in the bed we have no choice but to share. Why should I beat off when I could wake her up with soft, sweet kisses and whisper *I'm sorry* in her ear? Slip my hands beneath that thick robe and hope like hell I encounter bare, soft skin. Because I bet she is soft and bare beneath that robe.

And I'm suddenly eager to find out if it's true.

Turning the water off, I dry my body like I'm in a race

with myself, slipping my black boxer briefs back on but nothing else. It's not like I can just walk back out there naked. She'd probably freak the hell out if she found me like that.

I gotta take it slow with Chelsea. That's been my mantra ever since I met her. Slow, slow, slow.

So different from the guy who's always wanted it fast, fast, fast and now, now, now.

The heat of the shower and the steam-filled bathroom and smoking the joint earlier has left me dizzy. I stumble out of the bathroom and flick off the light, make sure the deadbolt is locked on the door, and then I approach the bed, where Chelsea is still sleeping smack in the middle. I flick off the lamp on the bedside table and tug back the covers, sliding beneath them, lying practically on the edge since Chelsea is pretty much hogging the entire mattress.

She doesn't even move when I get into bed with her, and I realize she's a damn heavy sleeper. Sweet and so innocent-looking, she's facing me, her hands tucked beneath her cheek. I lie there in the darkness, listening to her breathe, drinking in her features that are awash with the faint light that's shining from the crack in the otherwise drawn heavy curtains.

Reaching out, I touch her damp hair, slide a few strands between my fingers. She smells fucking amazing and I scoot closer, sharing the same pillow, desperately wanting to lean in and press my mouth to hers.

But I hold back. Not yet. Despite my fucked-up, high-as-hell state, I know I can't just barge in and make this happen. This is going to be subtle.

That last thought alone makes me laugh. Hell, I am high.

Chelsea stirs, a little sigh escaping her, and the sexy sound goes straight to my dick, making me even harder. And there's no way I can hide it, either. I'm in my underwear and everything is pretty much on display there. Hope boners don't scare her.

I laugh again because damn it, that shit is funny. Her eyelids flutter open and my breath stalls in my throat.

Damn it. I didn't mean to wake her up.

"Owen." She stretches, her arm brushing against me, and my cock stirs. Damn, she barely touches me and I'm ready to fire one off. "When did you come back?"

"A while ago. I took a shower."

She sits up with a wince, running her hand through her damp hair as she looks around. "I'm totally taking over this bed. Sorry." She scoots over and I follow her, thankful for more room since I felt like I was gonna fall off at any second. "My head feels better." She rubs at her forehead, runs her fingers through her hair, and I wish I could be the one touching her like that.

"Yeah, you sure? I picked up some stuff for you in the gift shop. Ibuprofen," I say. "I can go grab some and a glass of water if you want."

"Oh, you did? Thank you. You're so sweet." Her voice is soft, as is her gaze as she smiles at me, shaking her head. "I should be okay."

"Chels." I clear my throat, ready to get this over with. "I'm sorry about what happened earlier."

"What do you mean?" She frowns, looking confused and adorable.

"For what I told Fable," I explain. "I only said we were friends to get her off my back. It was nothing."

Her frown deepens. "So you mean we're nothing?"

"That's not what I said. I . . ." I shake my head. "What I told Fable meant nothing. But you, Chelsea? You definitely mean something to me."

She stares at me, her eyes wide, her lips parted. Damn, she's pretty. Lying here so close, I can see the freckles that dot the bridge of her nose. I'm tempted to lean in and kiss every single one.

"Thank you. I'm glad you told me the truth," she whispers, her voice shaky.

"You okay?" My hands literally itch to touch her.

"I'm just . . . really tired."

"Take off that robe and get under the covers, then," I say on purpose, curiosity making my mind spin with all sorts of images. Every last one of them is of Chelsea naked under the robe.

"Um . . ." She climbs off the bed to stand on the opposite side of it, closest to the wall. "I'm . . . not wearing anything under it."

I swallow hard. Exactly what I've been waiting to hear, but now that I know she's naked under the robe for sure, I'm not sure what to do next. What to say.

And this is a first. I always know what to do with a naked girl.

Just not a naked Chelsea.

Chelsea

I'd been dreaming about him. Owen. His big, rough hands all over my skin, his hot, damp mouth on my neck as we rolled around on the enormous hotel bed. In my dream, I was begging him for more and he was moving down my body as I lay flat on my back in the center of the mattress, his mouth on my chest, my breasts, his tongue licking, circling my nipple, and oh my God, I wanted more, more, more . . .

I jolted awake and found him lying there beside me, watching me, his green gaze glittering in the barely there light cast from between the curtains. He was gorgeous and damp and shirtless, his muscular chest gleaming, the dips and planes of his beautiful body making my mouth water. I said his name to ground me, to make sure he was really there with me and not some dream apparition put before me because I know my mind would probably play tricks on me. I felt so needy, so restless after the dream, I wanted to make sure he was real. When he answered, I knew I had to do this.

I had to be bold. I wanted to.

Then he went and apologized, telling me I mean something to him. How could I respond to that? My first instinct was to run, but I had nowhere to hide. And I'm tired of running, of hiding from men and what they could do to me. I can't live like this.

I want more. I want Owen.

Confessing I had nothing on beneath the robe sent a charge of awareness into the room that turned into this living, palpable thing, the tension nearly unbearable. We both stare at each other as I stand by the side of the bed, my confidence wavering, my body shaking with nerves. Maybe I can't say in words what I want and neither can he, but I can certainly show him.

Show him that I want to give him my body—and my heart—freely.

With shaking fingers I untie the belt and push the robe open ever so slightly, revealing a shadow of myself. My breathing's erratic, my heart is racing, and Owen scrambles up so he's sitting, his back against the headboard, his hot gaze locked on me, encouraging me to continue without saying a word.

So I do. I thrust my shoulders back, stand up straighter, and push the robe off, letting it fall to the floor in a soft heap at my feet. Until I'm standing there next to the bed, completely naked and on display in front of a guy for the very first time in my life.

"Fuck, Chelsea." He sounds pained and he shifts, his hand going between his legs as if he has to readjust himself and I swear, I break out in a blush all over my body. My skin is hot, between my legs I'm throbbing, and I . . .

Don't know what to do.

"Come here," he says, his voice low, the sound sending a fresh wave of tingles along my skin. He reaches out his hand and I take it, our fingers entwining as I get on the bed, which squeaks when he pulls me in closer so I have no choice but to climb on top of him.

Much like we sat together in the backseat of his car that first night we kissed, I'm straddling him, though this time I'm completely naked and there's only a sheet and a blanket between us since he's beneath the covers. His arms band around me, his hands spanning across my back, and I feel so exposed, unsure. Exhilarated.

"You're beautiful," he murmurs just before he devours me in the most consuming kiss of my life. He tastes like toothpaste. His hands are branding my back as he presses me close and my breasts are pushed firmly against his chest. The skin-on-skin contact feels so good I almost want to weep.

"So are you," I whisper when we break apart, his mouth at my neck, my hands skimming over his bared chest. I feel nothing but muscle and heat as I scratch my nails over his skin. His pecs are hard, as are his nipples, and when I rake my nails over them, he hisses in a sharp breath, then kisses me so fiercely, so deep, I swear I see stars.

His lips are firm, delicious, and precise. He kisses me as if he knows exactly what I like, knows exactly what I want. His tongue slides into my open mouth and dances delicately with mine, sending a flurry of shivers throughout my naked body.

I clutch him close, devouring him right back, and I hope he knows how much this moment, this kiss, in a dark hotel room with minimal barriers between us, means to me.

I grow slick between my legs with every thrust of his tongue, my nipples hard little points as they brush against his chest. I rope my arms around his neck and bury my hands in his damp hair, holding his mouth to mine, deepening our kiss even further if that's possible, as I tighten my bent legs at his hips.

"Chelsea." He whispers my name against my neck after he breaks apart from our kiss, his lips sliding down the length of my neck, his hands resting lightly at my waist. "You feel so fucking good."

"Please. Touch me," I encourage, shocked at my demand. But here in the dark, in a strange, unknown place, doing wonderful, unknown things, I feel strong. Bold. Different.

I like it.

His hands skim down over my hips, down farther until he's cupping my backside. A gasp escapes me as he strokes me, slow and sure, and his mouth is at my ear, panting, sounding so desperate a shiver moves through me. "Your ass has driven me crazy since the first time I met you," he admits, his voice rough.

I smile and lean into his palms, his fingers so close to the achy spot between my legs I will die if he doesn't touch me there soon. "Really?"

"It's fucking perfection, Chels." He skims his fingers along sensitive skin that no one else has ever touched before and a whimper forms in my throat. "Absolute perfection."

I love it when he calls me Chels. I love it more when he says such sweet, delicious things. No one has ever called me perfect before. And the way Owen touches me, so reverently, so sweetly, I know he means it.

His mouth burns a trail of kisses down my neck, along my collarbone, and I lean into him, my hands slipping to his shoulders so I can hold onto him tight. His lips and tongue are like magic, making my skin spark and heat wherever they touch. He grips my butt tighter, lifting so I have no choice but to lift as well.

And then he's pressing his lips to the valley between my breasts, skimming, tasting, licking. I tilt my head down, my hair falling around my face as I watch him, fascinated with what he's doing to me. How my body is reacting to his every touch.

His mouth travels to my left breast and he pulls away the slightest bit, staring at me. My nipple tightens when he breathes over it and then he's wrapping his lips around the hard bit of flesh, sucking, licking, driving me wild.

Oh God. I want to say it out loud but I press my lips together and lean into him, my arms winding back around his neck and squeezing him tight. The sheet is bunched between us, pooling in Owen's lap, and I grind down on him, feeling the unmistakable thrust of his erection against me.

"Jesus," he mutters, lifting me away from him with one arm bulging with muscle so he can push the sheet out of the way. Now there's nothing between us but his boxer briefs and I fall against him, wrapping my legs around his hips, slick and hot against his cotton-covered erection. I want more. I want it all, but he's holding me back. I can feel him pushing me away, his breaths harsh, his mouth against my forehead as he holds me loosely in his arms.

"I don't want to go too fast," he whispers. "You gotta tell me, Chelsea."

"Tell you." I swallow hard when I feel his mouth move along my jaw, his teeth nipping my flesh. "Tell you what?"

He cups my chin, forcing me to look at him. I blink, my

vision refocusing so I meet his smoldering gaze. His mouth is swollen, his eyes slumberous, and I don't think I've ever seen Owen look so sexy, so achingly beautiful. I want to touch his face, trace his every feature, but then his words penetrate my lust-filled brain and I'm left gaping at him.

"Are you a virgin?"

CHAPTER 15

It was not my lips you kissed, but my soul.
—Judy Garland

Owen

I wait for her answer, all the words I could ever say to ease her worries clogged in my throat. She stares at me, my bold, beautiful princess gone in an instant, replaced with my wide-eyed, lip-chewing, nervous Chelsea.

I'm familiar with this version but I much preferred the girl with no boundaries, the one who begged me. That had been hot. And I know she's still there, buried beneath the nerves and the expectations. I just need to coax her back out.

"I . . ." She breathes deep and closes her eyes, drops her head so her forehead is pressed against mine. "Yes," she admits, her voice small. "You're my first."

I knew it. I've always known it, pretty much from the first moment I met her, but to actually hear her say the words confirming my suspicions sends a bolt of possessiveness throughout my entire body. It's electric, this feeling. Vibrating beneath my skin, making me shake, and I tighten my arms around her, hold her close. Move my head so I can whisper in her ear, "We gotta make this good for you, Chels."

"It *is* good," she whispers back. "So, so good."

Closing my eyes, I hold her, convincing myself to calm the

fuck down. I'm not doing this. I'm not fucking her in a hotel room in an unknown city, Chelsea still edged with that hint of sadness that had consumed her earlier. I don't care how bold she is, how much she wants it, how good she feels, her naked body pressed against mine.

I'm high. I might not remember this clearly. Worse, I might mess up somehow and I could never, ever forgive myself for that.

"I just want you to touch me." She sounds restless, frustrated, and I lean away from her so I can look at her pretty face. Smoothing my hand over her hair, I push the stray strands away from her cheeks, my gaze locking with hers.

"I want to touch you, too," I admit, letting my eyes drop to her chest. God, she's perfect. I've never liked big or fake boobs, and I feel like Chelsea's were made just for me. Unable to stop myself, I curl my hand around her breast and squeeze, circling my thumb around her rosy nipple.

Her pretty little nipple reminds me of her middle name. The poem I wrote for her. How I could reenact that poem right here, right now. Slip my hand between her legs, searching those pretty pink folds, and have her crying out my name, shattering in an instant . . .

"Lie back," I tell her, removing my hand from her chest so I can guide her where I want her.

She goes willingly, her body trembling, her eyes wide as she stares up at me. I lean over and kiss her, taking it deep and hot in an instant, hoping she'll lose her head so she's not so focused on the moment and worrying what's about to happen to her.

"Have you ever touched yourself, Chels?" I move so I'm the one straddling her now, my mouth on her breasts, my lips wrapped around one nipple, then another. She arches into me,

195

a breathy little moan escaping her, and my cock is hard, heavy and aching as it presses against my briefs, desperate to get free.

Damn it, I can't take off my underwear. The moment I do, I'm done for. I'll be inside her so fast she won't know what happened.

"Hey." I lightly bite her nipple, making her yelp, and she glares up at me, shock written all over her face. "I asked you a question."

"A question I'm not going to answer, Owen." She slings her arm over her eyes and huffs out a breath. Indicating that yes, indeed, she has touched herself, and that particular image pops into my brain with so much force I have to take an imaginary crowbar to it and pry it out of there before I get too distracted.

"Hmm, that tells me a lot." I let my hand wander down the length of her body, trying my best to pay close attention to all the signs, the indications of what she likes, what makes her crazy, what doesn't do anything for her. She prefers a gentle touch. I've discovered that over the last couple of weeks, every time I've had her in my arms. A skim of my nails along her skin, or I'll rub circles in her neck, along her shoulders, kiss her softly, taking it deeper, licking her neck . . .

I keep my touch light, running my fingers along her arm, across her stomach, back up to circle her breasts, her nipples. She holds her breath, releasing it in a shuddery exhale before she holds it again, and I smile at her, loving how strongly my touch makes her react.

"Breathe, Chels." I dip my head and lick her nipple, making her gasp. "The only way you can enjoy this is if you're breathing."

"Trust me, I'm enjoying it, Owen." Her voice trembles and she closes her eyes when my fingers map the sweet curve of her stomach, circle the slight dip of her belly button. Her skin is so fucking soft. Everywhere. "So, so much."

She spreads her legs the slightest bit and my hand wanders farther, grazing her pubic hair, the heat of her branding my hand and I haven't even touched her there yet. I can smell her, though, lemony sweet, unique and musky, the scent of sex and woman and Chelsea.

I slip one finger down, encountering wetness. Heat. So much heat. I go farther and groan when I find her slick and creamy. Hot and wet. I search her folds at the same time I fuse my mouth with hers and swallow her cry.

She moves her hips against my finger and I add another, then my thumb, which I use to circle her clit. I keep it slow, my kiss slow, my brain slow as I bring her closer. Closer still.

Responsive. She's so responsive. I never want this to stop. I want to remember this moment forever and I'm afraid it'll slip right out of my brain when I fall asleep afterward. Sometimes when I'm high, I forget. And the shit I smoked earlier had been good. Too good. The kind of good that'll make you forget everything, because that's what you usually want to do when you smoke weed.

But I don't want to forget any of this. This moment is one of the most important of my life. I'm about to make Chelsea come for the first time by my hand.

Not necessarily a moment I can talk about in public, but it's mine. All mine. And I don't ever want to forget it.

"Owen." She breathes my name across my lips, the sound of her voice sending a spiral of heat throughout my blood, and I lick her lips, thrust my tongue in her mouth, silencing her.

I push my index finger inside her, her tight, velvety hot flesh clamping all around me. God, she would feel so amazing around my cock. Too damn amazing. I'd probably come in an instant.

I could almost come just thinking about it.

She moves against my hand, thrusting her hips, arching her back, trying to send me deeper. I add another finger, my thumb brushing her clit back and forth, over and over, and she lifts her hips higher, her feet planted on the mattress, her legs spread.

I'm watching her, fascinated by how she reacts to my touch. She's chanting my name, saying shit I can't even understand, and I hook my finger deep inside her, press my thumb hard against her clit. She stills, her lips parted, her eyes squeezed shut.

And then she's coming, her entire body shaking. I can feel her orgasm to her very depths, can feel the trembling and rhythmic pulsating deep within her body, all around my fingers.

It's like a fucking miracle. Her body responds naturally, beautifully. She sinks to the mattress, limp and sated, still trembling, her legs spread wide and all that pink, slick goodness still on display.

Hell. If I could sink deep inside her right now and lose myself, I so would.

But I won't. For once in my life, I'm not going to be selfish. I'll be the giver but not the taker. No matter how difficult it is.

Slowly I withdraw my fingers from her body, leaning in and giving her a kiss before I bring my fingers to my lips and smell her lingering scent. Taste her.

Next time I make her come, I think I should do it with my mouth.

"Oh my God, did you just lick your fingers?" She releases a shuddery sigh and I touch her lips with my hand, trace them with my index finger. The very one that had just been buried deep inside her.

"I promise, next time I'm going down on you. Taste yourself," I say, feeling like a dirty bastard but I don't care. Heat flares in my gut as she tentatively darts her tongue out and licks, her expression full of curiosity.

"Salty," she whispers.

I stretch out beside her, brush my lips against her forehead. "Delicious."

She loops her arm around me and nestles close, her face against my chest. The room is quiet, I can still hear her accelerated breaths, and I run my fingers over her tangled hair, again and again, hoping to soothe.

"That was . . ." Her voice drifts off.

"Good? Okay? So-so?"

Chelsea giggles and presses a kiss to my chest. "It was wonderful and you know it."

"Glad to hear it." My cock is throbbing, reminding me it has needs too, but I tell the greedy bastard to back off.

"But what about you? Don't you want to . . ."

"Come? Not tonight, Chels. Tonight is all about you." I kiss her forehead again, needing her to know how much she matters to me though I'm not sure how I can put it into words.

So I remain quiet, just holding her, trying to calm my racing heart, enjoying the blankness that still lingers in my brain. I could go to sleep like this.

If a certain naked Chelsea would stop wiggling against me.

"But aren't you . . ."

I love how she can't come right out and say it. It's kind of cute. "Hard? Hell yeah. You want to feel it?"

"No!" She pauses, and I muffle a laugh. "Yes," she says shyly. "I do. Really."

"Then go for it." I pull away from her slightly so I'm lying on my back, practically daring her to make a grab. I remove my arm from beneath her and fold both arms behind my head, going for casual, easygoing nothingness.

Inside, though, my nerves are rioting. My body's screaming for her to touch me. I doubt she'll work up the nerve.

Chelsea

There's no way after what he gave me that I'm not going to give him something in return.

My body is still a shuddery, limp mess. I've never been very comfortable touching my body. I've read books that have given me pleasurable tingles between my legs and I'd try a few times to touch myself there, but I never was really comfortable with it.

I've lived such a sheltered life. Parents who never talked about sex but a father who was out screwing every woman he could find. The contradiction there is a psychiatrist's dream, I'm sure.

I've read enough and watched enough TV and movies to know that sex can be amazing. Can feel so good. Usually it just scared me. Not with Owen, though. And the way he just touched me . . . *God*.

That had been amazing.

He thinks I'm not going to touch him in return, though. I can tell by the teasing tone of his voice, the smug look as he flops flat on his back, his arms behind his head, a little smirk on his face.

I prop myself up on my elbow and study him. Starting with his strong, muscular neck, his firm collarbone, his beautiful chest. His nipples are flat, brown, and small and his tanned skin is stretched taut over solid, beautifully shaped muscle. His stomach is ridged and flat, that dark brown trail of hair leading from his navel toward his erection fascinating. Without thought I reach out, drag my finger through the downy soft hair. Following down, down, until I brush against his erection.

It twitches and moves beneath the fabric of his boxer briefs, and I draw my hand back as if it just tried to bite me.

Owen laughs, and I turn a murderous glare on him. "Don't make fun," I say, my voice prim.

"Ah, Chels. Never. You're just too cute." He cups my cheek, his thumb gliding over my skin. "You've never touched a guy like this before, have you?"

"No." I feel silly, being so inexperienced, and I shouldn't beat myself up over it. When would I ever get a chance to do something like this? I've been alone and socially awkward most of my teenage years. Boys never paid attention to me.

Now I have the most beautiful boy I've ever met lying in a bed with me, telling me I'm beautiful, kissing me, bringing me to orgasm with his fingers.

It's a pretty heady feeling.

"Let's free the beast." He starts to tug down his underwear and I laugh at him calling it a beast, then help him, my hands brushing against his firm thighs, his knees, his hairy calves. Until his underwear is around his ankles and he's kicking them off onto the floor. Naked and bare before me, he resumes his casual position, and all I can do is stare.

I gaze at his erection, fascinated with the shape, the way it arcs toward his stomach. It's thick and veiny, the head plum-shaped, and a bit of creamy liquid leaks from the tip.

I wrap my fingers around the length of him, marveling at how small my hand looks. He's big, not outrageously scary or anything, but nothing small either, and I remember how un-comfortable it had felt at first when he slipped his finger in-side me.

And supposedly he could push that thing inside me? My body clenches tight just thinking about it.

"You going to hold it or do something with it?" His voice is strained, and he sounds like he's almost in pain.

"What do you want me to do?"

He reaches out and grips my hand with his, squeezing his erection, showing me how he likes it. He handles himself roughly, tugging and pulling, and I follow his lead, reaching down to caress his balls because you know, I've gone this far, so . . .

Why not?

"*Jesus*. Just like that," he encourages, removing his hand from the top of mine, and then I'm on my own. Stroking him hard, then touching him soft. Trying my best to drive him crazy the way he just drove me out of my mind. I trace the distended veins, mapping them with my fingertip. He trem-bles beneath my touch, his entire body tense, sweat forming on his skin. I can smell him. I want to taste him.

He likes it. I like it. I wish I had the nerve to draw him into my mouth, lick the tip of his erection with my tongue. I want to, but what if I do it wrong? What if I somehow screw it up and he ends up laughing at me?

I don't know if I could ever recover from that.

"There's no textbook on how to touch my cock, Chels."

His words, specifically the use of one particular word, make my entire face burn, especially when he's so close to figuring out what's running through my mind. I just flat-out don't know what to do or how to do it.

"What if I mess up?" I ask, my voice a mere whisper.

"Baby. You touch me and I love it." What I'm loving is

how he just called me baby. "Just do it. Touch me. I'm so close to exploding, I'll probably come all over your fingers within seconds, so be prepared."

Um. Wow. He's just so matter-of-fact about it. I wish I could be the same.

I hold him in my grip and start to move, stroking up and down, squeezing and releasing. He grabs my chin and lifts my face to his, kissing me until I can't breathe. I'm surrounded by him, can feel him all around me, his mouth on mine, his tongue tangled around mine. I'm stroking him, his hips are thrusting, his other hand comes down and shows me exactly how he likes it again and then he wrenches his mouth from mine, panting hard. I open my eyes, see the agony written all over his handsome face.

"Fuck. Chels, I'm gonna—"

And then he's coming all over my fingers, just like he said. My fist is slick and wet, and I watch with fascination as he falls apart right before me. Just like I fell apart right before him.

It's so intimate, so beautiful, that I'm stunned. I just shared something amazing with Owen. Something I've never done before with anyone else. I don't know what to say, how to react.

So I follow his lead. We both go to the bathroom to clean up in the dark so we don't have to see each other naked in the harsh lights. I think he knows I'm a little mind-blown and still feeling shy, despite what just happened between us. He pulls me to him after I wash my hands, kissing me so softly, so sweetly I melt into him, our naked chests meeting and making my heart pick up speed.

"We need to go to sleep," he whispers against my lips.

I nod. "I want to leave early. I need to get back home so I can turn in that paper."

"Always the conscientious student." He kisses the tip of my nose and takes my hand, leading me from the bathroom toward the bed. "Come on, Chels. I'll tuck you in."

I stand back when he fluffs the pillows and pulls down the covers, my gaze locked on his very firm-looking butt. Even in the dim light I can see it and I don't even care if he catches me totally checking him out.

If he thinks I have a nice one, he should take a look at his. I almost want to fan myself, he's so hot.

"All right, climb in," he says with a wave of his hand and I do as he says, lying still as he tugs the blankets up to my chin. Leaning over me, he drops a kiss on my forehead, then rounds the foot of the bed, crawling in beside me.

He lies on his side and pulls me close. I turn into him, resuming my position of before, and I close my eyes, listening to his heartbeat beneath my ear. His fingers tangle in my hair, his mouth whispers against my forehead, and I think he says something but I don't know what. I'm too sleepy, too far gone to understand him.

But I do know one thing. I've never felt so safe, so content, in all my life.

CHAPTER 16

*No matter whether you're a rose, a lotus flower or a
daisy. The important thing is that you blossom.*
—Osho

Chelsea

I wait for him, as usual. He's rarely on time. Only that first
official meeting we had, when he'd been trying to impress me,
did Owen ever make one of our tutoring sessions when he
was supposed to. Normally he runs about ten minutes late.

I forgive him. After all, he's pretty much my boyfriend,
right?

A secret little smile curls my lips as I check my text messages, scrolling past the endless list of the ones from Mom.
She can't stop messaging me. Thank God we're on an unlim-
ited program or we'd be spending a ton of money on the cell
phone bill every month.

She really needs to get a hobby. I'm tired of her worrying
about me. Lately she keeps referring to Dad and I don't know
why. He's not a part of our lives any longer. I thought she'd
filed for divorce.

I have a message from Kari, too, asking if I'm coming
home tonight. She says she doesn't feel well and I'd rather
avoid her since I don't want to get sick. It's Wednesday, and
normally I work the night shift, but I went in to the diner

yesterday morning, asking my boss if I could have a lighter schedule. He agreed, shifting it around so I wasn't working such late nights, and I only lost about four hours for the week.

That works out perfectly. I'm not a fan of working the late-night shift and I definitely know Owen isn't a fan of it either. So I changed my schedule to make him happy.

I'm not working tonight, so I think I might go to Owen's, I text her.

God, one night alone with him in a hotel room and now you've turned into a total whore.

Smiling, I shake my head. I know she's teasing.

You're right. I'm a complete whore.

Yay! I'm proud of you. Whores unite!

Laughing, I start texting her back when a big hand covers my eyes, rendering me still. I recognize the familiar hint of autumn and pine scent, but I go along with it.

"Guess who?" Owen's deep, sexy voice washes over me and I shiver.

"Hmm, I don't know."

He chuckles. "Did you just call yourself a whore in your text to Kari?"

"Ohmygod, you weren't supposed to read that." I try to jerk out of his hold but he won't let go. He's got the back of my head pressed against his chest, and he's so warm and hard. I try to be angry but I'm not. "Come on, Owen."

"I have a surprise for you. Ready?" His hand is still over my eyes, blocking my vision completely, and I cross my arms in front of my chest, slightly irritated. I've never really liked games like this. They always make me uncomfortable.

"I'm ready," I say, slightly exasperated.

"Keep your eyes closed until I say you can open them, okay?"

"They're already closed." I straighten my shoulders and clutch my phone in my hand, facedown. I so didn't want Owen to read that text, but I guess he kind of couldn't help it.

So embarrassing.

He removes his hand from my eyes and I hear a gentle rustling, then something is placed in front of me on the table. "Okay, you can open your eyes now."

I glance down to find a pretty pink rose lying on the table, its petals tightly furled, the flower not quite ready to bloom. I pick it up, careful to avoid the thorns, and bring it to my nose, inhaling the rich scent. Even in its budding state, it smells wonderful. "It's beautiful," I say, twirling the stem between my fingers.

He sits down across from me, his mouth curved into a small smile. "You like it?"

"I do." No boy has ever given me flowers before. "I love it."

"It reminded me of you." His smile grows and he looks downright wicked. "The pink is the same color as your—"

"Don't say it." I lunge across the table and slap my hand over his mouth to keep him from saying God knows what.

I will die of mortification if he says something dirty, I swear to God. I'm still having a hard time facing him right now. We haven't seen each other since we came home from our football game trip and I'm feeling a little shy.

He rolls his eyes at me and I drop my hand from his face, settling back down in my chair, sending him a warning look.

"I was going to say your *lips*." He stresses the last word. "What the hell did you think I was going to say?"

"You know." I wave a hand, my cheeks warm with embarrassment. "I was hoping we could get through this session without talking about what happened."

"Really? That's a damn shame, Chels. I was hoping to spend the entire hour talking about what happened. Reliving it a little. Maybe I could kiss you and convince you to come back to my place later tonight? Like after you're done with your shift at the diner?"

"You'd really want me to come by when I finish at two in the morning?" I'm shocked.

"Any time I can see you, I want to see you." He reaches across the table and grabs my hand, interlacing our fingers, pressing our palms together. "I already told you that, remember?"

I set the rose on the table and study it, smooth my fingers over the velvety-soft petals. "Owen. What were you really going to say about the rose?"

"I already told you. The color reminds me of your lips."

"Really?" I lift my head, our gazes meeting.

He smiles. "Yeah. Well, and your nipples. Since they're both the same shade of pink."

"Oh my God." I try to jerk my hand from his but he won't let me go. "I can't believe you said that."

"You asked." He shrugs, squeezing my hand in his. "So what do you say? Will you come over tonight? I don't care what time. I'll stay up and wait for you."

I'm sort of in shock at how easy he's acting around me. Like it's perfectly normal for him to invite me over at all hours of the night. That he'd speak so casually of lips and nipples, hold my hand, smile that secret smile of his at me.

All I can think is that he's had his hands all over my body. Inside of me. I've had my hands all over his body. I've touched him in the most intimate of places, witnessed one of the most intimate acts that can happen between two people, and here we sit like it's no big deal. Talking about work and school and nipples.

"I went into the diner yesterday morning and spoke with my boss." I take a deep breath, curl my fingers around Owen's. "I'm not working that late shift anymore."

"Well, thank God. I hated that you were out that late."

"I always had a ride from one of the waitresses who worked with me." I shrug, secretly pleased he was so concerned about my safety.

"Still. It wasn't safe." His eyes go soft, reminding me of the color of grass on a warm summer day. "So you can come over earlier, then."

"Don't you have practice?"

"Only till six. I don't work either tonight. I decided not to work as much as I originally thought I wanted. I'll add more hours at The District once the football season is over."

"Well, that sounds good." That sounds perfect. His schedule is so jam-packed, I've been afraid I'd never get to see him.

"I have something else I want to show you." He reaches down and pulls out a folder from his backpack and then sets it in between us on the table. "It's my creative writing portfolio."

"Okay." I slowly flip it open and see a nice, neat stack of Owen's writing samples. The list of assignments is stapled on the left side of the folder, check marks by the ones he'd completed. "It looks like you're pretty much caught up."

"I am." He pulls the folder closer to him and rifles through the papers until he finally finds what he wants and pulls it out. "Read this one."

I take the paper from him, notice the typed words but don't really see them. "What's it about?"

"You."

"Oh." I'm at a loss for words. He's being so tender, so sweet. I don't know what's happened to make him change.

Disengaging my hand from his, I grab the paper and pull it directly in front of me so I can read it.

Pink and soft
Damp and warm
My pretty little rose
Is my home
I cradle her close
Give her exactly what she needs
And when I'm finished
I'm the one who's pleased

My entire body is warm. I know what he's referring to. God, he's terrible.

In the absolute, most wonderful way a terrible person can be.

"Owen." I study the words before me, can feel his gaze on me. "This is . . ."

"Pretty good, huh? I'm not much of a poet and I'm definitely not a rhyming one, but I came up with this last night and I thought it was close. Not perfect rhyming but close enough, you know?"

I remain silent as I read the poem again. And again. On the surface, the words are seemingly innocent.

"Yeah, I was actually doing homework on my own last night after practice. Can you believe it?" I can hear the pride in his voice and I read his words yet again, lingering on the part where he calls his little rose his home.

Does he really feel that way? About me?

"It's very good." I finally feel brave enough to look up at him. He's leaning back in his chair, his legs stretched out in front of him, with a very pleased look on his handsome face.

"I thought so." He smiles, resting his linked hands on his chest. "You figure out what it's about yet?"

"Of course I have. I'm not dumb."

"Never said you were." His smile grows. "I'm starting to think you're my muse, Chels. My inspiration."

My cheeks turn as pink as the rose lying before me. "Don't you think your teacher will figure what this is about, too? And maybe be offended?"

"I don't care." He shrugs. "It's kind of fun, writing about such . . . personal things."

I want to both slug him and kiss him.

He sits up, pulls another sheet of paper out of the folder, and then slides it across the table toward me. "Read this one. I wrote it weeks ago."

She's shy. She's pink. She belongs to no one.
I vow to win her over with my touch.
Slow at first, my fingers gentle, searching as she opens
    only for me . . .
Caressing her, I bring her close.
So close.
Sending her over the edge.
Until I've completely destroyed her.
Petals scattered everywhere, her beauty wrecked.
All by my hand.
And now she's become everything.
To me.

"I had a couple of poem assignments," he explains, sounding so matter-of-fact while my mind is racing. He's writing about what's happening between us, the most intimate moments we've shared, and he's documenting them, immortalizing them. "One could be in whatever format we preferred. And the other one had to rhyme. I don't know which one I like better. I think they're both pretty fucking awesome."

211

"You said you wrote this one weeks ago?" I study him.

"Uh, yeah." He finally has the decency to look sheepish. "That night you came over to help me and we had Chinese for dinner."

"But we hadn't even . . ." Kissed? Touched? Nothing had really happened between us at that point.

"I have a very vivid imagination." The grin fades. His eyes darken, and this cloak of intensity seems to fall over him, the two of us, leaving me breathless. "What happened between us a couple of nights ago, I feel like that poem you just read describes it perfectly. Maybe I can predict the future, I don't know. I sound like I'm crazy."

Oh. My. I can't even talk, let alone form thoughts. What is happening between us? Only a few days ago I was devastated, thinking he wanted us to be just friends. Now he's writing poetry about our blossoming sex life and looking at me like he wants to tear my clothes off and have his way with me on the table.

"Say you're coming over tonight, Chels. Maybe we can do a few more things that'll inspire me to write." The grin is back, infectious and so cute I can't help but smile back at him.

"Fine. I'll come over." I try to sound all put out, but we both know I'm the biggest liar ever.

I'm dying to go over to his house and spend time with him. Alone.

"You'll be coming all night if you're lucky," he murmurs and I blink at him, shocked, yet not at his words.

"What did you say?" I want him to repeat it. Confirm that I really did hear that.

"Nothing." He puts on an innocent look, one that is so full of it, I want to reach out and smack him. Then pull him in close to me and kiss him. "Can you help me with my English? I have a test tomorrow."

How can I say no? After all, I'm still his tutor.

His girlfriend.

His rose.

His home.

Owen

I'm happy. The fucking happiest I've been in a long time, if ever. School is good. Football is good. I lightened my work schedule because holy shit, I couldn't take how heavy it was. I need at least a couple of free hours during the week so I can freaking relax.

And I plan on spending every one of those free hours with Chelsea.

I'm home, kicking it on the couch watching TV with Wade and waiting for Chelsea to come over. She sent a text about fifteen minutes ago, letting me know she'd be over in a half hour and she was bringing dinner.

Considering my stomach is growling and I'm anxious as all hell to see her, I hope she gets here soon.

"Des said the two of you argued," Wade says conversationally; his tone is light, but I know he's digging for information.

"Yeah." I shrug. I've got no major information to give. "It was no big deal. More like me telling him I'm sick of him mooching off of us."

"He's not a mooch and you know it, dude. He provides us with all the weed we could ever want, and sometimes he even brings beer. What more could we want from him?"

"Hmm, I don't know. Maybe I don't like having a drug dealer always hanging out at my house," I mutter, irritated I'm having this conversation again. "He fucking *deals* here, Wade. I won't have it. Not anymore. And I already went over all this with Des. I don't know what else you want me to say."

"So you don't want him hanging out here anymore."
Wade doesn't phrase it as a question. In fact, he sounds pretty
pissed.

Great.

"I never said that. It's just . . . I'm trying to clean up my
image." The guilt of messing around with Chelsea while high
still hangs over my head. "After all the trouble I've been in
lately, I don't want to have that kind of thing around here
anymore. I need to watch out."

"Come on, Owen. This has everything to do with that
little tutor of yours, right? At least, that's what Des said,"
Wade accuses.

Fucking Des. He needs to keep his big mouth shut. "Fine,
so it has something to do with Chelsea. But she's not the only
reason I don't want Des around here as much anymore."
How can I explain this without sounding like a complete
whiny little prick? "My mom . . . you know she's always coming around. Wanting to smoke a bowl with me or whatever. If
I kick the habit, then I'm eliminating half the reason she wants
to see me."

And that hurts. Knowing that Mom has only a couple of
reasons in the first place to want to see me, and both of them
suck.

"What's the other reason why she wants to see you?"

"Money. She always needs a handout. She can't save up
even a dollar. If she has change in her pocket, she rushes out
and spends it." I haven't heard from her in a while. Last time
I told her not to contact me for two weeks, and so far she's
holding to it.

But those two weeks are up soon and I don't doubt for a
second she'll be back in a hot minute, sniffing around and
looking for another payout.

"You know if you get rid of the weed, she'll just ask for

more money so she can get it somewhere else," Wade points out.

I've already thought of that. I've thought of everything. "That's fine, then at least it's not on my hands."

"Not completely."

Hell. Wade is right. I hate this. Hate what my mom's become, what she forces me to do. I'm mean to her and I despise it, but she's always mean to me first. She gives me no choice. This is our fucked-up relationship, and I'm jealous as hell of Fable. At least she doesn't have to deal with Mom. She was strong enough to cut the ties and walk away.

Why can't I do that? Why do I always feel so damn guilty when she looks at me, begging me for money, for drugs, for a light for her fucking cigarette, for Christ's sake?

Why does she have to be so fucked up? Why can't I have a normal mom like everyone else? I can't fucking stand her. And it hurts me to even think that, let alone say it out loud.

"Let Des know I'm not mad at him. Just tell him . . . I need him to stay back, only for a little while. I gotta try and get rid of my mom," I say, feeling like an asshole.

"I'll let him know. I just gotta tell you that if you're going to try and cut him out of our lives, it would piss me off. I like Des. He's one of my best friends, too, you know," Wade says.

"I get it, man. I like Des, too." Despite the fact that he's a drug dealer. But who am I to judge, with my white-trash mama and crazy-ass life?

There's a knock at the door and I leap from the couch to answer it. I find Chelsea standing on my doorstep, cute as hell wearing the 49ers sweatshirt I bought her and black yoga pants, her hair in a high ponytail. She's clutching a giant brown bag in one hand, a tiny smile teasing the corners of her mouth.

"Hi," she says softly, her eyes warm, everything about her . . . beautiful.

Shit. I am so gone over her. I wonder if she feels the same.

"Hey." I take her free hand and drag her inside, slamming and locking the door behind her. "You look good."

"I'm dressed like a bum," she says, rolling her eyes.

"Way to knock the sweatshirt I gave you." I bring her hand up to my mouth and kiss her knuckles, enjoying the way her eyelids flutter the slightest bit when my mouth touches her skin. "And way to show you're out to impress me tonight."

"Owen." She flicks her head toward where Wade's sitting on the couch.

I keep forgetting she's not 100 percent comfortable with us being together in front of someone else. I could care less what Wade says, but that's because I've known him forever.

But my poor, nervous Chelsea hardly knows Wade at all. So I guess I can't blame her.

"It's just Wade, Chels." I drop a kiss to her lips, then take the bag from her hand, surprised it's so heavy. "What did you bring for dinner?" Whatever it is, it smells damn good. My stomach is growing more demanding by the second.

"Indian food." She looks pleased with herself. I think she has me all figured out meal-wise. That my diet consists of pizza and fast food and . . . pizza. Beer and soda and beer and . . . that's about it. "I hope you like this place. I've only tried them once."

"I've never had Indian food," I admit as I carry the bag over to the dining table.

"Really?" She sounds incredulous as she walks into the kitchen. "Well, I brought a huge variety of dishes, so hopefully you'll like something." She's grabbing plates and utensils as though she lives here, and I like seeing her move about my house so comfortably. She fits in. I want her here.

I like having her with me.

"Wade, you can join us if you want. Do you like Indian food?" she calls from the kitchen as she pushes up her sleeves, turns on the faucet, and washes her hands.

"I've never had it either," he answers.

"We have so much. You need to come over here and try it. I think you'll like it." She shuts off the faucet, dries her hands, then grabs another plate before she brings everything to the table and starts setting it out.

I can't take my eyes off her. She's a completely different girl from the one I met only weeks ago. The first version of Chelsea had been shy, quiet, unsure of herself. This version is still a little shy, a little unsure, but there's something different about her now.

A confidence. It's in the way she moves, the way she talks, how she looks at me. I can feel it, see it, hear it, and I realize my sweet little Chelsea Rose has blossomed.

And I can't help but think I've been a huge influence in this change.

217

CHAPTER 17

Forgive my fingers
for when they find your body
they will lose themselves.
—Tyler Knott Gregson

Chelsea

"God, that was torture," Owen murmurs the minute his bedroom door shuts behind him. He pulls me into his arms, pressing me against the door as he leans in and kisses me.

I melt into him, curling my arms around his neck, burying my hands in his hair. His mouth on mine, firm yet soft, hot and damp, his tongue sliding against mine—relief mixed with desire floods me at the connection. I've waited for this, wanted it all night.

We spent hours out on that couch with Wade sitting right by us, watching some movie I really didn't pay much attention to. I couldn't. Owen kept touching me. Innocent little touches that should have meant nothing but instead meant everything.

Fingers on the back of my arm, his warm breath stirring my hair every time he spoke, he sat so close to me. The rumble of his laugh vibrating through me, making me shiver. His whispered words in my ear, griping about Wade being clueless, his lips brushing against my skin and sending a tremble throughout my body that I felt down to the very depths of my soul.

Dramatic. Silly. I know it, but I don't care. I'm in the throes of an Owen obsession and I've never been happier.

Though I'm scared, too. I'm just . . . me. And he's so . . . him. Easy to smile, easy to laugh, easy to show me exactly how he feels. Like now, being wrapped up in his arms, his big, capable hands sliding down my sides, I can feel him. Every hard inch of him pressing into me, and I'm scared and exhilarated and overwhelmed and ready.

So ready.

"I can't believe Wade didn't catch on I wanted to be alone with you," Owen murmurs against my neck, pressing tiny kisses there. "Thank God that shitty movie's over so we could bail."

His hands feel so good on my skin. He's slipped them beneath my sweatshirt, beneath the thin T-shirt I'm wearing under it, and his fingers dig into the pliant flesh at my waist. He's drawing little circles with his thumbs as he slowly kisses his way up the length of my neck. I close my eyes, my arms tight around him, my fingers tugging his hair as I lose myself so completely in his embrace.

"Fuck, Chelsea, you smell so good," he whispers just before he settles his mouth on mine. I open to him easily, gasping in surprise when he pushes me away so he can tear off my sweatshirt. He tosses it on the floor, irritation flashing in his eyes as he reaches for me again. "Who's the jackass who bought you that bulky thing anyway?"

Laughing, I shake my head. "I don't know. Some hot guy I just met who's the best kisser on campus?"

He raises an eyebrow. "Only on campus?"

"The entire town?" When he doesn't say anything I laugh even more. "The whole state of California?"

"Better." He kisses me again, soft and slow and so deliciously wonderful I swear my knees are buckling. Thank God he's holding me against the door. "Though I don't like the thought of you assessing my kissing skills in comparison to the other guys you've been with."

I say nothing. I can feel my cheeks flush, though, as he rears back slightly to study me. "The list of guys I've been with is embarrassingly small," I admit.

Both eyebrows are up now. "I know you're inexperienced, but . . ."

"Even with kissing," I finish for him, feeling inept. Totally out of my league, which is a feeling I absolutely do not like. He knows this.

The giant grin on his face tells me he sort of doesn't care.

"Is it wrong to admit I like that I'm a lot of your firsts?" He wraps his hands around the backs of my thighs and lifts so I have no choice but to let him carry me to his bed. He deposits me there, dropping me in the middle of the bed so I land with a plop, and I glance around, grimacing when I see the bed is a mess. The comforter's on the floor at the foot of the bed and there is no flat sheet, no blankets.

"Don't you ever make your bed?" I ask, bracing my hands behind me on the mattress.

He shrugs, then tugs off his shirt with one hand, yanking it over his head and tossing it on the floor. "Why bother? We're just going to mess it up anyway."

His words are full of wicked promise and anticipation skates through me, heady and strong. My nipples are hard beneath my bra and I press my thighs together to stave off the ache that throbs there. I let my gaze roam over the acre of bare skin on display just for me.

I'm dying for him to get closer so I can touch him.

"You know I promised you something the last time we were together," he says as he joins me on the bed, the mattress creaking from his weight as he crawls toward me.

"You did?" I scoot back as he comes forward, until my back is against a pile of pillows. He has a predatory gleam in his brilliant green eyes that both scares and thrills me.

"Yeah." He's over me, his knees on either side of my hips, straddling me. I stare up at him and curl my fingers around the waistband of his jeans, my knuckles grazing hot, bare skin. His eyelids flicker the slightest bit, his only outward reaction to my touching him. "I said next time I would make you come with my mouth."

I immediately let go of him, my cheeks so hot they feel like they could burst into flame. Closing my eyes, I hear him chuckle, feel him move over me, his spicy fall-like scent washing over me as I inhale deep.

"Don't be shy, Chels," he whispers against my lips right before he kisses me. "You know you want it."

He's right. I do. Oh God, I so do. I want everything Owen is willing to give me. There is so much I don't know, so much he could show me. When I'm with him I feel greedy. Insatiable. Completely and totally out of control.

And I like it.

"I want this to be good for you. I want to make sure you're ready," he says, his voice soft and solemn. My heart lodges in my chest and I'm at a loss as to how to respond.

But he kisses me before I can say anything, do anything, and it's as if his tongue knows just what to do to shut my brain down. It goes blank, until all I can focus on is his tongue swirling around mine, his gentle hands skimming over my skin, encouraging me to remove my shirt, which I do as if in a daze, opening my eyes so I can watch him. He's touching my chest, his mouth at my collarbone, his fingers drifting over the tops of my breasts. He's so patient, which shocks me. He's usually impatient and impulsive with everything else in his life, it seems, but not with me.

Never with me.

"I love touching you," he whispers as his fingers go for the front clasp of my bra. It unsnaps easily, the cups loosening, and then he's pushing them out of the way, his fingers, his palms brushing against my sensitive skin, and I shiver. "Your skin is so soft." He tugs the straps down my arms, pulls the bra off me, and then he's kissing my skin, his lips wrapping around my nipple and drawing it deep into his mouth. A jolt of electricity pulses between my legs and I smooth my hand over his hair, whimper when he sucks my flesh harder.

I love how he seems to savor me.

His impatience finally comes over him and he's pulling off my pants, taking my panties along with them. I kick them off, trying to fight off the embarrassment of being naked in front of him. I've done this before. He's *seen* me like this before, but not with the lights on. And that lamp sitting on his bedside table is distracting me.

"I'm not turning it off," he whispers, reading my mind as he kicks off his own jeans and underwear. I try not to stare but I can't help it. He's just so beautifully formed, so perfectly male. "I want to see you."

Before I can protest, he's kissing me again, his mouth working its magic, his hand trailing down my stomach until it's between my legs, testing me. Arousing me. He moans against my lips, a sound of utter male satisfaction, and then he's gone. Kissing his way down my shivering body, his lips hot against my skin.

"Cold?" he asks, right before he drops a kiss just below my belly button.

"Nervous," I admit, tilting my head down so I can look at him.

He's watching me, his hair a mess from my hands, his lips

quirked in the cutest little smile. "I'm nervous, too," he murmurs, holding out a shaky hand. "See what you do to me?"

I stare at him, dumbstruck. How do I answer him? I can't. I'm too overcome with emotion, foreign, powerful emotion that I could affect him this way. That I can feel his shaking fingers grip my hips and know that I did that to him. His hands slide down, along the tops of my thighs, farther down to part them, and I lean my head back, closing my eyes as I let myself be overcome by sensation.

His hair brushes against the inside of my thighs and then his lips are there, pressing soft, sweet, open-mouthed kisses. He grips my knees, keeping me spread wide open for him, and I can feel his breath against my slick flesh, then his lips . . .

Oh, God. A shuddery moan escapes me when he licks me there, his tongue doing a thorough search of my folds. He caresses my thighs with his fingertips, his mouth busy, his tongue circling in the most precise spot possible. All I can do is lie there and take it, my hands clutching the sheets beneath me as I lift my hips, wanting more but not quite knowing how to show it, let alone say it.

Owen seems to sense my struggle and he rests a hand low on my belly, stilling me as his tongue continues its thorough search. I'm writhing beneath his lips, my legs popping up of their own volition, my feet planted on the mattress. A ragged sound escapes as he slips a finger deep inside me and he sucks my clit into his mouth.

And that's all it takes. I'm already so keyed up, so turned on, I explode with a little cry, my entire body trembling as my orgasm rushes through me, leaving me breathless, boneless, mindless with pleasure. It's as if my entire system shuts down and he just killed me with his lips and tongue and fingers.

I'm lying in the middle of Owen's bed, just as I envisioned

the first time I went into his room. Naked and pale against the dark red sheets, sweaty and gasping for air, my arms and legs still trembling from the orgasm he gave me. My heart is racing so fast, I swear I'm going to have a coronary.

I've never felt better in all my life.

He's moving up the length of my body, his mouth brushing against my skin until his cheek is pressed to mine, his mouth at my ear, his hot breath making me shiver. "Did you like that?"

His deep voice is full of promise. Full of everything I could ever want and everything I never knew I needed.

My own voice has left me completely, so all I can do is nod. He kisses my ear, my cheek, until finally his mouth is on mine. His tongue meets mine and I can taste myself, but it doesn't bother me. Somehow, it kick-starts my arousal and I wrap my arms around his neck, my hands in his hair. Loving how he feels, naked and pressed tight against me, the heavy weight of his erection against my belly.

It's going to happen tonight. I know it is. I'm definitely giving up my virginity to Owen and though I'm nervous, I'm also excited.

"I thought you were going to rip my head off," he says after he pulls away from my lips. "Your thighs were clamped so tight around my head."

He just loves to embarrass me, doesn't he? I had no idea I'd even done that—that's how mindless he makes me. "Owen, stop." I let my arms fall from his neck, turning my face to the side.

Owen grips my chin with his fingers and makes me face him again. I stick my tongue out at him. "It was hot, Chels. I had no idea your thighs were so strong." Grinning, he reaches down and grabs one of my thighs and hikes it so my leg is draped around his hip, the heel of my foot pressing into his backside. He rocks into me, his grin fading, replaced with a look of pure, unfiltered pleasure. "Okay, yeah, this is perfect."

I don't want to close my eyes. I want to watch him. Watch all the emotions cross his expressive face, the way his lids fall at half-mast, his lips parted, his cheeks ruddy. His chest is gleaming with a light sheen of sweat and I rear up on my elbows, then press my mouth to the center of his chest so I can lick the spot just above his heart, in between his pecs.

"Jesus, Chelsea." He closes his eyes, his hand coming up to clasp the back of my head, and he just holds me there for a long, panted-breath second. "Can you feel what you do to me?"

I can. It's amazing, how little old me can make him react so strongly, feel so much. It's a powerful, heady feeling, one I don't ever want to let go of. I kiss his chest again, lick his skin, groan when he tightens his grip in my hair and pulls me away from him.

Blinking my eyes open, I stare up at him, see the greedy gleam in his eyes. He looks like he wants to devour me.

And I desperately want to be devoured.

"I need a condom," he says through gritted teeth just before he releases me.

Then he's gone, rising from the bed and padding over to his dresser, completely comfortable in his nudity. I stare at him unabashedly, drinking in the perfect lines of his broad, muscled back, his firm backside, his thick thighs. A little sigh escapes me as he pulls open a drawer and goes in search of condoms.

I am so lucky. He's so thoughtful, sweet, and funny. He writes me poems. Dirty ones, but I don't care. They're beautiful. *He's* beautiful. Not perfect, but he's mine.

And I am his.

He approaches the bed, what looks to be about ten condom packets clutched in his fist, and he drops them all on the bedside table, with the exception of one.

That one is in his hand and he's tearing it open, taking the ring and placing it at the tip of his erection.

I watch him, my eyes wide, my mouth dry. He's standing on the side of the bed, right in front of me, about to roll the condom on when he realizes I'm staring. "You're enjoying this, aren't you?"

I nod wordlessly.

His mouth quirks into a smile and he slips the condom on, then he's on me, pressing me into the mattress, pressing his mouth to my mouth, his tongue tangling with my tongue. His hands are everywhere and so are mine, and soft little sighs escape me, just as low, deep groans leave him.

I'm scared but I'm not. Owen has been so patient with me, I know he won't be too rough or quick. He wants me to feel good. He's told me that time and time again. It's why he wouldn't let me touch him when we first went into his room. He'd wanted the moment to be all about me and my orgasm and how good he could make me feel.

He wanted me ready, he said. He wanted this to be easier for me.

What he wants . . . he wants for me.

I spread my legs for him and he nudges his hips between them, the head of his erection brushing against my center. I'm slick down there from his earlier attention and I close my eyes, almost embarrassed by my own body.

"Damn, Chels, you're fucking soaked for me," he murmurs, his fingers sliding along my folds, teasing me before he inserts one long, perfect finger deep inside.

All my embarrassment disappears with his words. I spread my legs wider and hook one leg over his hip again, just like he'd positioned me a few minutes ago. I'm completely open to him and he moans against my neck, thrusting his erection against me slowly. It all feels so good, so wondrously right, and then he's right there. Nudging against me, the very tip of him entering my body for the first time.

I stiffen up all over, feeling like I'm going to shatter.

"Baby." He runs his hand over my hair, then cups my chin, tilting my face up. I open my eyes and stare at him, my heart racing for a different reason now. Fear of the unknown has left me quivering. "Don't be scared. Relax."

Nodding, I close my eyes tight, breathing slowly through my mouth. He drops tiny kisses along my neck, his lips light, his touch fleeting, just as I like it. His big hands are on my breasts, his thumbs tracing my nipples, his hips moving against mine languidly, and I lose myself. Let my mind float. Let my thoughts be free.

And then he's entering me. Slow, so slow. Just a nudge, a gentle push, the head of his erection broaching my body, and I let my thighs fall open. A willing captive to his body as he pins me in place.

"Put your other leg around me," he commands, and I do so, a thrill moving down my spine at the dark tone of his voice. "Relax, baby, this might hurt."

He presses forward, inch by thick inch, impaling me with his length. A gasp escapes me at the sharp pinch of pain and I close my eyes and tense my body, my muscles shaking I'm so rigid.

"Relax, Chels. I'm gonna make this so good for you—it's gonna be unbelievable," he whispers close to my ear. "Fuck, you feel amazing. Hot and tight. Just let it happen, baby. Trust me."

I trust him. I do. A ragged breath escapes me and I force my body to slowly relax. His hips rock, his erection pushes forward, and then he's inside me, thick and hot and throbbing. Filling me to bursting.

We move together, our bodies united, our limbs entwined, our mouths fused. He's kissing me, moving inside of me, pulling almost all the way out before he pushes back inside, and I open my eyes to find him watching me, his gaze so brilliantly green I'm momentarily dazzled.

"You're beautiful. You know that?" he asks, pressing his forehead to mine.

"You make me feel beautiful," I admit, because it's true. No one has ever treated me like Owen has. I feel safe with him. I trust him. He makes me laugh. He makes me want.

I think I'm falling in love with him.

Owen

I've had sex. Lots and lots of it. I would be embarrassed to tell Chelsea I was only fourteen my first time. Hell, Fable would die if she knew this, especially since it happened when I was under her watch. Mom was long gone, Fable was with Drew, and I snuck off with Wade to meet up with two girls from our history class. Girls we knew liked to smoke and party.

Girls we fucked in a bathroom at a public park not too far down the street from Wade's house.

Not a proud moment. None of my sexual encounters would be what I'd classify as proud moments. What can I say? I was young and dumb and horny. Only thinking with the thing between my legs, versus the thing that I'm supposed to be using when I'm thinking.

Never, ever did I allow my heart into the equation. Another embarrassing admission: I never felt anything for those girls. The majority of them are nameless. Faceless. They could have been anyone. It's not like I've been with hundreds of girls but for a while, there was an endless stream of them. All of them interchangeable, not a one of them special.

Until I met Chelsea.

We're wrapped all around each other and I feel like my body is permanently fused with hers. Her hair is spread out all over my pillow; her scent is embedded in my skin. I can still taste her on my tongue, still hear the little whimpers and whispers of my name when I made her come with my lips and fingers.

She was being quiet so Wade wouldn't hear us. She worried about that. She worries about everything. Her image. What she's doing, how helpless she feels when she doesn't understand what to do. Sex leaves her feeling helpless. She doesn't have to say it.

I can tell.

But I'm here to catch her. Here to teach her whatever she wants to learn. It all just comes naturally because after all, sex is an instinctive act. The most basic act two human beings can commit. And I can see that happening within her. Her hips are lifting, her legs wrapped tight around me. My cock feels like it's going to burst, and it takes everything within me not to just heave two sharp thrusts inside her tight little body and come.

I take it slow, though. I promised I would. I'm patient, infinitely patient with Chels.

Because she's worth it.

She's clutching my shoulders, her nails digging into my skin, and I welcome the bite of pain. I was so damn afraid I'd hurt her when I first entered her body and I'm pretty sure I did, though I definitely don't think she's hurting now. Whatever pain she can inflict on me I welcome, because then we're equal.

And I like being equal with her. With Chelsea. I like opening my eyes and watching her, learning a rhythm with her, our bodies in sync, my hands mapping her skin, learning just how to touch her to drive her wild.

She's mine. She might not know it yet, but I can't stand the thought of letting her go. The nameless, faceless girls—they're things of my past. Banished forever. I don't want to be with anyone else.

I just want to be with her.

"Owen." Her soft, breathless voice sends a shiver down my spine, and I drop a kiss on her forehead before swooping down and kissing her lips. She can barely keep up, her mouth slack from her out-of-control breathing; her breasts are crushed against my chest and her hands slide down my back, until they settle on my ass and she's pressing me deeper. "You feel so good."

Fuck, so do you, I want to scream at her. Too good. Too fucking good. She's too good for me. She's definitely worth it, but I'm not worthy. How did I end up with this girl, anyway? One minute I don't want to be near her because she's trying to force me to do something I most definitely don't want to do, and the next I'm chasing after her like a dog in desperate need of attention. I wanted her attention. All of it. All the time.

I still do.

"You close?" I ask, my voice rough, my entire body wanting to be rough. I need to ease her into this so I don't hurt her, but I'm desperate to unleash everything I have on her. Fuck her hard. Drive her out of her mind. Make her as addicted to me as I am to her.

She offers this tiny little nod and squeezes her eyes shut, as if she's focusing every bit of concentration within her to make herself come. Her teeth sink into her poor, ravaged lower lip and I bend down, suck her lip between mine and give it a gentle pull. Lick it. Savor her taste, the whisper of breath that gusts across my mouth. I swallow it, wishing I could swallow her.

I'm a man possessed—overwhelmed and confused and full of joy and scared out of my ever-lovin' mind. What's happening between us, I've never experienced before. I think I know what Chelsea's feeling and it's scary as fuck.

But at least we're doing it together.

Hesitating, I remain still and inhale sharply, goose bumps washing over my skin. A sure sign I'm about ready to blow, though she's not ready yet. I can tell she's not. The familiar tingling has formed at the base of my spine, insistent as all fuck, and my balls literally ache.

"Don't stop," she urges. The sound of her voice kills me and I drop my forehead to hers once more, trying to gain some control.

"I gotta stop," I tell her. "If I don't, I'm going to come. And you're not ready."

"I'm ready." She runs her fingers through my hair, and I really fucking love it when she does that. Her touch feels so good. I want to lean into her hand every time, like I'm a cat or something. "Do what you want, Owen. You won't hurt me. I'm not made of glass."

She's giving me permission to use her. And I don't really want to, because she's different. What we share together is so different from what I've done with other girls. "But . . ."

"I already came." She streaks her fingers down my cheek as shock courses through me over what she said. Look at my tentative Chelsea, saying I made her come.

"I want you to come again," I tell her just before I crush my mouth to hers. I increase my pace, using her because she gave me permission, but I'm also going to make sure she gets off, too.

Reaching between our bodies, I brush my fingers against

her clit. She hisses against my lips and I continue stroking her, keeping time with my thrusts, keeping time with my breaths. With hers. She shudders and moans, licks my lips with her tongue as if she can't get enough, and then she's thrusting her head back against the pillow. Her perfect neck is arched, her pink lips parted, but no sound is coming out beyond her sexy little pants of air.

I push harder, wanting her to reach for it. Needing her to reach for it. Because then it's too late. I've found it, my need consumes me as I push inside her once, hard, my orgasm taking over, washing over my skin, my thoughts, my brain, my everything. *Fuck*, I'm done.

Spent.

She's shuddering all around me, too, her body clenching around my cock, milking every last drop out of me until I can do nothing but collapse on top of her, exhausted. I think I shouted her name out loud but I can't be sure. Wade probably heard if I did.

I really don't fucking care.

Chelsea's arms are around me, her mouth at my ear. She's coasting her hands down my back, up and down, scraping her nails on my sensitive skin, and I shiver in her embrace, press my lips against her neck. She tastes amazing. She's whispering something in my ear that I can't really hear since my head is still buzzing, my ears ringing.

Fuck. That was intense.

"I'm too heavy," I tell her, bracing my hands flat on the mattress so I can lift away from her, but her hands press hard on my back, keeping me in place.

"A couple more minutes," she murmurs, her voice soft, her lids downcast. As if she's feeling shy again and well . . . fuck that.

I kiss her. A fierce, possessive kiss that's full of tongue and heat and demand. I need her to know she doesn't have to be shy with me any longer. We've done everything.

But she doesn't know everything. Not about Mom. How Des deals in my fucking house. How I'm one of Des's clients. And I smoked pot and was high as hell when I gave her an orgasm in a no-name hotel in a no-name city.

Shame washes over me and this time I do pull out of her embrace, offering her a brief smile when I find her studying me with concern etched all over her beautiful, flushed face.

"Where are you going?" she asks, sitting up, completely naked and comfortable with it. I stare at her breasts, those pink nipples that match her lips that match the rose I gave her, and I want to climb right back into bed. Clutch her close and never let her go, pretend that my problems don't exist and will never bother me again.

Never bother *us* again.

But that's just wishful thinking. I gotta get the hell out of here. At least for five minutes. I need some clarity.

I need a fucking hit.

"I'll be back. Gotta get rid of this." I peel the condom off and pinch the top, keeping it in my hand as I make my escape out of the bedroom, still naked, not caring. I dart across the hall into the bathroom and slam the door, flick the lock. Dispose of the condom, then search through the cabinet drawers until I find what I'm looking for.

A joint. We keep them everywhere in this house. I mean, what the hell? Was someone gonna sit on the toilet and pass the time by taking a few hits? I wouldn't put it past Wade to try something like that.

The idea disgusts me. *I* should disgust me because here I am, hiding away from Chelsea, contemplating smoking a joint rather than going back inside my room immediately so I can hold her close and show her how much she means to me.

I stare at the joint I hold pinched between my fingers. I can smell it, that strong, skunk-like scent that I love. Used to love.

Fuck it. Still love.

There's a lighter in the drawer, too. Of course. I pull it out and flick it once. Twice. Five fucking times before it finally catches and I bring the joint to my lips. Light the burned-out tip, hear the subtle crackle of the paper catching fire. Glancing up, I catch myself in the reflection of the mirror. Naked and sweaty and about to suck in a bunch of smoke that'll burn my lungs and clear my brain.

I don't want to clear my brain. It's full of Chelsea.

The lighter drops to the counter with a loud clatter and I stub the joint out in the sink, then rinse it out. I drop the half-smoked joint into the toilet and flush, watch as it disappears down the drain forever.

If my friends caught me flushing a joint they'd be pissed. But I don't care. I need to get this shit out of my life. I need to focus. I need to do the right thing.

I need to prove myself worthy of Chelsea. But no matter how much our relationship means to me, it also scares me.

Scares me so much I'm afraid I might do the wrong thing. And once I do that, I can never go back.

CHAPTER 18

*Only the truth of who you are, if realized, will set
you free.*
—Eckhart Tolle

Chelsea

I'm attending a college football game for the first time ever. Only took me three years to do it. Of course, I never had a reason to attend one before. I hated sports. I kind of still do. I can never understand exactly what's going on down on the field and that drives me crazy. I like knowing what's happening at all times.

As Owen teased me about last night right before we drifted off to sleep, I do wish there were a textbook for all of these things we're supposed to know and do and learn and watch. If I can't figure it out right away or read up about it, I'm lost. And frustrated.

I hate that.

But I'm letting all the anxiety go. It's the second half, our team is winning, Owen is out on the field, and I'm sitting with his sister and niece, bundled up against the crisp, cold fall air. The baby is adorable, sweet and content in her mother's arms, and when Fable offers for me to hold the baby, I take her, bouncing her up on down on my knee, cooing at her and saying the dumbest stuff that has probably ever come out of my mouth.

I don't care. Autumn likes it. She reaches for my face and my heart stops. She smiles at me and I want to make her do it again. Her eyes remind me of Owen's, green and clear and achingly beautiful. No wonder Owen goes on and on about how sweet his niece is. She's adorable.

"She likes you," Fable says, reaching out to readjust the little cap sitting on top of Autumn's head.

I cuddle the baby close to me, gazing down at her. "I like her, too."

"This game is sort of boring," Fable says, looking out at the field. "We're totally kicking their asses."

I muffle the laugh that wants to escape. "Yeah, we are."

"Thank goodness we're almost out of here. I need to get Autumn down for a nap soon before she starts getting cranky. You're going to dinner with us later, right?"

"Yes, definitely," I say, happiness filling my chest so full I feel like I'm going to burst. "What time did you want to meet?"

"I don't know." Fable shrugs, a little smile on her face. "After Autumn's nap, but not too late. I think I want to go to The District."

"Really? Didn't you used to work there?" I ask.

"I did." A wistful smile crosses her face. "I have a lot of fond memories at that place. Some not so fond, too. Most of them are pretty awesome, though."

"Is that where you and Drew met?"

"Oh, no." She laughs and shakes her head, then reaches for the baby and plucks her from my arms. "Daddy and I had an—unusual meeting, didn't we, princess?" She's talking to Autumn, who smiles and kicks out her little feet.

I'm almost afraid to ask how they met now. So I don't.

"You and my brother are getting pretty serious then?" she asks after a few minutes have gone by.

I glance around, thankful no one is really sitting by us. We're down on the bottom row of bleachers, close to the exit, because that's where Fable wanted to be. She was unsure how Autumn might behave while we're here and didn't want to take any chances. "Um, what do you mean by serious?"

"Boyfriend/girlfriend kind of serious?" She sends me a pointed look, one that says you'd better tell me everything, and quick. I swallow hard, suddenly intimidated.

"I—I think so." I shrug, feeling stupid. And I despise feeling stupid. "We haven't made an official declaration or anything."

"Ah." She nods. "I get it." She offers me a smile, cuddling her baby close to her chest. "Be patient with my brother. He might not be the best when it comes to relationships, but he's a good guy."

He's definitely a good guy, but I think we're both amateurs at relationships. I keep my opinions to myself. He's never really had a relationship and neither have I, but we seem to be navigating the course fairly well so far. And I don't want to rock the boat, asking him for something more that he might not be ready to give yet.

So I remain quiet and enjoy what we share. Ever since that night I went over to his place with the Indian food and we ended up having sex for the first time, I've spent every free hour I can spare with Owen at his place. So much that I'm starting to irritate Kari because she never sees me. I ignore Mom's texts, just occasionally sending her a one-word answer in the hope I can get rid of her for at least a little while.

It rarely works. I need to actually call her and find out what's really going on. I just . . . I don't have time for all that right now.

I'd rather spend all my time with Owen.

He's been edgy lately and I don't know why. Des never

comes around anymore. Wade leaves a lot, but we never protest. That just gives us the opportunity to be a little more
vocal when we're in bed together. And when we're alone in
the house, Owen has this way of looking at me, touching me,
that makes me lose all inhibitions. He can get me naked in
minutes, both physically and emotionally. He's made me
come so hard, I've screamed his name.

My body goes a little limp just thinking about it.

"You know, our mom was pretty screwed up," Fable continues.

I become instantly alert at the mention of their mom.
Considering Owen never, ever talks about her, I'm all ears.

"She was?" I ask, hoping she'll continue.

Fable's gaze meets mine and she rolls her eyes. "She's
awful. Just a terrible human being. I saw right through her
tricks. She didn't know how to take care of us and after a
while, she didn't want to, either. I was fine with it. Yeah, it
hurt my feelings, but I just wanted to get away from her forever."

I wait breathlessly for more information. Their mom
sounds like a nightmare.

"She abandoned us awhile ago. Well, she abandoned us at
first when Owen was just fourteen. Like, he came home one
night all alone and found our apartment empty. She'd taken
all of our stuff and just left."

I stifle a gasp. "That's awful," I breathe.

"I know." She nods sagely. "Then over a year later, she
tried to come back. Got an apartment in town, had Owen
half convinced to move back in with her and everything."
Fable shakes her head, her gaze growing distant. "That's a
time I don't like to think about. Neither does Owen. I almost
lost him. She was going to try and convince him to leave with

her. Leave the town, the state, go somewhere completely new and start over."

If that had happened, I would never have met him. My heart hurts at the realization. I can't imagine my life without him.

"I can't even comprehend what might've become of him if he'd done that. She would've ruined him. He'd be some high school dropout junkie living in the streets if he'd gone with her," Fable continues.

"So what happened to her?" I ask.

"I don't know." She shrugs, her gaze meeting mine. "I haven't heard from her in four years. Neither has Owen. Good riddance, I say."

Four years. I can't imagine not hearing from my mom in four years. Dad? That I can see, but I don't want to hear from him and there's a difference. Sounds like Fable and Owen don't want to hear from their mom either.

"She sounds like a despicable human being," I finally say.

Fable laughs, and the sound makes baby Autumn smile. "Great word. So true. She *is* a despicable human being. That's why it's nice to see Owen with someone so . . . normal. Not some over-the-top cheap-looking girl with her tits hanging out of her shirt and her hands all over him."

Ugh. Just imagining that makes me want to throw up. I hate thinking of Owen being with anyone else, and it's a reality I kind of have to face.

He's been with a lot of someone elses.

"Our mom screwed with his head. He had all this guilt over her. Always thought he was responsible for her well-being or whatever. She put it on him. So when she finally left and disappeared out of our life for good, he'd go out with girls, but none of them were worthy of him. They were all kind of trampy." Fable gives me the once-over but her eyes are kind. "You, Chelsea, are not a tramp."

"Um, thanks?" I say, laughing nervously. I have no idea how to respond to that assessment.

"It's a compliment. Trust me." She smiles, and we both glance at the football field when the crowd cheers. My gaze snags on Owen and I can't help but go all dreamy-eyed at seeing him running across the field in his uniform, the number 26 and his last name emblazoned on his back.

He looks good—big and broad and indestructible. He's quick on his feet and can catch a ball with a preciseness that impresses. No wonder his coach was so eager to get him back on the team as fast as possible.

"He reminds me of Drew." I look over at Fable and she's watching Owen with the same sort of wistful expression I must have. "Different position but same determination, same natural ability. He could go far. As far as Drew has, if he wanted to."

"You really believe that?" Football hasn't been up for much discussion between Owen and me. I know it's import-ant to him. But we'd focused on his grades so much we hadn't discussed anything else. And if we weren't talking about school, we were busy flirting.

"I do. Drew wants to talk to him. See if that's what Owen really wants. Though I'm not sure what Owen really wants."

I don't think Owen knows what he wants, either. He's just cruising through life without a plan. Without a net. Whereas me, I like to plot and plan and figure out my next step. After graduate school, I'm going to teach, most likely at college level. That has been my plan since I was a little kid. Mom had instilled it in my brain that it was the best possible future for me. The only option I had.

But now . . . I wonder. It sounds so boring. Teaching.

Doing the same thing, day in and day out. Would I want that? Would I be happy? Would I really be fulfilled? If you'd asked me this question a few months ago I would have answered yes without hesitation.

Now, I'm not so sure. Meeting Owen, spending time with him, letting him take me off track and actually learn how to have a little fun, changed me.

For the better.

Owen

It felt good to be out on the field and winning the game knowing my girl and my sister and niece were in the stands watching me. I caught sight of them a few times, chatting with each other more than keeping their eye on the game, and I could forgive them for that. Fable's probably seen enough football games to last her a lifetime and Drew's career is really only a couple of years in. And Chelsea isn't big on football.

Plus, they're getting to know each other, and that's important to me. If Chelsea is going to become as big a part of my life as I hope she will, then I want them to like each other.

I'm at home with my girl now, kicking it in the living room, waiting for her to finish taking a shower. I'd tried to get in the shower with her but she'd shoved me out of the bathroom, giving me that look—the one that said no way, asshole—while whispering, "Wade's right out there. He'll *know*."

I didn't push. Hell, I'd cleaned that bathroom like crazy to ensure she'd even want to take a shower at my place. Guys are pigs. I'm no exception. But when we made plans for Fable to be here this weekend a few days ago, Chelsea had said she might stay the night and take a shower at my place. She even asked if that would be okay.

Took a lot for me to play it off and act like that was no big deal. While inside I was dying to tell her, *move in with me forever.*

How I feel about Chelsea is just . . . fucking ridiculous, in the most awesome, unbelievable way.

"Going out with your girlfriend?" Wade's tone is kind of snide, a little joking. I think he's still mad at me about the Des thing, but what can I do? It's too late to back down now, and I kind of like not having Des here all the damn time, bringing his posse of druggies with him.

"Yeah. My sister's here, you know."

"Right. I talked to Fable after the game." She's always liked Wade. Though she'd probably hate him if she ever discovered all the trouble we got into numerous times throughout our high school years. Thank God we hadn't been caught.

That hadn't been all Wade's fault. We were a bad influence on each other.

A knock sounds on the door and Wade goes to answer it. I'm feeling too lazy to even move from the couch. I played a hard game today. Truthfully, I was trying to show off for Fable and Chelsea. I'm going to pay the price tomorrow, especially if I get what I want later tonight.

Chelsea, naked in my bed. Beneath me, making her cry out my name when I first enter her.

Yeah, I'll gladly suffer through sore muscles for that.

"Uh, Owen."

I glance up at the sound of Wade's voice to see him with the door partially shut, his head tilted toward it and his expression one of pure panic.

Shit. I think I know who's waiting on the doorstep. I gotta get rid of her, quick.

Pushing up from the couch, I rush toward the door, Wade backing away so he's not in the middle of the family drama. Because there *will* be drama if I let her linger for any length of time. Fable is supposed to meet us here with her car before we head to The District for dinner. I can't have her see Mom.

That is the absolute last thing I need.

"What are you doing here?" I say the moment I step out onto the front porch and slam the door behind me.

Mom glares at me, her arms wrapped around herself. She's wearing raggedy old jeans, those same damn Nike shoes that have probably been around for ten years and look it, and a freaking T-shirt.

It's like 50 degrees outside. She must be freezing.

You don't care, man. You. Don't. Care.

"It's been almost two weeks." Her expression turns pleading in an instant, but the hard glare is still in her eyes. I'm trying to look at her and see nothing, but it's so damn hard. She's my mom. I always feel like I owe her. "I need money, Owen. I need a smoke. I—I need to come down."

Come down? Shit. "I don't have any weed in the house."

Her mouth hardens. "Don't lie to me. You always have weed in the house."

"Not this time."

We stare at each other in silence, neither of us moving. We're at a standoff and we're both too stubborn to give in first. All I can think is the clock keeps ticking, bringing us closer to Fable showing up here soon, and Chelsea coming out of the shower and going in search of me.

"I need money," Mom finally says, caving first.

"I don't have much of that either. I'm taking less hours at work."

Her mouth drops open. "Why would you do that?"

"Football season is eating into my time. Plus my school-work."

"Still trying to pretend you care about school, huh? You can tell me the truth. I know how you really feel."

"Yeah, when I was fifteen and always wanting to skip," I say, glancing behind me. The blinds are open; I can see Wade pacing the living room but no Chelsea yet. Hopefully he'll distract her for me.

"Like you've really changed. You're the same ol' Owen. My baby." She reaches for me like she's going to hug me, and I step out of the way, shocked that she'd do it. I can't remember the last time she's touched me with any sort of affection.

Her arms drop at her sides, her mouth turned into a deep frown. "Come on, Owen. Give me some money. I need at least twenty dollars. I have nowhere else to go."

She almost sounds like she's going to cry, but I don't remember the last time I saw her do that either—if ever. So I call bullshit on the pathetic act. "You need to go, Mom. I—I can't have you hanging out here."

Her eyes narrow. "Why not? You got something to hide? Why won't you smoke with me? What's going on?"

"I don't have any weed on me, I swear." I really don't. After I flushed the first joint down the toilet, I got rid of the rest. I haven't had a smoke since that night at the hotel with Chelsea. Whatever Wade might have is on him. But me?

I've got nothing.

"What about your roommate? Let's go ask him what you have. I remember that boy, you know. I used to talk to his mom sometimes. Real snob, that one." She tries to dodge around me and grab the door handle but I'm quicker than her. I block the door, slapping my hand against the handle.

"Wade's mom took care of me when you couldn't," I remind her. "She's definitely not a snob."

"That was your sister's deal, not mine. She's the one who always passed you off on that woman. Too busy out fucking around to worry about her baby brother." Mom sneers.

Anger boils in my gut. "Don't talk about her like that."

"I can talk about her any way I want. She's *my* goddamn daughter. Not that she knows how to act like one." Mom points her thumb at her chest and stumbles, almost falling right off the porch. I lunge for her, grabbing her by the elbows so I can set her back on her feet.

It happens so fast, she takes total advantage, darting beneath my arm and going straight for the door. I run after her, slap my hand against the door to keep from opening it, and she tugs on the handle, putting all her weight into it, though that's not much. She's like a shadow of her old self. Thin and frail-looking, her fried blond hair wispy and dry, her jeans bag off her body, and when I get close to her, I realize she smells. Bad.

"I want to talk to your roommate," she says, her teeth clenched as she puts all her might into tugging the door handle again. "Stop trying to block me, Owen."

"Where the hell are you living, Mom?" I wince. She doesn't really like it when I call her Mom. She doesn't want me to call her anything.

"What do you care?" She tosses over her shoulder. "I don't have a home. Not that it matters to you or that bitch sister of yours."

"Stop insulting Fable. I can't stand it."

"Good, because I can't stand her and I can't stand you! Always passing your judgment, acting like you're so much better than me! You're just the same, Owen Maguire. You and me, we're exactly the same."

I push away from her, staring at her in disbelief. She's expressing everything I've always worried about but never put into actual words. Hearing her actually say it is . . .

Devastating.

"No we're not," I protest weakly, but she laughs.

Actually laughs.

"Oh yes, we are. It's why I loved you best. You're just like me, Owen. Whether you like it or not, you're going to end up like me. Wandering through your life with no goals, no success. Every time you build yourself up, someone will kick you back down. That's what always happens. They've all held me down through the years. Everyone. No one ever gave me a break. No one will ever give you one, either."

I try to fight against her words but it's hard. So hard. I feel like I'm ten years old again. She used to scare the hell out of me when she went on her drunken binges, cursing me and Fable and whoever happened to be the boyfriend of the month. It was always some loser who'd live with us for a little while, using her up only to spit her out.

We saw it happen time and again, to the point where Fable tried to run away more than once, the summer she was fifteen.

We never talk about that, though. We don't talk about a lot of stuff. Those types of memories are best left forgotten.

"And if you think you can find love, you've got to be kidding." When I open my mouth to say something, she laughs again. "I saw you come home with that silly girl. Hanging all over your arm and looking at you like you're her hero. You're nobody's hero. Does your stupid little girlfriend know you smoke weed with your mom? That you're nothing but a worthless drug addict? That you give me all the weed and money that I want? That you hide me from all your friends and your sister because you're ashamed of me? You should be ashamed of yourself. You make me sick."

"I have no idea what you're talking about." The words come out stiff. I don't even sound like myself. "I don't have a girlfriend," I tell her, because that's the last thing I want Mom to know. Somehow she'll use it against me, and God, she might even . . . even approach Chelsea.

And no way can I have that.

"Don't lie. I saw her."

"She's no one. Just a friend." It pains me to even say that. She's more than just a friend.

Chelsea is . . . everything.

"Owen?"

I turn to find Chelsea standing with the door open, her hand clutching the handle. She's wearing jeans and a black sweater, looking like my every dream come true with her wet hair piled into a bun on top of her head, her face freshly scrubbed and her skin glowing. But her expression is one of ice-cold shock. She's looking between my mom and me like she can't quite figure out what's going on.

Dread sinks my gut to my toes. She had to have heard what Mom said. And what *I* said. She'll know. All of it.

And she'll hate me for what I've done.

CHAPTER 19

If you correct your mind, the rest of your life will
fall into place.
—Lao Tzu

Chelsea

"Chelsea." He says my name but I can hardly hear it. The words this woman—his mother—said are still ringing in my ears, clanging through my mind. Harsh and ugly, growing bigger and bigger inside my head until they're all I can hear. All I can think about.

Does your stupid little girlfriend know you smoke weed with your mom? That you're nothing but a worthless drug addict?

And Owen's devastating, horrible reply.

I don't have a girlfriend.

She's no one. Just a friend.

"Well, lookee here, there's your not-a-girlfriend right now. And aren't you a plain little thing?" His mom sneers at me, her thin lips curled, her face worn and faded and so full of hatred I take a step back, surprised that she's aiming all of that anger at me. "You really think my handsome boy would want to be with you? Look at you. You're *nothing.*"

"Shut the fuck up," Owen says, his voice low. He sounds so angry. His hands are curled into fists and his jaw is tight.

He looks ready to beat someone with his bare hands. "Don't talk to her. She's not a part of this."

"*You* shut the fuck up," his mom retorts, her face scrunched and ugly, her cheeks red as she glares from me to him and back to me again. "And she's definitely a part of this. She's trying to steal you away from me. You're my baby boy, Owen. I need you. You can't leave me. A boy always needs and loves his mama."

God, what is she saying? She hates me. And no one has ever really hated me. I'm always well liked. I work hard at being liked. By my professors, by my employers, by what few friends I have.

This woman doesn't even know me and she hates me on sight.

"I—I should go." I stumble backward, practically smacking into Wade, who's standing right behind me, and then I turn. I'm running down the hall to Owen's bedroom, where I slip inside and grab my small overnight bag and my purse off the floor, slinging them both over my shoulder so I can make my escape.

I can't stay here. Owen told his mom he doesn't have a girlfriend. I don't exist. So what does that make me to him? His piece on the side? Some dumb girl he's just . . . *fucking* until he's finished using me and ready to move on to someone else?

The idea is so painful, I can hardly stand the thought.

Blindly I walk through the house, noticing that the front door is still hanging wide open and I have no choice but to leave the way I came. Wade isn't in the living room. He's nowhere to be found. I don't see Owen or his mother, either.

Oh my God. If Fable knew Owen was still in contact with their mom, she'd probably flip out.

249

I step out onto the front porch to find Fable already there, glaring at her mother as though she wants to tear her throat out, and Owen is grasping hold of Fable's shoulders to keep her from lunging.

"You need to leave," Fable is saying, her voice so low, so dark, it sends a shiver down my spine.

I'm frozen, standing by the door, watching the three of them.

"Why does she hate me, Owen?" their mother sobs before she turns into Owen's chest, crying all over the front of his shirt. He wraps his arm loosely around her shoulders, looking uncomfortable.

"Please. You're so pathetic," Fable mutters. "Quit the act and get away from him. Stop trying to ruin his life."

They hardly notice me and I make my escape, slipping past them and down the short steps, running down the sidewalk without a backward glance. My feet slap against the concrete, my breaths coming fast and full of panic. I can't stop hearing Owen's denial that he has a girlfriend, the horrible things his mother said to me, about me. She doesn't even know me. How could she hate me so much? What did I ever do to her?

And why didn't Owen defend me?

"Chelsea!"

I hear him call my name and it only makes me run harder. Faster. Tears stream down my face but I don't bother brushing them away. They flood my vision, make it hard for me to see, and when I trip over a raised crack in the sidewalk, I go flying forward, throwing my hands out and ready to eat concrete.

Only to be caught by Owen, hauled back into his arms with my face pressed against his chest. I can smell him—

apples and the outdoors and pine, the scent of fall, of Owen. "Jesus, you're fast, Chels. Good thing I caught you."

"Don't call me that." I wrench out of his grip and take a step back, nearly tripping on the same spot again, but I gain my footing. He's talking to me as if nothing's happened. How can he do that? Everything's happened. It's . . . it's over. Just like that. "Get away from me."

He frowns, trying to take a step forward, but I only take one back. "I—let me explain. My mom . . . she's crazy. She has a lot of problems."

"Clearly," I retort through chattering teeth. I'm freezing. It's so cold out here and my hair is still wet. "Is it true?"

Owen frowns. "Is what true?"

"That you smoke pot with your mom. That you give her—marijuana and money?"

He sighs and hangs his head, runs a hand over his hair. I feel his despair. See it clinging to him like thick tendrils of smoke, wrapping all around his body, choking him. I ache to comfort him. To take him in my arms and tell him everything's going to be all right, but I don't. I can't.

His earlier denial sliced my heart in two.

"There's a lot you don't know about me. About my mom," he says, keeping his head downcast.

"I know. Because you never tell me what's going on. I'm completely in the dark here, Owen."

"Really? You feel that way? Because you don't tell me shit either, Chels. I know nothing about you. *Nothing*. Beyond you being some sort of child prodigy and graduating high school when you were sixteen—that's all I got. And that's not enough," he says, his angry words flowing out of him like a dammed river that's finally been let free.

"So you're saying *I'm* not enough. That's why you told

251

your mother that you don't have a girlfriend." I wrap my arms around my waist and rub my hands on my arms, but there's nothing I can do to ease the shaking, or the cold, dark ache that's consumed my chest, the weight so heavy I can hardly breathe.

"Now you're just putting words in my mouth."

"I heard you say it. 'I don't have a girlfriend.' Those words came out of your mouth. Oh, and my favorite, 'She's nothing.' That sentence hurt the most, Owen. Can you deny you said them?" I approach him, stretch my arms out so I can shove at his chest. He goes stumbling backward, his expression one of total shock, but it doesn't make me feel any better. None of it does. I'm hurting too much. "No, you can't. So guess what? You don't have a girlfriend? And I'm nothing? Then you're right. You don't have me."

"I had to say it. I had to tell her that." His voice is ragged, his expression full of anguish. His eyes are dark and full of so much . . . too much emotion. I can hardly stand to look at him it's so painful. "If she knows we're really together, she'll try and talk to you. Ruin you. Use you. She uses everyone. It's what she does best."

"She hates me." I pause because I'm finding it hard to breathe. "She doesn't even kn-know m-me." My teeth are chattering and I will them to stop. I refuse to fall apart in front of him. He shouldn't matter so much.

But he does.

"She hates me, too." He exhales roughly and hangs his head. "And I don't think she really knows me either," he mumbles.

I stare at him, dumbfounded. I wonder if *I* really know him. Did I ever? I believed I did. Only a few minutes ago, I thought I did. "Where's Fable?"

"Back at my house, chasing our mom out of there." His

expression crumples and I swear, he looks close to crying. My already broken heart threatens to crack deeper and I take a sharp breath, trying to keep everything together. "I should've told her Mom was back," he says. "I've kept it from her for months."

"You should've told the both of us. You should've been honest with me, Owen." I turn on my heel and start to walk but he doesn't chase after me. Not that I expected him to, but . . . well. Fine.

I *did* expect him to.

Turning, I look at him. He's still standing in the same place I left him, in front of someone's house, standing next to a white picket fence and staring at me as if he can't believe I would leave him.

But he leaves me no choice.

"So you're a drug addict, too," I whisper, wrapping my arms around myself.

He winces. "I smoke pot sometimes. It's no big deal."

"You smoke pot more than I think you let on." I pause. "Is it a problem for you?"

He says nothing, which is answer enough. We both remain quiet and I want to walk away, but I can't.

I'm not strong enough. Not yet.

"You haven't been honest with me either and you know it." His voice is so cold. "You have your secrets. Just like I have mine."

I say nothing because he's right. I do have my secrets. But he wouldn't understand. Not now. If I confessed everything to him about Dad, he'd think what he did for his mom was okay. He'd think I understand because of my no-good father. That I'd have no problem with Owen for enabling her. Giving his mom drugs, giving her money, keeping their relationship from Fable, from everyone. It wouldn't be fair.

My secret will remain my secret.

"You can't walk away from me like this, Chels," he says. "Give me another chance."

"I don't want to be with someone who gets high all the time," I murmur. "You're just trying to escape your reality. And that makes me feel like you're trying to escape *me*."

"Never," he whispers. "So I get high. So what? It's no big deal, right? I can quit whenever I want. I haven't smoked much this past week."

Only a week. I just . . . I don't even know what to think.

"You're not who I thought you were, Owen Maguire. Not at all," I say.

"Neither are you."

I flinch. Those three words lash at my heart. Tear at my soul. I waver, my knees threatening to buckle, and I press my lips together to stifle my cry.

And with that, I turn and run. Escaping my troubles, my problems, the boy I love.

Same difference.

Owen

"It's been a week, man." Wade's voice reaches deep within me, grabbing at my insides and trying to wake me up. "You need to get the fuck out of bed and start living again."

No. Hell, no. That sounds like a nightmare. I'd rather stay in bed and sleep. Or wake up and drink. Smoke a little. Get high. Forget the pain. Forget Mom is mad at me. That Fable's mad at me and won't talk to me. Forget that Chelsea hates me.

"Where's Des?" I croak, reaching toward my bedside table and knocking over the half-empty beer bottle that was sitting there, the golden liquid spilling all over the carpet. "*Shit.*"

"He's gone. I kicked him out last night. Told him I was sick of how he's keeping you on the shit when we should be getting you off it. I was wrong about him and you were right. Des is our friend but I'm tired of dealing with his . . . dealing." Wade walks farther into my bedroom, his nose wrinkling in disgust. "It fucking stinks in here."

It does. Like beer and weed and sweat and desperation. "I need Des."

"You don't need anything Des can give you, trust me." Wade strides toward my window and yanks the blinds open, letting in the early afternoon light. I hiss like a fucking vampire, my entire body recoiling as though I'm going to disintegrate into a pile of dust the moment sun makes contact with my skin.

"Why the hell did you do that, asshole?" I sit up in bed, squinting my eyes against the brightness while rubbing the back of my neck. It aches. Everything aches. I've hardly left this room, let alone the house, since the night Mom ruined my life.

Correction. Since the night *I* ruined my life.

"Because you need to see some light instead of sleeping the day away. After you put in all that time trying to get your grades up and you actually fucking did it, you let it all go straight to hell over a *girl*." Wade says the last word with disgust.

"Three girls, really," I say, thumping the back of my head against the wall. Mom, Fable, and Chelsea.

"Whatever." Wade waves his hand. "The fact that you're letting a bunch of women ruin your life when you had everything going good is what's tripping me up."

"You wouldn't understand." I groan and slide back down, under the covers, pulling the comforter over my head. "I fucked up."

"You constantly fuck up. What else is new? You usually just keep moving on. That's what I always liked about you. Shit would go down, you'd handle it, and then off you went. Ready to tackle something else if it came your way. You always acted like you didn't have a care in the world. Nothing bothered you."

"I'm real good at faking it," I mutter. *Everything* bothered me. All the time. When I was younger, I'd absorb it, hold it in, and slowly let it take me over until the anger and the hurt consumed me. The pain, the guilt of having a fucked-up home life with a crazy mother did a number on me, especially when I was younger and had no outlet.

Until I discovered drugs and girls and partying and drinking. I could lose myself in those things. Forget my troubles. Forget everything.

Fable would always pull me back on track. Drew, too. I'd try my best to do right, to be good and make the right choices.

But those right choices are hard when you're always staring temptation right in the face.

"Yeah well, what's that saying? Fake it until you make it? That's what you usually do. Until now." Wade yanks the comforter from over my head and I find him glaring at me, his expression fierce. "You need to get up and take a shower. You'll have a visitor here in an hour."

I frown. "Who the hell is coming to see me? Des?" I ask hopefully.

Wade shakes his head, his mouth set in a grim line. "No more Des for a while, bro. He's bad news for someone like you. You can't hardly function because of all the weed you've smoked the last seven days."

Good shit, too. Kept my mind hazy and thick with smoke, perfectly blank. So I wouldn't slip and think about Chelsea.

Whoops. Just slipped. "There's gotta be a joint around here somewhere, right? Where's my bong?"

"I hid it."

I tumble out of bed, nearly falling to the floor before I catch myself. I'm standing on wobbly feet, clad only in my underwear, and I wrinkle my nose. My skin feels grimy, my mouth tastes like a sewer, and I bet I smell like one, too.

Wade doesn't even flinch. He stands there, the calm in my storm, his arms crossed in front of his chest, his expression firm. I see the sadness in his eyes, though. And the worry.

He's sad and worried about me.

"Give me my bong," I say, because it's all I can focus on. All I'd rather focus on, because facing my reality is just way too difficult to contemplate.

"Fuck your bong. Fuck your weed. Go take a shower." He shoves at my shoulders, pushing me toward my open bedroom door, and I let him. Give in because it's easier and he's right. I'm rank, and I need to take a shower before I stink myself out.

I go into the bathroom and shut the door behind me, turning the lock. Start digging through the cabinets, hoping to score a joint like the last time I looked, but I'm out of luck. I turn on the water in the shower, letting it warm up as I brush my teeth. The bathroom is cold as ice, but the steam from the shower starts to up the temperature. I think of Chelsea taking a shower in here. When my life was normal and good and everything was going my way.

But that's ruined. I ruined it.

Way to feel sorry for yourself.

I take a quick shower, thankful that Wade pushed me into it because I feel semi-human again. His words are on repeat in my head, reminding me that I am acting like a mopey, good-for-nothing asshole. I need to pull my head out of my ass and get back to living. Fuck it if Mom's mad at me. If Fable won't speak to me. If Chelsea won't ever look at me again. I can't let that shit get me down.

Fake it until you make it.

After I throw on some clothes, I check my phone, ignoring the text messages from Des, and from some girl in my English class who has the hots for me and somehow got my number. There's a voice mail from my coach, and another from my boss at The District, but I choose not to listen to them right now. They're probably full of nothing but bad news.

I can't handle that. Not right now.

Then I see Drew's number. He left me a voice mail. I hit the play button and hold the phone to my ear, the sound of Drew's familiar voice filling my head, making me sit on the edge of the mattress and nervously bounce my knee. I dread hearing what he'll say.

What if he hates me?

"I don't know what the hell you think you're doing, but ignoring your sister isn't doing you or me any favors. She's mad, but more than anything, she's worried about you, Owen. Call her. You two need to talk."

That was it. That was all he said. He didn't beat me up, didn't tell me I was a rotten, no-good asshole brother who'd ditched his sister. Just simple and to the point. *Call your sister. She's mad. She's worried.*

The end.

Taking a deep breath, I stare at my phone's screen, contemplating giving Fable a call. But I can't do it. I'm scared to hear her voice. Hear the accusations, the questions. She's got plenty to say, I'm sure. She always does.

Instead, I text her. Two simple words I should probably send to Chelsea as well, but I'm not ready for that confrontation yet.

I'm sorry.

One step at a time. Fake it till you make it. I can do this. Approaching Fable is the first step. Figuring out what I'm going to do with Mom is the second step.

Begging Chelsea's forgiveness will be the third and final step. The scariest step of all.

"You dressed?" Wade asks as he barges into my room.

"Would it matter if I was, considering you just busted right in?" I stand and shove my phone into the front pocket of my jeans, pretending it's no big deal that I haven't heard back from Fable after my text. She's usually so quick, texting me back as fast as I answer her.

My phone is silent. Mocking me. Making me feel like a failure.

"Come on." Wade flicks his head toward the front of the house. "Your guest is waiting."

I follow Wade out into the living room, nerves gnawing at my gut, making me almost nauseous. I haven't eaten much this last week either, so that could contribute to the queasy feeling I'm having.

The nausea hits me tenfold when I see who's sitting on my couch.

"Coach." I stop when he stands, big and wide and intimidating as hell. He played football all his life, had gone to the pros only to have to bow out due to an injury two months into his first season. So he turned to coaching and is one of the best coaches in the state, if not the entire country.

Everyone has mad respect for Coach Halsey. And I've shit all over it practically the entire season.

"Son." He nods, his mouth grim. "You've missed practice."

I stand up straighter as I watch Wade wander off into the kitchen. "I know. I'm sorry."

"Got any excuses you want me to hear?"

"No, sir." I shake my head. Coach hates excuses. He thinks they're nothing but a bunch of bullshit and lies.

"Good." He approaches me, stopping just in front of me so he can poke the center of my chest with his index finger. "This is your last chance. You screw around again, miss one practice, screw up your classes, whatever, I'm dropping you for the rest of the season."

Swallowing hard, I meet his gaze, grimacing against the pain in my chest when he pokes me there again. "I understand."

"For whatever reason, that brother-in-law of yours thinks you have a lot of potential. I was just on the phone with him last week. Right before you ditched us."

"You were?" I rub my chest, surprised that Drew would bother to call him.

"I was. He thinks you could go pro. I agree with him. But if you're going to blow it every time you get your panties in a twist or your heart broken, you're never going to make it."

Coach Halsey is right. He gives me another ten minutes of the same speech and I take it, bowing my head, saying "yes sir" and "no sir" in all the right places. Until finally he claps me on the shoulder, tells me to show up tomorrow afternoon for practice or else, and then leaves my house as if he'd never been there in the first place.

I am a lucky bastard, that he's giving me another chance. I don't deserve it.

"Did that work?"

I turn to find Wade studying me, his expression completely neutral. Right about now, Wade would make a most excellent poker player. "If you mean did Coach set my head on straight, then yeah. I think so."

"You'd better do more than just think so. One more screw-up and you're gone. Don't fuck up."

"I won't," I promise, but I know that's going to be near impossible. I fuck up all the time. Even Wade said so.

"Stop faking it and actually make it for once," Wade continues, his gaze level with mine. "I think you can do it if you just let yourself. You're stronger than you think, dude."

I wish I believed in myself as much as Wade does.

CHAPTER 20

As soon as you stop wanting something, you get it.
—Andy Warhol

Owen

"You shouldn't do it."

I glance up to find Wade studying me, his jaw tight, his eyes narrowed. He's let his dark hair grow out since the beginning of the semester and it falls around his face in downright curly waves. I've told him more than once he looks like a pussy with all that hair in his face.

But the chicks fucking dig it. He's had more tail than I ever did. Big bad football player with the shaggy hair and pretty face gets all the ladies, which doesn't make sense to me, but whatever.

That's what we're doing now. Having yet another party at our house. But this one is legit. We're celebrating the big win, the one that's taking us to the playoffs. Practically the entire team is in our house, spilling out onto the front porch, the front yard, the backyard. The neighbors are tolerant, the majority of the houses on our street are filled with college students, but still.

We're loud. The party is getting semi out of control and it's not even midnight. There are girls everywhere. The place is crawling with them. Even Des is here. Wade reluctantly let him come over since for whatever reason, Wade has decided to become my personal bodyguard, detective, and bouncer, all in one.

This is how he's caught me, all alone in the bathroom with a joint in one hand and a lighter in the other. I'm happy as fuck, thrilled we're on our way to the playoffs, but I'm plagued with thoughts. Bad thoughts.

I swore I saw Chelsea this afternoon at the game. Same hair, same style of clothes, same long sexy-as-hell legs, the girl had been with her friends, both male and female, and she kept distracting me. Especially when the guy sitting next to her slung his arm around her shoulders and pulled her in close, kissing her.

Jealousy had torn at me and I ripped off my helmet, glaring at her. Glaring at him. Could she really be ballsy enough to show up at a game and make out with some jackass right in front of me?

Turned out it wasn't her at all, but it was too late. My brain was fucked. Chelsea was in there. Insistent and sweet and pissed and sexy and naked and smiling, and *hell*.

I couldn't shake her.

"Come on, dude, give it to me." Wade holds out his hand, waiting for me to drop the joint in his palm, but I don't.

Instead I flick the brand-new lighter and the flame appears. I spark the joint up, take a long, slow drag, and let the harsh smoke fill my lungs, holding it there until I finally can't take it anymore and exhale.

"Bastard," Wade mutters when I drop the joint in his palm after that one-and-only hit. He shoves the joint in his jeans pocket. "I thought you were laying off the weed."

"Something fucked with my head today," I tell him as we emerge from the bathroom together. Three scantily dressed girls stand in our hallway, bursting into laughter as we push past them, the noise grating on my nerves.

"Something or some*one*?"

I shrug. "I don't want to talk about it."

"So you'd rather pretend it never happened by smoking. Gimme a break."

"Who are you to judge? You never refused when I offered you a hit." He's been my partner in crime for years. He's my best friend. We've always been in this together.

Since when did he grow up and turn into the responsible one?

We stop outside the kitchen, the two of us just taking it all in. The place is a madhouse. Loud music, louder people, lots of beer, and the living room is filled with smoke, the pungent smell of marijuana permeating the entire house.

Fucking great. Maybe this wasn't such a good idea.

"I know how to control myself. You don't. There's the difference." He gives me a shove on the shoulder. "We're not kids anymore, Owen. It's one thing to fuck around, get in trouble, and smoke it up all the time when you're a kid. It's another thing entirely when you fuck around and do all those same things as an adult. You get arrested, and suddenly you've got a permanent record."

Valid point. One I never really thought of before, but shit.

"Don't let weed control you. Or your guilt, 'cos I know you have a lot of that, too," Wade says, his voice firm. "Now, I'm gonna go find a girl, feel her up, and drag her back to my bedroom where if I'm lucky enough, I'll get her naked. You game for finding one for yourself?"

I shake my head, disgust filling me at the thought of finding some girl I don't know and dragging her back to my room. "Hell, no."

I only want one girl and she's not here.

"You still not over her?" Wade's voice is gentle, like he's afraid I might freak out if we talk about her for too long, which is probably pretty accurate. Just thinking about her hurts.

And he doesn't have to say her name for me to know who he's talking about. "She's the reason I needed to take a hit," I admit. "I thought I saw her at the game earlier, but it wasn't her."

"I saw her, you know," he says nonchalantly.

"Where? At the game?" *Bastard.* Why didn't he tell me? Not that I would know what to do when I *did* see her. Still, I'm jealous.

"Saw her on campus. She ran right by me like she didn't see me, but I think she did." Wade rubs a hand along his jaw. "She looked sad."

I blow out a harsh breath, training my gaze on the party going down in my living room. Some chick has already taken her top off and all the guys are yelling at her, encouraging her to take off more. She does nothing for me. Her tits are way too big and the bra she's wearing doesn't do her any favors. Not that any of those guys are protesting. "Don't tell me that kind of shit, man."

"Whatever. Thought you should know." Without another word Wade leaves me where I stand and merges into the crowd, plucking a red cup from some random chick's hand and taking a long swallow before he hands it back to her, a giant smile on his face.

Just like that, the girl is caught under his spell. Shaggy hair and all. That used to be me, minus the hair. I walked in a room, flashed a smile, said a few words, and I had girls surrounding me. It was easy. *Too* easy.

I finally meet a challenge, fall for her, and I mess it up. Can't find the courage to go back to her and make it right. She was the best thing that ever happened to me and I'm still hiding from her.

Still.

Wandering outside, I go to the keg Des brought and pour myself mostly foam, then head out into the yard, away from the party and the noise and the girls. There's a couple making out behind a tree not too far from where I'm standing, but I ignore them. I pull out my phone and check my texts, pulling up Chelsea's name. I down the beer in one gulp for courage, realizing the single hit I took off that stupid joint didn't alter my state of mind much whatsoever.

I'm still a nervous, bumbling fool, my head filled with thoughts of nothing but Chelsea.

Dropping the empty cup onto the ground, I hold my phone in both hands, my fingers shaking. My thumbs hover above the keyboard, my heart's beating about a million miles a second, and I swear I break out in a sweat.

But I'm doing this. I'm going to message her and tell her the truth. Tell her how I really feel.

It's the least I can do.

Chelsea

I'm alone. I don't know what I'm going to do. Kari left almost two weeks ago after she came down with a major bout of mono. Who gets mono anymore? I blame her stupid non-boyfriend Brad. It is, after all, the kissing disease.

Her mother wanted her to withdraw for the rest of the semester and Kari protested big time, but she was so tired and feverish, her parents made her come home. So she did, worried about leaving me all alone in this stupid apartment I can't afford, but what else could she do? She's sick. Not severely, but enough that she's out of commission for a while.

Trying to figure out a way to make this work, I took on extra shifts at the diner. I've also found more students at school to tutor, but with all the extra work my grades are starting to suffer.

I'm exhausted. And I'm still broke. I tried to find a roommate but couldn't, not this late in the semester. Gave notice to my landlord a few days ago, and now he's anxious for me to move out because he already has new tenants lined up.

I'm screwed. I have nowhere to go. And I refuse to go back home, though Mom is begging me to on an hourly basis.

It's a Saturday night and I'm not working. I already did a graveyard Friday-night shift and my feet are killing me. I have another shift tomorrow, the breakfast rush, and I'm not looking forward to it.

My life sucks. I don't know what happened. One minute everything was perfect and bright and filled with happiness and a boy and sex and hope.

Now I have nothing but darkness and exhaustion and work and studying. It's colorless, sad. Dim.

My cell rings and I answer it, listen to Mom rattle on about how we have no more money and she's been so worried over what to do. I don't know how to answer her, don't know what sort of advice to give. I've always been her rock, the one who offers comfort when she's fallen into despair.

Now I'm the one who feels like she's lost all hope and Mom's so focused on her own troubles, she doesn't even see mine.

And I have a ton of them, not that I've told her anything. I've turned into a completely different person and she doesn't even see it.

"I talked to your daddy," she finally says, and I realize she's been leading up to this the entire conversation.

I curl up on the overstuffed chair in the living room, soaking up what Mom just said. Kari's parents took all of her furniture, including the couch. I don't have much. Kari feels awful, she's constantly texting me asking if I'm okay, and I wish I could be mad at her.

But I can't. She got sick and her overprotective parents whisked her away.

"Why are you talking to him after everything he did to you?" I ask, though I'm dreading the answer.

"He wants to help, sweetheart. He understands we're in a tough predicament and he wants to be there for his family."

A little too late for that, if you ask me. "How can he do that when he's in a prison cell?"

"Chelsea! Don't talk about your daddy like that," Mom chastises.

I hate it when she calls him my "daddy." I haven't called him that in years. I rarely refer to him as anything other than my father. He's never been a real dad to me. He never really cared.

"Whatever," I mumble. "I don't want his help."

"He's told me where some money is that he stashed before he went to jail. I'm going to withdraw it from the bank and hold it for him. He said I can go ahead and use part of it now," she explains, sounding perfectly fine with this arrangement. "Don't you think that'll be a big help?"

Unease settles in my stomach, making it turn. "That's dirty money, Mom."

"It is not," she says, her voice prim. She believes what she wants to believe. That's how she's always been with her husband.

My father.

He's a horrible person. Right up there with Owen's mom.

My mother, for all her man-hating and constant warnings about how men will treat me awful, how I can't trust them and I'm better off alone, can't believe her own hype. My father is her absolute weakness.

And she can't even see it.

"It's dirty money. He has some secret account he wants you to clean out so he doesn't have to do the hard work and possibly get caught after he gets out. You'll save it for him and when he's released from prison, you'll give it to him, think everything will be wonderful and perfect between the two of you, and then he'll leave you. Again."

She's sputtering, sounding like a plugged-up faucet right before it blows and spits water everywhere. "How *dare* you say that, Chelsea. He is your *father*. He may be in prison doing his time, but you shouldn't judge him for that. Everyone makes mistakes and now he's paying his dues. He has redeemed himself."

"Right. He's a model citizen. Paying his dues by encouraging you to pull out his dirty money from his secret account." I pause, wondering if my words are even sinking into her brain. "He's a real prize, Mom. I refuse to get involved with that sort of thing."

"That money will help you survive, which you're barely doing, might I remind you."

Way to rub salt in the wound, Mom. "I don't want it. He stole it."

"We don't know that," she starts, but I cut her off.

"Sure we do. He took it. I don't want it." How many times do I need to say it? "I want nothing from him. Absolutely nothing."

"I'm not abandoning my husband in his time of need, Chelsea." Her voice is like ice. "If you're going to make me choose, be careful. You might not like my decision."

She's threatening me. Letting me know she'd choose him over me. I don't understand her. I never really have. She's always such a contradiction, her thoughts, her whims moving with the shift of the wind. Dad wronged her? Men are evil.

Dad's now wooing her with sweet words and endless promises? She needs to stand by her man no matter what.

I'm sick of it. Sick of the back-and-forth and depending on a man who doesn't give a crap about us. It's exhausting.

They both are.

"I won't take the money." I lean my head back and close my eyes, swallowing hard. "I don't want you to see him."

"Too late. I've seen him, many times. We talk on the phone daily. We write each other letters. He'll be getting out of prison by the end of the year and we'll be together again." She sounds happy, so falsely pinning all her hope on this, and I want to smack her. Tell her he'll disappoint her again. She's forgetting all of that. Just believing his lies and his empty promises.

And when he disappoints her yet again and leaves her alone, what will she do? Turn to me?

"He told me that he's tried to contact you," she says, her voice full of disapproval. "And that you hang up on him every single time. You shouldn't do that, Chelsea. He just wants to talk to you. You're his daughter, his only child."

They won't have to worry about it any longer because I shut off the house phone, depending only on my cell. Couldn't afford to keep the landline, which we had only because Kari's parents insisted on it for safety reasons, whatever that means.

And cell phones normally can't take collect calls.

"I refuse to allow him back into my life, Mom. I'm sorry." I hang up on her before she can say another word and I stare at my phone screen, wondering if she'll call back. Counting on her to call back. At least text.

But she doesn't. That hurts more than I care to admit.

Leaning back in my chair, I stare at the ceiling, feeling . . . hopeless. The beginning of the semester I felt like I had everything. With two jobs and the perfect school schedule, finally out of the dorms and living with my best friend, I was on top of the world.

Then I meet Owen, and my world is flipped upside down. Everything's changed. I can't blame him for all of the changes, but he's part of it. A *big* part of it.

I wish he were still a part of it.

Closing my eyes, I try to shut off my churning thoughts, my overactive imagination. I can't go home. I can't stay in this stupid apartment. I have nowhere. Nothing. No friends, no possibilities. Maybe I could rent a room. Sell what pitiful amount of furniture I have and move in with someone. That could work, and the rent would be way cheaper.

First thing tomorrow I'm looking for someone with a place to share. Tonight . . . tonight I'm too tired and too depressed.

My phone buzzes and I crack open my eyes. I hold it up so I can see who texted me. Probably Kari, crying the blues that she can't go out on a Saturday night. Or that her parents treat her like she's on her deathbed when she's really only sick with stupid mono. Those had been her complaints last night when she texted me.

These messages aren't from Kari, though. There's an endless stream of them, one after another. One heartbreaking sentence at a time.

I miss you.

I think about you all the time.

I dream about you.

I lied to you and I'm sorry.

I was embarrassed.

Ashamed.

I want to earn your forgiveness but I don't know how.

I hold my phone with trembling hands and tears forming in my eyes. I haven't cried since that night I ran away from

Owen. I told myself I was stronger than that. He couldn't break me. I refused to let him.

But now, with the truth typed out for me to see, I cry. Quiet, continuous tears that slide down my cheeks, drop from my jaw onto my chest, dampening my shirt. I don't care. The release feels good. It frees me from everything I've held so tight within me for weeks.

Sniffing, blinking past the tears, I text him back.

One pitiful sentence at a time, just like the ones he sent to me.

I miss you, too.

And I think about you all the time.

You come to me in my dreams and I don't want to wake up.

You lied to me but I lied to you, too.

Because I was embarrassed.

And ashamed like you.

Maybe someday I can tell you about it.

I wait for his answer, my breathing short, my chest aching. What if he doesn't reply? Maybe he's drunk. Maybe he's . . . oh God, maybe he's high and he's trying to con me into going back to him.

Maybe, just maybe, I want to be conned. I want to go back to him. I miss him so much. I need him.

Does he need me?

My phone buzzes and I look at the screen, my heart in my throat.

Tell me about it now.

It would take me forever to text him everything. Before I can reply, I get another message:

Come over. I want to see you.

Can I? Am I brave enough? I don't know. I want to see

him. I'm desperate to look at him, smell him, feel his arms come around me and hold me tight.

Please Chels. I need to see you.

I need you.

His last text tells me that I am.

CHAPTER 21

Being deeply loved by someone gives you strength,
while loving someone deeply gives you courage.
—Lao Tzu

Owen

I wait out by my car for her, wishing for about the ten thousandth time that I'd offered to come pick her up. She probably would have turned me down. I don't want to push, but I hadn't expected her to answer my text messages.

She did. Her words mirrored mine but reflected her own troubles. The secrets she kept from me. I want to hear them. I need to.

I need to see her.

Girls approach me outside, one after another, all of them asking if I need anything, do I want something to drink, something to eat, maybe I could take them back to my room and they could help me out in other ways. So many girls are here, looking to score with a football player. Ready to brag to their friends that they snagged one. I don't want to deal with the groupies and the obvious girls who want nothing more than to get laid.

I used to be one of those guys who wanted nothing more than to get laid. It didn't matter with whom or where, I was happy to be getting some.

I'm not that guy anymore. I want my sweet, smart girl. I need Chelsea.

Whipping my phone out of my pocket, I check for a message from her but there isn't one. My head is clear, the faint haze from my earlier buzz all gone. I'm focused. Centered. She feels close. I can sense her presence, I swear, and when I glance up I see her. Walking across the street, headed straight for me. Her hair is in a sloppy knot on top of her head, she doesn't have any makeup on, and she's wearing the sweatshirt I gave her when we went to Drew's football game and black leggings that make her legs look like they're a mile long.

She's the most beautiful thing I've ever seen.

"Hi." She stops directly in front of me, her hands stuffed in the pocket on the front of her sweatshirt, her expression wary but her gaze . . . hopeful.

"Hey." I want to reach out and touch her so bad it's killing me. "You, uh, walked here?"

She shrugs. "I've had so much crap happen to me lately, I figured I may as well live dangerously and walk. What else can go wrong?"

Damn. She doesn't usually talk like this. She's the positive one in this relationship. "What's going on, Chels?" I give in to my urge and reach out, tuck a strand of hair behind her ear, let my index finger trace the curve of it.

She releases a shuddery breath and closes her eyes, exhaling softly. "Are you high?"

"What? No." *Fuck.* I need to tell her the truth. "I took one puff on a joint earlier. Wade caught me. I stopped."

"Owen . . ." She shakes her head, the disappointment clear in her voice, and I'm so scared she's going to leave me for good I don't know what to do.

"I was feeling sort of fucked up," I confess. "I thought I saw you earlier."

"Where?" She frowns.

"At the game. Some girl who looked a lot like you was hanging all over some guy." I take a deep breath. "I was jealous."

"You thought it was me."

I nod. "And I just wanted to forget, you know? That's why I lit up. Then Wade saw me and called me out on my shit. Made me realize I can't run away from my problems. I need to face them head on." I stare at her, hoping she realizes what I'm saying.

I'm willing to face our problems and make them right. I want this to work. I want *us* to work.

"I can't be with you if you keep smoking weed," she murmurs. "I just . . . I can't deal with it."

"I swear I won't, Chels. For you, I'll give it up."

"You have to want to give it up for yourself, too, you know," she points out.

Damn, my girl is smart. "Yeah, I know. You're right."

She stares at me for a moment, her gaze dark, her expression sad. "I have to move out of my apartment," she blurts out.

Shit, she's leaving? Panic races through me and I stifle it down. I don't know if I can stand the thought of her gone. "Why?"

"Kari got a bad case of mono and her parents freaked so hard they withdrew her from school, packed up all her stuff and brought her back home. They never really wanted her to leave, to go away for school. This is their way of getting her back under their control."

Controlling parents who actually care. I have no idea what that's like. "You can't find another roommate?"

"No. Kari's parents took all of her furniture and I only have a few things. I've been alone in that little apartment for almost two weeks." A tiny sob escapes her and she hangs her head, kicks at the sidewalk with her booted foot. "I've been working extra shifts. I-I've even skipped class."

"*What?*" I must have sounded extra startled because her head jerks up, her eyes wide as she stares at me.

"I said I've skipped class."

"But you *never* skip." I'm incredulous.

"I had no choice. I was either working or passed out in bed after an extra-long shift at the diner."

"Why do you need to work all the time, Chels?" I want to get to the heart of the matter. I'd invite her to my room so we could discuss this in private but she'd probably accuse me of trying to get in her panties, and I just . . . I'm too exhausted to deal with that right now. Another fight, another loss. Because I would lose.

I always do.

"My dad's a thief. He embezzled money from his job for years. They trusted him. We all trusted him." Her voice is small, barely above a whisper, and I lean in closer to hear her. "He's also a cheater and a liar. He's in jail. Prison, really. He's used my mom forever, always promising he'll take care of her when really he just stomps all over her heart and leaves it to bleed. I hate him. I also . . . I hate it when she believes him. When she talks about how bad men are and how much she hates them, then turns around and takes him back. Every single time, she does that. I don't know why. I don't get it."

My heart aches for her. I hear the pain and anguish in her voice and it's fucking killing me.

I grab her by the upper arms and pull her in close, hold her to me as she presses her face into my shirt. She feels so good, so damn right back in my arms, but I hold her loosely. Not wanting to scare her or make her run.

I need her here. With me.

"Mom always says men shouldn't be trusted. That she's pushed my father out of her life forever. But of course, she's talking to him again and he wants her to withdraw money out of some secret account he has. It's probably more money he stole. He embezzled hundreds of thousands of dollars, Owen. He did it for *years*. And he cheated on my mom, had endless affairs with an endless list of women. I hate him so much."

She's crying, getting my shirt wet, and I let her. Let her get it all out as I hold her to me, one hand in her hair, the other smoothing down her back. I can't believe she's here, standing with me outside in front of my house while inside, all around us, there's a party raging on.

"Why does she keep doing that? Why does she trust him when he's done nothing but lie and cheat and steal? He doesn't love her. He doesn't love me. My dad only loves himself."

I could get that. Mom is the exact same way. She's the most selfish person I've ever known.

"I want you to trust me, Chels," I tell her, my voice soft as I press my hand to the small of her back, pushing her in closer. I want her to feel safe with me and never doubt me again. "I swear on my life I'll do whatever it takes to earn back your trust."

When she slips her arms around me, offering the smallest nod as her answer, I almost want to shout with relief. She belongs with me and I need to prove that I'm worthy of her. That I love her.

Because I do.

"Let's go inside," I whisper in her hair, my arms tightening around her.

"Nice party, Owen," she says, the sarcasm thick, displaying a hint of the old Chelsea. "I bet there's someone in your room right now."

"There's a lock on the door. No one is in my room. And if someone is, I'll kick them the fuck out." I thread my fingers through her hair and tilt her head so she has no choice but to look at me. Her cheeks are streaked with tears and I wipe them away with my thumbs. "Come inside with me, Chelsea. We can talk more now or we can talk more tomorrow. Whatever you want. I just . . . I really need to be with you tonight."

She stares at me, seeing right through me I'm sure but I don't even flinch. Everything I am, everything I want to be for her, it's showing. I can feel it. I'm vulnerable as fuck and I don't care.

"All right," she finally says, sounding reluctant, which of course fills me with worry. I don't want to ruin this or somehow fuck it up beyond repair.

I need to be careful. I need to make this work. For my sake and for Chelsea's.

We need each other. I don't know if Chelsea's aware of it yet, but I know I am. Having her here with me makes everything right again. Makes me feel like I can breathe again. These few weeks apart from her have nearly killed me.

There's no way I can let her go now.

Chelsea

Everybody at this party is beyond obnoxious. I see the way the girls look at Owen as we walk by them and they make me feel possessive. I want to shout at all of them, *Back off, he's mine!*

But I don't. I have at least some sort of control.

I grab hold of his hand when we enter his house and let him pull me through the crowd. The girls are all dressed to impress, their hair and makeup perfect, the tight or skimpy outfits they're wearing meant to intrigue and entice.

I'm in leggings that have a hole in the inside seam and the sweatshirt Owen gave me, with a tank top and no bra on underneath. I look plain and boring, as if I just crawled out of bed after a night of no sleep. Tired and sad, with a tear-stained face and red eyes. Not that I think anything's going to happen between Owen and me tonight, but . . .

You never know. If he tried something, I wouldn't stop him.

Everyone looks at me as if I don't belong with him, but I know the truth. We belong together. He's mine and I'm his. Somehow we're going to break down each other's last, thick walls and be honest with each other. I already told him so much, pretty much all he needs to know. What more can I say about my father?

Nothing. I don't want to talk about him. I just want to forget.

The house reeks of beer and weed and I wrinkle my nose, raising my brows when we pass by Des. He has a knowing smile on his face and his arms around two girls, and I almost want to laugh. It's all just so . . . weird. Owen's life. Mine. And how they intersected. We are complete opposites.

Yet it feels so right to be with him.

"Well, well, look who showed up."

I glance over my shoulder to see Wade standing there, a big grin on his handsome face. His hair is a mess and there's a girl hanging on his arm with a satisfied smile curling her lips, her eyes kinda hazy. Like maybe she was the one who just had her hands in his hair.

"Hey," I say, just as Owen's fingers tighten around mine.

"Leave her alone," Owen warns and I look at him, wondering what his comment is all about.

"Just saying hey." Wade leans forward, as if he's about to

tell me a giant secret. "He's been a whiny baby for days. He missed you."

My heart swells. Owen missed me. Hearing someone else say it somehow makes it feel even more real.

"Shut up," Owen mutters, solidifying that real feeling.

That this is real between us. What we share, what we have, isn't all one-sided. We're definitely in this together.

"Don't fuck up with her again," Wade says, pointing his finger in Owen's direction before flashing me a gentle smile. "She actually tolerates your ass, so don't let her go."

I release Owen's hand and go to Wade, pulling him into a quick one-sided hug since the girl still hasn't let him go. And he doesn't seem too upset about it, either. "Thank you," I murmur as I pull away from him.

"See how sweet she is? You don't deserve her, man," Wade says, gesturing at Owen, who looks ready to rip him apart with his bare hands. "She even hugged me."

"Consider yourself lucky I didn't chop your hands off for touching my girl." Owen slings his arm around my shoulder and steers me away from Wade. I can hear Wade laugh, hear the girl ask what all that was about, but the buzz in my head slowly takes over, until all I can focus on is Owen.

Holding me, guiding me through the mess, getting all jealous and calling me his girl.

I love it. Maybe an hour ago I felt like I was at the end of my rope. Everything about this night is exaggerated and crazy and over the top. I feel like I'm on a ride at Disneyland or some crazy amusement park and I'm begging them to let me off. It's all just too much.

Finally we're in Owen's room and he closes the door. Turns the lock. That subtle click rings loud in the quiet confines of his room and he faces me, leans against the door so he can study me.

"My mom is a drug abuser. A drunk."

His words are flat, his tone impassive. I wait for him to continue.

"She's never been there for us, not really. I always wanted her approval. When we were alone, she told me I was her favorite. I was her baby boy. And I wanted to be her baby boy. I wanted her to love me. I don't think she ever did."

My heart hurts and I can feel tears forming in my eyes, but I blink them away.

"When I was fourteen, she left. Just one night packed up all our shit, left only my clothes and Fable's and took off. We didn't hear from her for a year." He takes a deep breath, as if he needs it for strength. "She called me one day. Out of the blue. Begged me not to tell Fable. Asked me to come live with her. I wanted to. Despite everything she'd done to me I wanted it so bad.

"First she just said she wanted us to live together here in town. Then she started talking about moving away. Out of the state. Across the country. She wanted a fresh start. The idea of leaving Fable like that, and Drew . . . it scared me. I went to Fable and told her everything. They got in a huge fight and Mom left. Four years later she finds me. I don't know how, but she showed up awhile ago and I . . . I've been helping her the only way I know how."

"Owen." My voice cracks and his gaze meets mine, his green eyes shimmering with unshed tears. "You can't blame yourself for any of this. It's all on her. It's not your fault your mom is so hateful and selfish."

"Try telling that to my fourteen-year-old self." He thumps the back of his head against the door and gazes at the ceiling. "She's in jail now, you know. Like your dad. Well, county jail. Fable called the cops that night. Turns out she had warrants out for her arrest. I was so pissed at my sister for doing that. She put our mom in jail."

Their mother put herself in jail, but I decide not to point that out. "Are you and Fable not talking?" I ask. It would hurt me if I knew he wasn't communicating with his sister. Just break my heart.

"We've talked. I texted her, though she made me sweat for a few days. It's not—perfect, but we're trying. She's still mad at me for dealing with Mom on my own. That I gave her drugs. That I gave her money."

"You did what you thought you had to do." I inhale deeply, then let it all out, trying to gather my thoughts. "I hate that you kept it from me, too. But I had my own secrets to hide. I can't . . . I can't be mad at you for that."

He closes his eyes, presses his lips together. "I don't deserve your forgiveness."

"Yes, you do." My simple answer feels so freeing it lightens my heart.

His eyes crack open and he looks at me. "I don't deserve you."

"If you don't deserve me then I don't deserve you."

"Chels . . ." His voice drifts off and he sounds so sad, so defeated, I can't take it any longer.

I stand in the middle of his room, wondering if I should just go for it. I missed him so much these last few weeks. My body still aches for his and now it's even worse. When he held me outside, my knees had grown wobbly and I thought I would collapse, it felt so perfect to finally be back in his arms.

Now he's suffering and it feels like he's doing it alone. He's too far away from me. I want to touch him. I *need* to touch him.

Deciding to hell with it, I reach for the hem of my sweatshirt and pull it up and over my head, tossing it onto the floor. I've done this before; this very moment reminds me of the night in the hotel room, our first night together. When we were naked and vulnerable and afraid, but still happy that we were in this together. We had each other.

He needs to know he still has me.

Owen's eyes are wide after I threw off my sweatshirt, but he doesn't move from where he's standing. Doesn't say a word, either.

He just watches. And waits.

Leaning over, I pluck off my boots, tossing them near the bed. Standing straight, I grab hold of the waistband of my yoga pants and shimmy out of them, letting them fall to my feet so I can kick them off.

"Chels." Owen says my name again, then clears his throat, his expression full of slumberous, hungry desire. He wants me. I can see it. I can practically smell it. "You don't have to do this."

"I've missed you." I say nothing else, just let those simple words hang in the air as I whip off my tank top and expose my upper body completely. A strangled noise falls from his lips and heady, powerful pleasure swamps me, makes my knees weak.

I'm clad in only my turquoise-blue panties, with a little white bow at the center of the waistband. When I wear them I usually feel like a little girl, but I definitely don't feel like one now. Not while standing in the middle of Owen Maguire's bedroom with nothing else on but these panties, my breasts heavy, my nipples hard, and between my legs I can feel myself grow slick and hot.

"I've missed you, too," he finally says, his voice rough. "So damn much."

"I want you." Glancing behind me, I start to make my

way to his bed and suddenly he's right there before me. His big hands grasp my waist, fingers pressing into my skin as he guides me down onto the bed, before he whispers against my lips.

"I want you, too. You're my fucking everything."

His words wash over me and I close my eyes, my breath catching in my throat when he kisses me. His full, delicious lips are finally on mine again and I want to cry.

But I don't. I wrap my arms around his neck and hold him close. Spread my legs and feel him settle between them, his jeans rough against my bare skin, his belt buckle biting into the tender flesh just above my panties.

I help him shed his clothes and he takes off my panties, slipping them down my legs with shaky fingers that skim along my skin, his mouth on my breasts, his hand settling between my thighs. I'm so wet for him it's almost embarrassing, but before I can push him away or say something stupid, he rears up on his knees, leans over me, and pulls a condom from the bedside table drawer.

"I can't wait. I want to be inside you too much." He rolls the condom on and then he's over me, inside me, filling me completely.

This is what I want. What I need. He feels so good inside me, so right. We're not perfect, but we're a perfect fit for each other. It's all or nothing with Owen and me—and nothing is too hard for us to bear.

So I want it all. Everything. With Owen.

He rolls us over so I'm on top and he tugs the band from my hair so it falls past my shoulders in a riotous mess. "Ride me," he whispers, his eyes glowing, his expression full of an unnamed emotion I don't want to label.

Not yet. It's too soon. It all feels like too much.

I do as he asks, sitting up and resting my hands on his hot, hard chest, my hair spilling all around me, the ends tickling my naked skin. I press my lips together and lick them as I slowly, surely start to move. Hesitant at first, but then Owen's gripping my hips, showing me how to move, helping me establish a rhythm.

He reaches up to cup my breasts and I arch my back, sliding up and down his erection, my eyes closed. I'm lost in the feel of him. His hands on my breasts, his cock in my body, and I know without a doubt at this very moment, I'm scarily in love with Owen.

"Fuck, you are beautiful," he whispers as he moves his hands down from my breasts to my waist, then my hips. "Your skin is so smooth, so soft."

I open my eyes to find him staring up at me, wonder filling his gaze. I slow down, clamp my thighs tight at his hips, and slowly roll my body into his, sending him as deep as he can go.

He closes his eyes, a ragged moan escaping him, and I increase my pace, eager to find my orgasm and give him his, too. I want it. I want mine and I want his. Together.

I want it all.

Falling on top of him, I pump my hips, my mouth at his ear as I whisper how much I want him, how much I need him.

"Chelsea." His hands are at my back, holding me tight, and then I feel him tense beneath me, his hips lifting. I know he's close. So, so close and so am I, but I want to help him along.

"I'm in love with you," I murmur just before I kiss his throat, his jaw, his cheek. "I love you, Owen. So much."

A choked sound escapes him and he grips my backside, pulling me in so close to him I cry out, my orgasm coming out of nowhere as my clit brushes against the length of him, setting me on absolute fire. My body trembles, my belly clenches as I cling to him, as he clings to me.

This moment . . . I never, ever want to forget. Making love with Owen in his room while a wild party rages on in his house. We're locked away in our own little world, where the only things that exist are him and me.

That's all that matters. Owen and Chelsea.

Chelsea and Owen.

Together.

CHAPTER 22

Find the adventure,
I'd rather be lost with you,
than found all alone.
—Tyler Knott Gregson

One year later

Owen

It's hot as hell outside as we sit under the blazing sun, watching the graduation ceremony. Autumn keeps toddling off, fast as can be on those chubby legs of hers, little screams of joy emitting from her rosebud lips as Drew or Fable chases after her.

I just sit there, a smile curling my lips, occasionally reaching out to snag her into my arms when she buzzes by me. She laughs and shoves at my chest, wanting out of my arms, but I know it's just a game. She loves me.

At this very moment, for once in my life, I feel surrounded by love. Nothing nagging at me, reminding me I'm a terrible son or making me feel guilty.

Is it wrong that my mother died while in jail and I didn't mourn her death for long? I was sad—sadder for the loss of the opportunities she'd wasted more than anything. She could have been someone. She could have had Fable and me as her family. She could have had Drew and then Autumn, too. Hell, even Chelsea.

Instead, she died alone, her heart giving up after too much drinking and drugs and bad choices. Fable was completely emotionless when she told me. She was the one who got the call from the county jail and in turn, she called me. I found out over the phone that Mom died without anyone.

It hurt, but mostly I was numb. When had she ever been a real part of my life? A meaningful part? Not in years, maybe not ever.

That night, I let Chelsea comfort me. She held me close and told me how much she loved me. Then she got naked and showed me how much she loved me, too.

I am one lucky motherfucker.

The people sitting around us are irritated with Autumn, but they keep their mouths shut because there's a superstar in their midst. Freaking Drew took his team to the Super Bowl again . . . and they won. Again. Two years in a row. The man is a god. Cover of *Sports Illustrated*, cover of *People*, cover of . . . I can't even remember, he's been on so many magazine covers. Fable's been on a couple of covers with him, too.

Crazy. My pain-in-the-ass sister is freaking famous.

The ceremony announcer drones on, and he's only on the R's. Sweat forms at my neck, in my hairline, and I breathe deep, trying to pretend I'm somewhere cool, but it's not working. I'm wearing a button-down shirt and the nicest pair of jeans I own, and I rub the back of my neck, grimacing. I wanted to look nice for Chelsea. It's a special day for her, one I'm so thankful we're all a part of.

She's graduating. It's a huge step and I'm so freaking proud of her. She's not going on to graduate school, though, not yet. She's taking the summer and the fall semester off because she wants some time for herself, for us, but I know she's scared. She told me so.

I told her as long as we have each other, we'll be just fine.

The announcer has kicked into the S's and I sit up straight, craning my neck around the crowd of people that surround me. The bleachers are packed, as are the chairs down on the field. We're on the field, since I'd pulled some strings with Coach Halsey and got us decent seats. I wanted to be close, so I could run up to Chelsea after the ceremony and hug her. Kiss her. Congratulate her and tell her how much I love her right before I give her her present.

It's pretty simple, but I think she'll like it.

"She's going to drive me nuts," Fable mutters under her breath as she comes back to her seat for about the hundredth time, a wiggling Autumn clutched in her arms. Drew takes his daughter and cuddles her close, holding her so her head rests on his shoulder. Her hair is dark like her dad's, but her eyes are green like Fable's and mine. She's a perfect combination of her parents, bold and fast, pretty and strong. "And to think I'm going to have another one."

"You're pregnant?" I whisper loudly, causing more than a few heads to turn.

Shit. Word gets out like that about them and it makes front-page news.

"*Sshh.*" Fable glares at me, though her lips are curved in a tiny smile. "Yes, I am," she admits.

Well, holy shit. Aren't they just building the perfect little family? "I'm happy for you, Fabes," I tell her truthfully.

"Thanks." She smiles, resting her hand on her stomach. "I'm exhausted, sick half the time, but I'm the happiest I've been in my life."

I agree. So am I. We're fucking lucky, Fable and I. On paper, we should have been a disaster. At certain points in our lives, we were. The fucked-up siblings with the even more fucked-up mother and absent fathers. We should be losers. In jail. No jobs. No education. Nothing. We'd been told that time and again growing up.

Now look at us. We proved everyone wrong.

"I already promised Fable I'd hire ten nannies if the next one is anything like this little girl." Drew jiggles Autumn in his arms, making her giggle as she keeps her head on his shoulder, her little thumb between her lips.

"Give me a break." Fable rolls her eyes. "I told him five would be plenty."

Drew leans over and kisses her, and I swear I just heard a collective sigh sound throughout the crowd.

These two can't go anywhere without people watching them.

"Kayla Shroeder," the announcer says, and I realize we're getting close. I shush Fable and Drew, hoping like hell the baby doesn't decide to start squalling at this particular moment, and I keep my eyes glued to the stage. Ready to watch her walk across.

"Brian Siebert . . . John Signorelli . . . Jessica Simerson . . . Chelsea Simmons."

I stand up, unable to stop myself, as I watch her walk across the stage. She's wearing a white graduation gown and one of those silly little graduation hats—I don't know what the hell you call them. Her hair has grown a lot since we've been together and it flows almost to the middle of her back, straight and sleek this morning. She shakes the dean's hand and accepts her diploma and I yell and cheer for her. So do Fable and Drew.

So does the rest of the crowd.

Chelsea glances out toward the audience, a smile on her face. She looks so damn happy, I want to grab her right now.

Drag her away and tell her in private how proud I am of her. How much she means to me. Then I want to show her how much she means to me, too.

The rest of the ceremony happens in a blur. Autumn falls asleep on Drew's shoulder, drooling all over it, which makes him laugh. Fable's starting to fade, her skin growing paler from all the heat and the new baby growing inside her. As the ceremony is winding down, Drew tells me he's going to take them back to the hotel. Fable needs to rest and Autumn needs a nap.

"Tell Chelsea we're sorry we can't congratulate her right now, but I gotta get my girls out of here," Drew says, his gaze serious as he gathers up the heavy diaper bag one-handed, Autumn still drooling on his shoulder. Fable stands next to him, her smile wan, her eyes heavy with sleep. "But we'll see her later tonight at the restaurant, right?"

We're having a graduation party for her at The District. "Absolutely. I'll let her know what you said." She'll understand. And she'll be excited to hear about Fable's news.

Drew leaves with Fable and Autumn, and I wait, standing on the sidelines as the ceremony comes to a close. All of the graduating students toss their caps up into the air at the same time, screaming and shouting, their voices loud and strong. They did it. They're done with school.

I know the thought would have sent Chelsea into a panic not even a year ago, but now, I think she's relieved. I'm relieved, too. Our lives are going to change, and for the better.

I can't fucking wait.

Chelsea

I glance all around me, looking for a sign of Owen, but I don't spot him anywhere. It's so hot, the mid-May air is stifling even in the morning, and I use my graduation cap to fan myself, clutching my diploma in my other hand.

No one else is here for me. I called Mom and told her the date and time. I even sent her an invitation, asking her to come. When she texted me that the only way she'd attend my graduation was if she could bring Dad with her, I flat-out refused. Told her not to bother. I don't want him here. I don't want to see him.

That was my choice, and no matter how much it hurt, I had to stand strong. Owen told me I did the right thing and I needed to hear that, because the doubt creeps up on me still.

So Mom stayed away today, and it made me sad. She sent me a graduation present and signed the card from Mom and Dad, which irritated me, but I told myself to get over it.

I have to accept the fact that no matter what, Mom is always going to choose Dad first. Her behavior disappoints me, but I can't change her and I can't change him. It is what it is.

At least I have my new family here. Owen and Fable and Drew and Autumn. They've embraced me fully into their clan and I love every one of them so much. They're always there for me no matter what, and that's more than I can say about my own parents. I've grown so close to them, especially Fable. She's like the big sister I never had. She's so busy, what with Drew's career and fame and her own celebrity, but she drops everything to talk to me. And Owen.

She loves us unconditionally.

The last year hasn't been easy for them either, what with Owen and Fable's mother dying in jail just after the new year. A heart attack, brought on by all the drug and alcohol abuse she'd done over the years.

No one was surprised and they really didn't outwardly mourn her, but I know it was hard on them, Owen more so than Fable, only because of all the guilt he carried with him from the number his mom did. She'd worked him as hard as she could, since Fable didn't fall for her manipulations.

And it worked. He still held on to that need to please his mom no matter how much he knew it was wrong. It was a waste of his time. So when he discovered she'd died, I comforted him as best I could and helped him deal with it, letting him talk, letting him be alone—whatever he needed, I tried to be the best girlfriend I could.

Despite everyone wanting him to try for the pros once he graduates, Owen is tempted to give up that dream. He says he doesn't believe he has the skill level or the discipline that Drew has to make it. Owen gets distracted and he's the first to admit it. I both admire his decision and worry for him, wishing he didn't feel that way. I try to subtly encourage him that he shouldn't give up on his dream.

Fable, on the other hand, is constantly pushing him to reconsider, which is her prerogative as his sister. He tells her he might, but I'm not sure. I think he's afraid he'll fail in Drew's shadow and somehow disappoint us all.

I'm hoping this summer I can convince him he can do whatever he sets his mind to. He's so strong, so smart, and so stubborn. All that determination wrapped up in his charismatic package, I don't see how he can go wrong.

I plan on helping him realize that, though I'm not sure Owen knows what he wants to do. He just lives in the moment. That sort of attitude used to scare me to death.

Not anymore. Lately I've embraced living in the moment, too.

It's rather liberating.

I'm postponing graduate school to gain back some time for myself. I've always done what everyone else wanted me to. I accelerated through elementary school, high school, and now college. Always working, always doing what I was supposed to. I'm finally taking some time for myself. I'll work, I'll spend time with Owen, I might even pick up a hobby.

I'm excited about all the unknown possibilities. I'll be fine as long as Owen's with me.

"There you are." One warm, strong arm slips around my waist from behind and pulls me in. I lean my head against Owen's chest for the briefest moment before I turn in his embrace, gazing up at his handsome face.

He's smiling at me, his gaze soft, his hair a bit of a mess, as if he's run his fingers through it again and again. Leaning down, he presses a tender kiss to my lips, then pulls away. "Congrats, Chels. I'm so proud of you."

"Thanks." I grin, so happy I feel like I'm going to burst. I still can't believe he's mine and that we're together. That this beautiful, sweet, funny, irritating, sexy man loves me as much as I love him. "Are you ready to get out of here?"

He raises his brows. "Are you?"

"Definitely. It's so hot." I nod, glancing around at everyone else starting to leave the field. "We're all dying to get out of here."

"I have a gift for you first." He holds up a bouquet of pink roses, the same shade as the one he gave me oh so long ago, and my heart melts. He thrusts them toward me and I take the bouquet, the clear wrapping crinkling in my hands as I bring the flowers up to my nose and breathe deep their familiar fragrance. "They always remind me of, well . . . you know." He's smiling so big and my love for him nearly overwhelms me.

"I love them," I whisper, tears threatening, really meaning that I love *him*. He's so sweet to me, so good. I remember how I once was, all tangled up in knots over everything and nothing. Worried that I was doing the wrong thing, needing to be a good girl, accomplishing my work, my assignments, desperate to keep everything under control but not really happy.

Not really living.

Owen has untangled all my knots. Smoothed them out and made me see there's more to life than order and control and being good and seeking approval. There's beauty and pain and love and sex and happiness and anger. And it's okay to have all of that, to feel all of that. *He* makes me feel.

And I know I'm loved.

"Where to now?" he asks, his gaze warming when I unzip my graduation gown and shrug out of it, then drape it over my arm. I'm wearing a pale yellow sundress, and his eyes zero in on the little straps that tie on each of my shoulders. I can only think he's imagining untying those bows and slowly peeling the dress off of me.

I'm imagining the same thing.

"I don't know," I say as he slips his arm around my shoulders and we start walking across the field toward the campus, where his car is parked.

"Feels kind of good to say that. Don't you think?" He plays with the bow on my shoulder, his finger tracing the loop of fabric, and I shiver.

"Feels good to say what?" He's distracting me. I can hardly focus when he touches me like that, even in a crowd of hundreds of people, like right now, because we're surrounded completely.

Somehow, it still feels as though it's just me and him.

"That you don't know. We don't know what we're really doing next, do we? The entire summer is open for us to do whatever we want." He smiles down at me, the sight of it making me a little dizzy, and I suddenly stop, causing him to stop, too. People brush past us, some of them grumbling irritably since we're standing right in the middle of everyone's path, but I don't care.

I don't think Owen cares either.

"I'd rather not know what I'm doing with you, Owen, than have everything plotted out for the rest of my life with someone else." I mean it. He's the only one I want. The only one I need.

"I feel the same, Chels. Exactly the same." His voice is as soft as his touch upon my face, his fingers drifting across my cheek, and I close my eyes, in that moment so completely lost in him . . .

That I'm also completely found.

Acknowledgments

This has been by far the most exhilarating and wonderful and stressful year of my life. What started out as a little idea about a broken boy and a broken girl turned into this series that completely changed my writing career. I'm so thankful to everyone who's been there for me every step of the way. There are a lot of people who I want to acknowledge and thank, so here we go.

First to my agent, Kimberly Whalen, for believing in the series and for helping me find its home at Bantam. To my editor, Shauna Summers, who helps me go deeper with every book and who's so encouraging and enthusiastic. It's been a joy working with you. To Sue Grimshaw, who is always so helpful and responsive. To everyone at Bantam/Random House for helping me with the endless questions and emails, and for the support.

A big thank you to Kati Rodriguez for all the help with . . . everything. To KP Simmon for the endless amounts of hard work you put into every book release and for the friendship.

I've made so many new friends in this self-publishing turned traditional publishing venture since January 2013. What a wonderful, supportive group of women I've met, and I'm so lucky to call them my friends. An extra big shout-out to Lauren Blakely for the hilarious emails and the scarily correct predictions—you're amazing.

To my critique partner Katy Evans, who is a busy bee just

like me, so thank God we have each other. This has been a wild ride and extra fun because we've done it together.

I have to mention my friends from the other side. The ones who've known me forever, who've been there for me through thick and thin, who know me as I really am (and that would be as my other writer self, Karen Erickson). So to Shelli Stevens, Kate Pearce, Loribelle Hunt, Stephanie Draven, Lisa Renee Jones, Gwen Hayes, Stacey Jay, and Tracy Wolff, thank you.

I must thank my family because, hello, they deal with me never being around, or sitting at my desk all the time, or with my head in the clouds because I'm working through a plot point. To my husband for his never-ending support—I absolutely could not have accomplished what I did this past year without you. To my children, who are extra proud of the fact that their mama is in Target, their favorite store. To my parents, my grandma, and my brother- and sister-in-law for cheering me on.

Finally, I must thank the readers and the bloggers and the reviewers. Do you guys know how awesome you are? I would be nothing without you all spreading the word, supporting me (supporting all of us authors!). Thank you for taking the time to make (awesome!!!) graphics, for writing reviews, and for talking about my books and my characters like they're real people. I know you've waited a long time for this book. I appreciate your patience and hope like crazy you loved reading Owen and Chelsea's story as much as I loved writing it.

I never planned on Owen having his own book. He was just Fable's brother, a secondary character Fable needed to ground her and give her something to love before she met Drew. He was a total pain in her ass that she had to deal with, but she loved him so fiercely. So did I.

Then he grew into this . . . thing. He became this man-boy

who punched Drew in the face, who loved his sister just as fiercely as she loved him and had all of this guilt to deal with because of his mom. He *demanded* a story. So here it is. And dare I say I love Owen just as much as I love Drew? Yes. I do.

I hope you do, too.

PHOTO: COLBY RAIMER

New York Times and *USA Today* bestselling author
MONICA MURPHY is a native Californian who lives
in the foothills of Yosemite. A wife and mother of
three, she writes new adult contemporary romance
and is the author of the One Week Girlfriend series
and the tie-in novella, *Drew + Fable Forever*.

monic
amurphy.com
missmonicamurphy@gmail.com
facebook.com/MonicaMurphyauthor
facebook.com/DrewAndFableOfficial
@MsMonicaMurphy

Read all of **MONICA MURPHY'S** Addictive New Novels

One Week Girlfriend: Available Now

An utterly addictive and sexy story about a fierce, determined young woman who's just trying to make ends meet, and the hot college football quarterback who makes her an offer she can't refuse.

Second Chance Boyfriend: Available Now

The exhilarating conclusion to Drew and Fable's story as Drew fights to show Fable why they're destined to share a love that lasts forever.

Three Broken Promises: On Sale December 2013

Colin feels responsible for his best friend's death in the Iraq War, and vows to make it up to the one person who was devastated the most: his friend's sister. Colin takes Jennifer under his wing, but Jennifer isn't interested in Colin's charity or his guilt. Instead, she wants his love . . .

Four Years Later: On Sale Spring 2014

About to start college, Owen Maguire is stunned when his mother waltzes back into his life four years after having abandoned their family. Owen's afraid that he'll revert to his bad habits under the burden of his mother, until he meets a girl who's ready to show him how to love.

Visit Monica's website: **MonicaMurphyAuthor.com**
Join Monica on Facebook: **Facebook/MonicaMurphyAuthor**
Follow Monica on Twitter: **@MsMonicaMurphy**

BANTAM TRADE PAPERBACKS AND EBOOKS